# THE EX WHO

# WOULDN'T

# DIE

**Sally Berneathy**

This book is a work of fiction. The names, characters, places and incidents are products of the writer's imagination or have been used fictitiously and are not to be construed as real. Any resemblance to persons, living or dead, or to actual events, locales or organizations is entirely coincidental.

The Ex Who Wouldn't Die
Copyright ©2012 Sally Berneathy

ISBN-10: 1939551102
ISBN-13: 978-1-939551-10-8

Original cover art by Cheryl Welch
http://www.mywelchdesign.com/

# Chapter One

Amanda accelerated around a sharp curve, leaning her shiny black Harley Night Rod so low the toe of her boot touched the road. Coming out of the curve, she watched as the speedometer climbed...70...75.

She leaned forward, letting the wind flow over her rather than against her, savoring the sharp curves of Highway 259 as it wound upward through the Kiamichi Mountains, letting the thrill of speed and danger crowd out anger, desperation and frustration.

Eighty-five and still climbing. The trees along the roadside flew by in a rush of green.

Too fast.

She knew that.

Ninety.

It was better than getting drunk to escape her problems. No hangover the next day.

She could handle the speed. She'd been riding since she was a teenager. She could handle the motorcycle and her demanding mother and her ditzy sister. She could handle everything life had thrown at her except Charley Randolph, her almost-ex-husband. He'd held that title for fifteen months and counting. Today his scumbag lawyer had finagled another postponement of the final divorce hearing for his scumbag client.

Charley had sworn he'd never let her go, and she was beginning to believe that might be the only time in their two-year marriage when he'd told the truth.

She veered around a particularly sharp curve, leaning so far over she fancied she could feel the heat of the pavement through her thick leather pants. Adrenalin suffused every cell in her body. This was great. Another hour or two and maybe she'd calm down enough to stop plotting Charley's demise.

She'd planned this weekend getaway to a log cabin nestled deep in the Kiamichi Mountains to celebrate the divorce she thought would happen and to mourn the marriage that had never really happened. Now she could only hope the peace and serenity of the mountains coupled with the exhilarating ride getting there would soothe her murderous anger.

She gave the throttle another twist.

Ninety-five.

One-hundred.

Blow out the cobwebs, focus on the joy of speed, of the wind rushing past her and the trees along the roadside turning to a green blur.

A sharp curve twisted to the left just ahead. She pushed gently on the foot brake, and a chill darted down her spine. The pedal was mushy. The bike didn't slow. Something was wrong.

Not a good time or place for the brakes to go out. Her muscles tensed as she feathered the hand brake. The bike gradually slowed as she swept into the curve. She let out a long breath and ordered herself to relax. Everything was going to be okay. She'd check the brake when she got to the cabin. The hand brake controlled ninety percent of the braking anyway.

But everything wasn't going to be okay. Something was wrong besides the brakes.

The back wheel wasn't gripping the road the way it should.

She hadn't noticed any sand or oil on the highway, no irregularities in the smooth surface. This shouldn't be happening.

But it was.

Refusing to allow herself to panic, Amanda held the bike steady as she continued around the curve, slowing as quickly as she dared, making a Herculean effort to maintain control of herself and the bike.

It wasn't going to be enough. The bike slid toward the side of the road, the side of the mountain.

She lost control—of the motorcycle and of her own pounding heart.

She slid toward the side of the mountain.

The adrenalin was gone. The euphoria was gone. Even her anger at Charley was gone. Her entire focus became survival. A blanket of calm fell over her, shutting out sound and scenery, bringing her world down to nothing but the bike and her.

Feeling as if she was moving in slow motion, she thrust away from the cycle, leaving the beloved bike to roll on its own down the hill, anywhere but on top of her body.

She tumbled, freefalling helplessly down the mountain, blue sky replaced by green grass replaced by blue sky, over and over. A tree slammed against her shoulder and sent her in a different direction. A large mossy rock filled her vision. Pain exploded through her head, her body, all around her. She embraced the enveloping blackness.

డిౚ

"Amanda! Wake up, damn it! Do you hear me? Get up! You have to get up!"

Charley. Of course it was Charley. Who else would be demanding that she wake from a pleasant dream?

"Go away," she grumbled.

"No, I won't go away until you get up. You have to get to the highway."

*The highway?*

"No, I don't." She tried to go back to her dream, to the most amazing bright light she'd ever seen, a light that promised the fulfillment of all her dreams, but Charley continued to yell.

And now he'd ruined it all. She was awake and her head ached abominably. In fact, her whole body hurt.

She put a hand to her head, a gloved hand that touched something smooth and hard instead of flesh and hair.

She opened one eye and, through a fog, peered at her hand. Motorcycle gloves. And she was wearing her helmet which was fogged from her breathing with the faceplate closed and no air being forced through as she rode.

Why had she gone to sleep in her riding gear?

"Get up, Amanda. You're hurt. You've got to have help."

"I'll hurt a lot less if you'll leave me alone and let me go back to sleep."

"No! You can't do that. Listen to me. Look at me and listen to me."

She pushed her faceplate up and lifted her gaze to see him kneeling beside her, streaked blond hair shining in the sunlight, blue eyes concerned, his khakis and white Polo shirt immaculate as always. In the background she saw trees and rocks and grass and sky.

Huh? Where the hell was she and why had she been sleeping outside in her riding gear?

*The accident.* She'd lost control of her bike, skidded going around that last curve, skidded as if she'd hit sand or oil.

She lifted herself painfully on one elbow. "What are you doing here? I *knew* you had something to do with it! You were following me, weren't you? This is your fault! Somehow, this has to be your fault!"

"I didn't. I wasn't. I swear. I think I'm here to save your life. You've got to make it back to the highway so you can get help."

4

Amanda blinked and looked around her, trying to focus through the fog inside her brain that couldn't be dispelled by anything as simple as opening a faceplate.

"All right." She'd learned to agree to Charley's irrational demands to shut him up, then do as she pleased. "Okay. I need to get to the highway."

"Good." He rose and stepped backward.

"Go on," she urged. "I'll be there later."

"Damn it, Amanda, this is no time to be stubborn! You're hurt. You'll die if you don't get help."

Amanda had to admit, she didn't feel so hot. She'd taken quite a tumble, and her desire to go back to sleep probably wasn't a good sign considering how hard her head had hit that rock. With a sigh, she tugged open the zipper of her jacket pocket and fumbled for her cell phone. With her gloves on, she couldn't work the touch screen. "Call 911," she said, offering it to Charley.

"Great idea!" He reached eagerly then drew back with a strange sad look. "I can't."

"Oh, for crying out loud!" She pulled off her gloves and started to punch in the numbers, but of course there was no signal so far into the mountains. She shoved the phone back in her pocket.

"Fine. You get your way again. I'll walk back to the highway." She tried to rise, but pain shot through her left ankle and she fell back with a groan. "I'm just going to lie down here for a minute and take a short nap. Then I'll have the energy to walk."

"No!" Charley shouted. "You'll die!"

"And you can't stand for me to escape from you even in death. Well, I can't walk. I think my ankle might be broken."

"Then you'll have to crawl," Charley declared.

Familiar fury rose in Amanda's throat. "You could give me a hand!" she snapped. "You could carry me. You could at least let me lean on your shoulder."

Charley grinned, looking like a mischievous boy. Which he was. A 32-year old child. "You always want to be independent. You're always saying you don't need any help. Guess you'll have to prove it now." He took another step backward, up the mountain.

"Why, you worthless..." Her words ended in a groan as she again tried to get to her feet. Every muscle and bone in her body protested, registering their complaints with sharp stabs of pain.

"Worthless what?" Charley taunted, moving farther away and still grinning—triumphantly, she thought. "Come on, Amanda, you can do better than that. Remember the time I hocked our wedding rings to pay off my gambling debt? You had some pretty colorful names for me then."

Amanda unleashed a few heart-felt invectives, but Charley continued to step backward.

"What? I can't hear you. Did you say you still love me?"

"You are the most despicable creature on this earth! I only thought I hated you before this. What kind of monster forces an injured woman to crawl?" She crammed her hands back into her gloves, grasped the nearest bush and pulled herself upward. Using her arms and her uninjured leg, she inched her way toward him, every movement an agony. Each time she gripped something with her right hand, a pain knifed through her shoulder. Fortunately her anger at Charley provided something of an anesthetic.

"You're going to pay for this, Charley Randolph." The rock she'd wedged her right foot against gave way and she clung to a small tree with only her right hand, the pain in her shoulder excruciating. Blackness crept around the corners of her mind, but she shoved it away, replacing it with righteous fury.

"All deals are off," she panted when she'd stabilized her position. She reached upward, dragging herself along as Charley continued to move backward, away from her, up the hill. "I'm no longer offering to give you two-thirds of our property just to get away from you. I'm taking half of everything and all of my business. I earned ninety percent of everything anyway. I'll fight you in court if it takes another ten years."

"I won't sign the divorce papers, Amanda. I won't give you half. I won't let you divorce me. If you keep trying, you'll end up with nothing. Not even the cat." And still he smiled that infuriating smile.

"Damn you to hell! Damn you to living with my mother and never going deaf for all eternity!" The bush she grabbed hold of had stickers so sharp they pierced her glove and her palm, but she ignored that relatively minor pain and continued to move. "We don't even have a cat. That's just like you to take something we don't even have. I hope the next woman you sleep with gives you leprosy."

"What was it you threatened to do with that rusty serrated knife when you caught me with Becky? Cut some flowers for a bouquet?"

"Cut off your penis and put it down the garbage disposal. And it was Megan! I didn't know about Becky until now."

Charley continued to taunt her, and Amanda continued to climb, determined to reach him and throw him back down the mountain. So much for moving past her desire to kill him.

After an eternity of pain and torment, he stopped, and she realized the highway was inches from her face. With a gargantuan effort she pushed herself erect, careful not to put much weight on her left ankle.

Charley beamed. "You made it, babe. I knew you could do it."

She lunged for him—and fell onto the surface of the highway.

"Amanda, get up. We have to talk about something," he said, his tone suddenly serious, but she was already drifting into the blackness, her last ounce of energy expended. "Amanda! You almost died. He tried to kill you! He'll try again! You're in danger!"

# Chapter Two

Somebody was moaning, making an awful fuss. Being totally obnoxious.

Bloody hell. It was her.

Her head throbbed. She lay still, trying to remember what she'd done last night to deserve to feel so bad.

Oh, yes. The motorcycle wreck, skidding out of control, tumbling down the mountain, expecting to die.

Then Charley. He'd made her crawl up that blasted mountain to the highway, hadn't given her even a little bit of help. She could have died, but he wasn't about to get dirt on his hands or grass stains on his Dockers. Same old Charley.

She opened her eyes. Even without moving her head—which she didn't dare attempt—she could tell this was a hospital room. Small, gloomy, an IV pole beside the hard, uncomfortable bed.

Apparently Charley had gone for help then probably gone for a drink. Even as she cursed his lack of responsibility in leaving her, she was glad she didn't have to contend with him *and* a vile headache.

"You're awake!" Her younger sister's always-excited voice came from the other side of the bed, and Amanda smelled the floral perfume before the small, perky face appeared above hers. Jenny was always perky. Petite with short, dark hair framing delicate features, she was Amanda's opposite in every way. Amanda, tall, red-haired and rebellious, had often wondered if she might be a changeling in the family that fell short of perfection only by her presence in that family.

Jenny lifted one dainty hand and touched Amanda's cheek. "How do you feel?"

"Rotten. How do you feel?"

9

"Worried! We've been so scared ever since Mother got the call that you'd been hurt on that terrible motorcycle. We always knew eventually you'd have a wreck. Just the other day we saw a motorcycle wreck on the news, and Davey said, that could be Amanda. Thank God you're okay. Well, I mean, you will be okay. Of course you're not okay right now, not with your ankle sprained and your shoulder out of socket. It's not out of socket anymore, but it was, and you have a lot of bruises. At first they thought they'd have to operate on your head, but they gave you some kind of medicine that made the swelling in your brain go down. It's a good thing those people in that van found you when they did. Much longer and you might have died. Daddy tried to give them a reward—"

"Jenny, slow down." If she had to listen to the babbling much longer, her head would surely explode. "In short, specific sentences, tell me where I am."

"In a hospital."

Amanda sighed. "And in which city or state does this hospital reside? I was in Oklahoma when I crashed."

"Yes, you were. But Daddy pulled some strings and got you moved to a private hospital in Dallas as soon as we found out you weren't going to die. You're in Graham General. Daddy's friend is your doctor. He—"

"How long was I unconscious?"

"Two whole days. They said you'd probably be out longer, but look at you! Wide awake! You're—"

"I know, I'm okay. What time is it?"

Jenny checked the diamond-studded watch on her wrist. "Seven minutes past one. They brought your lunch." She indicated a tray with a glass of milk, bread and a stainless steel cover hiding something on a plate, something that likely should remain hidden. "I made them leave it because I had a feeling you were going to wake up today, and I knew you'd be starving—"

"What about the motorcycle?"

Jenny blinked rapidly, never a good sign. "The...motorcycle?"

"Shiny black machine with two wheels. Makes this loud VROOM VROOM noise. Where is the motorcycle? They did bring back my bike, didn't they?"

Jenny folded then unfolded her hands and fluttered nervously. "Yes. The police have it."

"The police? What are they doing with my bike? This has something to do with Charley, doesn't it?"

Jenny's nervous look changed to startled distress, her small eyes widening, one hand flying to her mouth. "Oh, Amanda!"

Amanda groaned. She had been a little surprised that Charley wasn't looming at her bedside, especially after that scene on the mountain. Her accident and confinement to a hospital bed would have been the perfect opportunity for him to prove his devotion, try to convince her to drop the divorce proceedings. But if one of his scams had landed him in trouble with the authorities again, he'd be hiding out. Or in jail.

Her father, a local judge, had managed to keep Charley out of jail during their marriage. However, there had been plenty of close calls, plenty of times the police had shown up on her front porch and plenty of times Amanda had hoped her father wouldn't intervene. But Charley had always appealed to his father-in-law who didn't want to "see the family's reputation blackened."

Charley had been caught at the scene of her accident, so the cops had confiscated her bike. It was the prettiest, hottest bike she'd ever owned. Now, *thank you, Charley,* the cops had it. They'd take it apart, looking for evidence. It would never be the same.

But something had gone wrong with the bike even before her accident. The horrifying details washed over her in a rush—the loss of control, the sensation of sliding

11

on a slick surface that hadn't been slick, falling over the side of the mountain then abandoning the bike to save her life.

Had Charley tampered with it? She'd left it outside when she went into his third floor apartment for the latest in a series of confrontations that had, as usual, ended with her storming out, jumping on the bike and riding hard and fast to get away from everything.

No, that wasn't possible. Not that she thought him incapable of it, but he'd been inside with her the entire time she was away from the bike, arguing with her, shouting at her.

Still, it was a huge coincidence that he'd suddenly appeared right after she crashed. She'd been riding fast for a couple of hours. The only way he could have been there was if he'd followed close behind her for the entire trip.

Damn him! She was going to get her bike back, fix it, and then she was going to kill Charley.

"Where's a nurse? Jenny, get me a nurse. Please," she added before Jenny could upbraid her for her lack of courtesy.

"Oh, dear! Are you in pain? Do you need more medication?"

"Yes, I'm in pain. No, I don't need more medication. I need my clothes. I need to get out of here. I've got things to do." *Kill Charley.*

Jenny fluttered, one hand touching her cheek then drifting to her hair. "I don't think you can do that."

Amanda had a few doubts of her own what with her left leg swathed in bandages and that IV stuck in her arm, but she was going to give it her best shot. "Jenny, please, get me a nurse or, better yet, get me Dad's friend, the doctor." She rolled to the side of the bed, putting her good foot on the floor. The process was painfully reminiscent of her climb up that blasted mountain.

"I have to call Daddy," Jenny said. "I told him I'd call him as soon as you woke up."

The old *I'm going to tell on you!* Jenny had always been good at that one. She was the obedient daughter. She did whatever their parents told her to do. She graduated college with a 2.5 GPA in education then promptly married a young lawyer and took her place in Highland Park society. David Carter, Esq.

Jenny, and only Jenny, called him "Davey." Well, Amanda called him that sometimes to annoy him. To the rest of the world he was "David" or "Mr. Carter." He was as boring as day-old white bread. He was the perfect son-in-law. Jenny was the perfect daughter.

Amanda loved her little sister, had since her unexpected birth when Amanda was seven and their parents were already in their early forties. But her life would have been a lot easier without Jenny's staunch alliance with their parents. As she listened to Jenny on the phone to their father, Amanda thought it would have been nice to have a rebel sister, someone who would have "forgotten" to call their father until she'd made her escape.

But no one got to choose their relatives. If they did, Amanda would likely be the one not chosen for inclusion in this family.

Jenny ended the call.

"Is Mom coming with Dad?" Amanda asked.

"No, she had to speak at a charity luncheon, and you know how much everybody depends on her. She's been very worried about you, but I told her I'd take good care of you." Jenny smiled and patted Amanda's arm.

"I understand. She would have hated being here when I was unconscious and couldn't hear her criticisms. On the other hand, I couldn't have argued with her, either. She may have just missed her big chance."

13

"Oh, Amanda! You know how much Mother loves you. We all do. But we don't understand you, especially about—oh, dear! Daddy said we couldn't talk about him!"

"We can't talk about Dad?" Amanda asked, the misinterpretation deliberate.

"No! We can't talk about—" she lowered her voice to a whisper— "Charley!"

"Like we'd want to."

"Amanda, I'm so glad you're awake." The deep, resonant voice announced Emerson Caulfield's entrance. Her father was an average-size man, but he always loomed as large as his voice. His full head of steel-gray hair, his penetrating brown gaze and immaculate dark suit completed his imposing courtroom presence no matter where he was, even in a hospital room.

Brian Edwards, an associate from her father's old law firm, came in behind him. He was handling her divorce, but they weren't buddies. He wasn't on her birthday party list or her hospital room visitors list. Why was he there?

Brian stood quietly, deferentially. Though he seemed as imperturbable as always, something wasn't right. His erect posture bordered on rigid. He clutched his briefcase with a white-knuckled hand.

Had Charley filed a new motion of some sort, something so bizarre her father felt the need to bring her attorney to her even as she lay in bed tethered to an IV?

"Jenny," Emerson said, "would you please stand outside your sister's room and make sure no one disturbs us?"

"Of course." She gave Amanda a perky smile then left the room and closed the door behind her.

Amanda groaned. "Is this about Charley?"

The two men exchanged glances. "Yes," Emerson replied, his dark gaze softening. In spite of her status as black sheep of the family, Amanda knew her father loved her and would always be there for her no matter how

14

much he might disapprove of her actions. Sometimes she wondered if he might even envy her freedom, just a little bit, once in a while. "Mandy, whatever happened, we'll fix it."

Amanda frowned. "*Fix it?* Don't you think we're a little past fixing every little problem for Charley? Have you ever heard of the concept of *actions have consequences*?"

Her father looked uncomfortable, not a normal state for him. "Of course they do, but sometimes there's a question as to what those consequences should be. When you feel up to it, I'll go with you to the police station, but if anything should come of this—and I'm quite certain it won't—we need to have Brian involved from the beginning."

"So Charley's in jail. Did he do something to my bike? I can't believe he would want to hurt me. Physically, I mean."

Again the men exchanged worried glances.

Emerson moved forward and took his daughter's hand in his. "Mandy, sweetheart, Charley's not in jail. He's dead."

"What?!" Amanda half rose from the bed then fell back with a grimace of pain. Charley couldn't be dead. He was a lot of things, most of them bad, but everything about him was alive and vibrant. She couldn't imagine him any other way. "Dead?" she repeated. Well, that would explain why he hadn't come to stalk her in the hospital. "Are you sure? What happened? I didn't even know he was sick. Did he overdose on something?"

Her father looked down and drew in a deep breath. "Somebody entered the apartment—apparently somebody he knew since there was no sign of a break-in—and shot him."

"Omigawd! Was it a robbery?" Not that Charley had anything to steal after so many visits to the pawn shop. More likely a jealous husband.

Emerson shook his head. "They don't think so. Nothing seemed to be missing."

"The gun," Amanda whispered, guilt washing over her.

"What gun?"

"Charley called and asked me to bring him that gun he bought me. Said he'd sign the divorce papers if I would. I went to his apartment, but I didn't take the gun. I thought he wanted to sell it or hold up a liquor store or something awful. But maybe he wanted it to defend himself."

She looked at her father, hoping he'd say something to relieve her feelings of guilt.

"You didn't take the gun with you?" he asked. "Where is it?"

"Home in a box in the back of my closet where it's been since he gave it to me." Amanda's eyes fill with unexpected tears. "I wanted him out of my life, but I didn't want him dead." Okay, maybe she'd thought of making him dead a few times, had fantasized about things like stripping him naked, tying his hands and feet, pouring honey on him and leaving him on a fire ant hill in west Texas in the middle of August or beating him with a black jack wrapped in barbed wire then squirting acid on him at thirty-second intervals for a few hours. But those were just pleasant fantasies, on a level with dreaming about winning the lottery. "He saved my life," she said quietly.

Her father's gaze sharpened. "What do you mean, he saved your life?"

"The accident. I passed out somewhere down the side of the mountain. Charley found me and wouldn't let me go back to sleep. He forced me to crawl up that mountain to the highway so somebody could find me." It was the truth—refined and honed, omitting the ugly part about his refusing to actually help her. He had, nevertheless, forced her to help herself.

Her eyes overflowed, and a tear trickled down each cheek. She felt benevolent at being able to remember Charley in a good light. "No matter what he did in the past, I'll have that as my last memory of him."

"Amanda, that's not possible. Charley's body was found at nine o'clock Sunday evening with time of death approximately three hours earlier. You were picked up just after eight o'clock Sunday evening in Oklahoma. The motorist said he saw you stagger onto the highway and fall...alone."

Amanda stared at him for a long moment, trying to comprehend and make sense of her father's words. "What are you saying? Charley did not die two hours before my accident. I saw him after the accident. He was rude and mean, but he made me crawl up that mountain. He taunted me until I did it. If he hadn't been there, I would have lain down, gone to sleep and died. When I reached the highway, he was with me."

Her father shook his head. "I'm sorry, Mandy. It was a dream. Sometimes when people are involved in traumatic accidents, they have strange dreams."

"You mean hallucinations. Great. Other people see bright lights or angels. I almost died, and all I saw was my ex-husband."

*You almost died. He tried to kill you. He'll try again. You're in danger.*

She struggled to sit up as the memory of Charley's last words hit her. "He said somebody tried to kill me."

Her father's brow creased with concern. He took her hand. "Sweetheart, it was a dream. Charley wasn't there. He was already dead."

Of course he wasn't there. He hadn't saved her life. He hadn't warned her she was in danger. Just a dream.

17

The last time she saw him was their violent argument at his apartment. She hadn't brought him the gun that might have saved his life, and he'd been angry. She'd shouted that she hated him, and he'd told her to go away. That was her last memory of Charley.

She lay back on the pillow and turned her face to the side. "I guess," she agreed, suddenly too depressed to argue about it.

Her father, still holding her hand, took another deep breath. "Someone saw you race away from Charley's place on your motorcycle around 5:30 Sunday afternoon. The police want to question you."

"Question me? I can't tell them anything. I don't know anything." She wished everyone would go away and let her deal with Charley's death. "I didn't see anything."

Brian cleared his throat. "Mrs. Randolph, the police want to talk to you about your husband's murder because you're the prime suspect."

# Chapter Three

For two days Amanda lay in the uncomfortable hospital bed, eating the dubious food served in ugly dishes on cold stainless steel trays and wondering if this was similar to prison except they probably wouldn't give her pain meds in prison.

The police thought she killed Charley.

Okay, she had motive. And she'd threatened him a few times. A lot of times, to be precise. But how could anyone think she'd murder him? At one time she'd loved him.

Even now she had errant thoughts of how Charley, if he were still alive, would have come to visit her in the hospital, would have joked about her injuries and made her laugh. He'd have smuggled in pizza for her, brought her pastries from the little German bakery across town.

But when he wasn't bringing her treats, Charley would have been out drinking, gambling, chasing sleazy women and participating in any other activity, legal or illegal, that caught his fancy. She felt a little irreverent thinking those things about someone who was dead, but Charley's death hadn't turned him into a saint.

When she was finally released from the hospital, she didn't protest her father's suggestion that she stay at her parents' house for a few days. She still had a limp and ached all over, not quite ready to tackle motorcycle repairs. Dawson could handle the place on his own a few more days. Besides, the food would be excellent, much better than either the dismal hospital fare or the frozen dinners and peanut butter sandwiches she typically ate at home. Her mother employed housekeepers who were good cooks.

As they drove across Dallas, Amanda leaned back in the leather seat of her father's Mercedes and watched the familiar scenery slide past. She'd spent her entire life in this area...born, lived and attended school in Highland Park then college at SMU until she'd dropped out her junior year to ride a motorcycle cross country. She knew the best restaurants and the worst, went to the Texas State Fair every year, strolled the restored brick streets of Uptown. This was home. But now things seemed to have shifted ever so slightly, become strange and unknown.

Charley was dead. Her husband—still legally her husband, thanks to his stubborn refusal to become an "ex"—was dead. She was, technically, a widow.

Her lips curved into a faint smile at the thought of such a respectable term being applied to her. *The Widow Randolph.*

"Good to see you smile," her father said. "You'll be surprised at how fast you'll get through all this, put it in the past, and move on with your life."

"I want to change my name back to Caulfield," she said. Erase all traces of Charley.

"Easily done. Your mother will insist we wait a proper amount of time, of course, then we'll file a Request for Name Change, and you'll be Amanda Caulfield within the week."

"If I ever decide to get married again, I'm keeping my birth name." She considered that for a moment then amended, "If I ever decide to get married again, I'm going to have myself committed to a mental institution."

Her father laughed, a robust, hearty sound, and she found herself joining him. Charley was gone. Death, if not divorce, had parted them. She was free. It felt good.

≈∙≈

That evening at dinner her father sat at the head of the family dining room table with her mother at the other end, Jenny and "Davey" on one side, and Amanda on the other.

The oak table with seating for eight was her mother's idea of a cozy family table—as opposed to the rosewood version in the formal dining room that seated sixteen before the addition of leaves. Amanda had lived in this house all her life and had never found anything "cozy" in any of the fourteen—or maybe it was fifteen—rooms. Today was certainly no exception.

"Lucinda."

A young dark-haired girl in a uniform appeared immediately from the kitchen.

"My quiche is lukewarm. Could you please heat it for me?" Beverly Caulfield's gestures were slow and graceful, the silk fabric of her light green blouse flowing with her movements. She was slim and small-boned, her hair still brown, though Amanda suspected her hairdresser had a hand in that.

"Mine needs to be warmed too." Jenny leaned back so Lucinda could reach her plate. "Just a little bit. I don't like it so hot it burns my mouth, but just a little hotter would be good." She held thumb and forefinger a millimeter apart. "Just this much." She giggled and fluttered.

Her pale blue summer dress set off her delicate features perfectly. In appearance, she was a younger version of their mother, though Amanda couldn't imagine that their mother had ever fluttered or giggled.

Lucinda took Jenny's plate then looked at Emerson Caulfield whose quiche was already half-consumed. "I'm fine." He waved his fork.

"I'm good," Davey added.

"Me too." After the cardboard hospital food, Amanda relished every bite of her lukewarm quiche, savoring the rich cheese and egg flavors.

In stark contrast to the well-dressed members of her family, Amanda wore the faded jeans and T-shirt in which she'd tumbled down the mountain in Oklahoma. Her mother had sent a sedate, blatantly expensive dress of blue silk with matching heels to the hospital. Amanda refused to wear it.

Had the doctor given her mother the wrong baby? The only thing that kept that from being a certainty was the knowledge that her mother, had she had any doubts, would surely have returned her in the same way she returned clothes, shoes and purses upon finding any minute flaw—and Amanda's flaws were much larger than *minute*.

Lucinda returned with the quiches and set them in front of Beverly and Jenny.

"I've spoken to the funeral home and made arrangements for Charley's funeral just as soon as they release the body," Beverly said. "I suppose we can use one of the family plots for him. He's still family." She gave a faint shudder, visible in the rippling silk of her sleeves, then took a bite of her quiche. "This is much better, Lucinda." Thus she disposed of Charley's body and the warmed quiche, events of equal importance, in one fell swoop.

"I don't know what you've got planned," Amanda said, "but Charley would have hated an elaborate event with flowers and organ music and his body crammed into some suit he'd never have worn in life."

Silence. Her comments often had that effect at family gatherings.

"The civilities must be observed," her mother stated in a tone that allowed no argument.

That tone never stopped Amanda. She toyed with her salad, flipping a slice of cucumber to the side of the plate. "Charley wanted to be cremated." He'd never actually said that, but he might have if he'd ever considered the possibility of dying. "He wanted to be cremated then have his ashes tossed into..." A bar? A sleazy motel room? "Into the air. From a plane. So he can fly."

More silence.

She glanced at her dad.

He met her gaze briefly, and in that instant she knew that he knew, but he also understood. "Then that's what we'll do," he said with finality.

"Emerson!" Beverly exclaimed.

"Daddy!" Jenny added her disapproval.

"Would you pass the bread, Beverly?"

Judge Caulfield had ruled in her favor...this time.

That evening Amanda settled into the room where she'd grown up. It was cool and dark, the heavy curtains trapping the coolness inside and keeping the heat out. Those curtains also kept out the moonlight and the night sounds and any contact with the outside world. Amanda threw them open and lifted the window then drew in a deep breath of the night air. She'd have to remember to close it in the morning or listen to a speech from her mother about the ills of dust and heat and insects.

She took her cell phone from her purse. Time for her daily check-in call with Dawson.

"Everything's fine," he assured her. "We got a Honda Gold Wing in for some big time repairs. Looks like it got in a fight with a semi and lost. And I got another custom paint job." He spoke the last sentence with pride.

As a part-time college student studying art and computer technology, Dawson Page had seemed an unlikely candidate when he'd applied for the job as her assistant. But he did own a motorcycle and had made minor repairs to his own bike, plus he was the only applicant with no missing teeth and no tobacco tin in his back pocket. She'd hired him, and he'd immediately become invaluable.

23

"If I take off a couple more days, are you going to be able to handle it and keep up with your classes?"

"Of course. You don't have that much business. I mean..."

Dawson was blushing. Amanda didn't have to see him to know that, and the thought made her smile. She rather liked his tendency to say whatever popped into his mind. No filter between brain and mouth. Complete honesty.

"It's okay," she assured him. "I know what you meant."

"Take all the time you need. I've got everything here under control."

"Great. You know where to reach me if you need me."

"One thing, Amanda. Some guy called for you, and when I told him you weren't here, he wanted to know when you'd be back."

"Oh? Well, if he calls again, give him my cell number."

"I'm not sure that would be a good idea. He blocked his number so I couldn't see who was calling. I didn't like the sound of his voice. I think he might be one of Charley's...um...acquaintances."

Even dead, Charley continued to cause problems. "You're right. Don't give him my cell phone number."

She disconnected the call and lay back with a sigh. Was she never going to be completely rid of Charley? The cops thought she killed him, and somebody, probably somebody he'd conned, was looking for her.

Who knew those two little words, "I do," would lead to so many nightmares?

She slipped into an old T-shirt, settled into bed and was drifting off to sleep when a voice woke her with a start.

*He tried to kill you. He'll try again. You're in danger.*

24

She sat up, wide awake, heart pounding, peering around the room for the speaker.

*Oh, for goodness sake!* she chastised herself, lying back down. *Nobody's here. Nobody spoke. It was all in my mind, just like the first time. Charley didn't say that. And the stranger who called the shop was just somebody trying to get his money back from me now that Charley's dead.*

But she got up and closed her bedroom window.

సారా

Three days in the house where she grew up. Three days of eating good food, relaxing in air-conditioned comfort, sleeping on a plush mattress, and letting her body heal. Three days of listening to her mother and Jenny. Amanda was ready to run away from home.

When she proclaimed herself completely healed, her father set up her interview with the police for the following day. The thought of being grilled by the cops felt infinitely preferable to being criticized by her mother for everything from her hair style to her unpolished toenails.

The next day she prepared for her visit with the cops by putting on the dress and heels her mother had sent to the hospital, taming her red curls with a lot of hair goo and even applying on makeup. When she emerged from her bedroom, her mother smiled.

"You look so pretty. You should wear a dress and do your makeup more often. Why don't you and Jenny and I go shopping tomorrow?"

It was, Amanda thought, a nice gesture. Controlling, but nice. "Thanks, Mom, but I have a lot to do at the shop. Dawson needs a day off." And she needed to find out what the mysterious stranger wanted, the man who'd called anonymously a second time to check on her whereabouts. If it was somebody expecting to get back money Charley had taken from him, she'd tell him where he could go to find that money. "Are we ready, Dad?"

"Brian should be here any minute."

Brian. Her attorney. *You have the right to remain silent, you have the right to an attorney…*

Brian arrived, and the three of them drove to the police station. Her father spoke to the receptionist, and they were led immediately to a room which was spectacularly mundane, nothing to suggest an appropriate place for the discussion of murder. The large rectangular space contained a rectangular table and five wooden chairs that echoed the rectangular theme.

Based on her knowledge of police stations—such knowledge gathered entirely from television crime shows—Amanda assumed the mirrored wall was a one-way mirror through which various detectives would be watching the interrogation, looking for signs of guilt. The room smelled of old wood and stale sweat and gave her the creeps in spite of its ordinary composition.

Amanda fell into one of the scarred wooden chairs with her father on one side and her lawyer on the other. Protected. Surrounded by her own personal warriors.

In spite of all that, while sitting in the creepy rectangular room she had an uneasy feeling, as if she were hanging over the side of a cliff with a brutish cop stepping on her fingertips.

*Ridiculous,* she chided herself. This wasn't a television crime show with *good cop, bad cop* characters trying to bully an innocent person into confessing to something she hadn't done. This was real life where the cops only wanted to ferret out the facts, discover the truth, find out what really happened.

The door opened, slammed back against the wall, and the bad cop strode inside.

# Chapter Four

Amanda flinched.

So did the man who stood in the doorway. "Sorry," he said. "Guess somebody finally oiled those hinges."

So maybe he wasn't the bad cop. All Amanda's knowledge of good cops/bad cops also came from TV crime shows, but she was pretty sure bad cops didn't apologize for slamming a door.

This guy didn't look evil either. He was tall, wore a rumpled shirt with a button missing, no tie and gray slacks that had seen better days. His brown hair was tousled and several days overdue for a visit to the barber. He was a few hours overdue for a shave too. She probably would have liked the man had they met under different circumstances. But these were the only circumstances they had, and she was fairly certain this cop wasn't her friend.

As if to negate his apology, he strode forcefully into the room, slapped a file folder on the table, then sat down across from Amanda.

"Detective Jake Daggett," he said, his words clipped and no-nonsense.

"Amanda Randolph." Brian nodded in her direction. "Her father, Judge Caulfield, and I'm her attorney, Brian Edwards."

The detective nodded, pushed a hand through his already mussed hair and opened his folder. "Mrs. Randolph, sorry about your loss."

For an instant, Amanda thought he was commiserating with her on the loss of her motorcycle, and for that instant, she liked the man, almost smiled at him.

Then he continued, "You were in the middle of a divorce, right?"

Charley. Of course. That's who they were here to talk about.

"We—" Amanda started to reply, but Brian cut her off.

"That is correct."

Detective Daggett did not seem to find this act of ventriloquism unusual. "You went to his apartment on the day of his death?"

"I advise you not to answer that," Brian said.

Daggett sighed and leaned back. "You went to his apartment on the day of his death." This time it was a statement, not a question. "The neighbors identified you. A lot of neighbors. They'd seen you there before. A lot of times."

"They were going through a divorce," Brian said. "Communication was necessary."

Amanda met the detective's gaze and shrugged. She didn't see any point in denying what was blatantly true. Judging from what she'd seen, most of Charley's neighbors were as gainfully unemployed as he and as soon as she appeared outside his door, sidled from their apartments, making no attempt to hide their interest in whatever she and Charley said. Cheap entertainment. They probably didn't have cable.

"Loud communication," Daggett emphasized. "The neighbors said the two of you fought a lot, and you had a doozy on the day of Mr. Randolph's death. What were you fighting about that day?"

"I advise you not to answer," Brian said.

She glanced at her lawyer. His usually benign, boyish features were set in concrete. This was serious business. She could be going down for murder.

"I didn't kill Charley!" she blurted.

Amanda's father patted her hand. "Nobody's saying you did, sweetheart."

Daggett lifted an eyebrow. "Somebody killed him. Any idea who?"

Amanda's head jerked in Brian's direction as if she expected him to protest her answering the question. He remained silent.

"Charley had a lot of enemies. He was always scamming somebody," she said.

"For instance?"

Amanda threw up her hands. "You think he shared that information with me? Charley and I haven't exactly been close lately, and even when we lived together, it's not like he brought these people home to dinner and introduced me."

"Any information you can give us would be appreciated."

"I wouldn't count on it. For instance, Jack Scott. A few months before I left Charley, this guy came to the door in the middle of the night. Charley went outside to talk to him. I could hear enough to know they were arguing about money. Most of the time, it was my money Charley was throwing around, so I went out to join them. Introduced myself. Charley said the man's name was Jack Scott."

Daggett scribbled in his notebook.

"Same man was there a couple of weeks later. Charley introduced him as Ben Parker."

Daggett paused in his writing and looked up.

"I asked the man if he had a twin named Jack Scott. He didn't answer. Most of Charley's acquaintances had no sense of humor."

Daggett sighed and leaned back in his chair. "Okay, I get the picture, but we're going to need every name you can give us, whether it's a real name or not, descriptions of anybody you met, anything you know about Charley's business activities, legal or illegal. When you say *scams*, can you be more specific?"

Amanda slid her gaze toward her father. He'd worked so hard for so long to hide Charley's activities from the world, but today he gave her a slight nod.

So it was okay to have a member of the family involved in nefarious activities if that member was dead.

She exhaled in a long sigh and prepared to trash Charley. Somehow this didn't feel as good as when she'd complained to friends, telling them in graphic detail about the outrageous things Charley had done.

"Nothing huge," she said. "Nothing you'd ever hear about on the ten o'clock news. But Charley had a certain charisma along with the ability to get into people's heads and figure out their dream then offer that dream to them." She was only too familiar with that aspect of his personality.

"Go on."

"He'd meet somebody in a bar and next thing you know, Charley has a new best friend. The two of them are going to buy a boat and go to Alaska fishing for King Crab or travel to South America where Charley, a renowned archeologist, has discovered ancient Mayan treasure. The friend, of course, would make a financial investment in the non-existent boat or the rights to the Mayan treasure or whatever happened to be the victim's dream."

"I see."

"Sometimes I think Charley actually believed he was going to do these grandiose things. He was very convincing."

She'd believed him when she first met him, throughout their two-month whirlwind courtship and even for a couple of weeks after their marriage. She'd wanted to believe. Her parents had hated Charley immediately, so that had gone a long way toward validating him and ensuring that she'd marry him.

30

The motorcycle repair shop he'd promised to help her open had happened, though the "partnership" element had never materialized. He hadn't produced the financial backing or the clientele, but, to give the devil his due, he had helped her find the courage to do it, to quit her latest default job as a real estate agent.

Daggett's left eyebrow lifted again. "So," he said, "the deceased was a small-time con artist. Did he have a day job?"

*A small-time con artist.* "Yes, he was a con artist who never made the big-time," Amanda admitted. "And no, he didn't have a day job. He worked at being a con artist twenty-four seven. He was dedicated to his career."

The detective made a few notes then directed his stern gaze to her. Apparently there wasn't going to be a *good cop.* "Was Charley involved with another woman?"

Amanda stiffened, but waved a hand as if the matter was of no import, was not totally humiliating. "*Women,* not *woman.* Yes, Charley's charm and lack of morals extended to other women."

"Can you give us names?"

"We were never formally introduced."

Daggett's lips almost curved into a wry smile, but he caught it just in time. Yeah, she might like him under different conditions. "Did you catch him with another woman?"

"He came home smelling like cheap perfume and wearing his shorts backward. If we went out together, women would come over and flirt with him. A couple of them called to ask me to let him go. One even came by our home. I felt kind of sorry for her. She stood at the door and cried and begged me to let her see Charley. I told her I'd toss his sorry ass out and let her have him but he wasn't home. He wasn't home a lot."

"Were you jealous of these women?"

31

"Of course." The first time, she'd been insanely jealous, but after that initial betrayal, she'd simply hated—the women, Charley and herself.

"So you've had personal contact with some of these women, but you don't know their names."

Amanda shrugged. "I can give you first names and descriptions. None of them were around for more than a few days. Charley wasn't into long-term relationships." *Except with her. She was the one who wanted to get away from him, and he didn't want to let her go. Typical Charley.*

Daggett blew out a long sigh and rubbed his square, stubbly jaw. "You know, you're not being very helpful. It's in your best interest to give me another suspect."

Amanda opened her mouth to protest, but Brian interrupted her. "May I remind you that our presence here is on a voluntary basis? If you've finished questioning my client, we'll leave now."

The cop scowled at Brian then forced a pseudo-smile. "I appreciate your coming in," he said, his voice dripping with honeyed sarcasm. "And while I don't want to be a nuisance, I do have a couple more questions, if you don't mind."

Brian gave a curt nod.

"What did you and the deceased fight about the day he was murdered?"

"I advise you not to answer that."

Daggett dropped his pen on the table and looked frustrated. "We've already taken statements from the neighbors. It's not exactly a secret that Mr. and Mrs. Randolph were arguing about their divorce. I'd just like to get a few details so we can find out what happened in that apartment on the day of the murder."

Amanda didn't want to discuss her problems, but she didn't want to look guilty either. She'd already admitted most of the sordid details. What difference did a few more make?

She clenched her hands in her lap and ignored her attorney. "That morning we had another court date for the divorce. I thought it was finally going to happen, and I planned a motorcycle trip out of town as a celebration. But his freaking lawyer got another freaking continuance. I decided to take the trip anyway, even though there was nothing to celebrate. Then Charley called and said he needed me to bring him the gun."

Daggett's eyes widened slightly. "*The gun*?" he repeated.

"Amanda, I advise you not to say anything else," Brian said, his tone adamant.

Amanda looked at him and shook her head. "This is all going to come out. I'm not going to say anything that will make me look guilty because there isn't anything that could."

Brian and her father exchanged worried glances.

Amanda rolled her eyes then turned her attention back to Daggett. "Charley gave me a gun when we got married. Said it was for my protection. I thought that was a little strange at the time, but it made sense when I realized what he did for a living."

"And he wanted you to bring this gun to him?"

"Yeah. Said he'd sign the divorce papers if I'd bring him the gun. I didn't believe him. I figured he just wanted to sell it. He persisted." She frowned. "He sounded funny, kind of tense, stressed. I could tell he really, really wanted that gun, and I thought maybe, if he wanted it badly enough, just *maybe* he might sign those papers. So I went to his apartment."

"You told him you were bringing him a gun?"

"Yes."

"But you didn't?"

"No way. If he'd signed those papers, I would have taken it to him. But I know better than to give him what he wants and expect that he's going to give me what he promised."

"So you went to his place without the gun?"

"Yes. My bike was already packed for the trip, so I rode over to his place. He opened the door a crack and asked me if I had the gun. I told him he had to give me the signed papers first. He freaked out, started yelling at me, and I started yelling at him. I tried to get inside so we could yell at each other in private. He blocked me, and that made me really mad."

"He wouldn't let you come in? Did he have company? Somebody he didn't want you to see? A girlfriend?"

"Possible. But usually when I catch him red-handed, he gets..." She spread her hands, searching for the right word. "He turns into Super-Conman. Ultra slick. Really lays on the charm."

"He didn't do that this time?"

"No, he just kept shouting at me to go home and get the gun, and he was adamant that he wasn't going to let me into his apartment. Naturally I kept trying to get in."

"You thought he was hiding something in his apartment?"

"He didn't want me inside his apartment so I was determined to get in."

"You threatened him."

"I advise—"

Amanda interrupted her attorney's admonition. "Brian, there's no point in my denying it. Yes, I threatened him. I'm sure all the nosy neighbors heard me, that time and a hundred other times. I threatened him on a regular basis. But I never actually threatened to kill him. It was always something like pouring hot wax in his ear while he slept or drilling a hole through his forehead, inserting a peg and hanging a potted plant from it, stuff like that."

Daggett grimaced. "And you don't think those things would have killed him?"

"Obviously I didn't do any of them. They were just fantasies." That probably didn't sound right. "Anyway, I never threatened to shoot him. That's far too quick and easy, not enough suffering."

Her father cleared his throat. Amanda refused to look at him. She didn't have to. She could envision his reproving expression.

"So after you threatened Charley, he let you into his apartment?"

Amanda shifted on the hard, wooden chair. "Sort of. I stomped on his foot with my motorcycle boot, and when he bent down, I shoved past him."

Daggett flinched as if he could feel Charley's pain. "When you were inside his apartment, did you see anything unusual?"

"Greasy pizza boxes, dead French fries, empty beer cans, dirty socks. The usual."

"What happened after you got inside?"

"Nothing. We yelled at each other some more. He was obsessed with that stupid gun, and I was obsessed with getting him to sign the divorce papers. I finally gave up and left."

"This gun Charley gave you, was it a .38 revolver?" Daggett asked.

Amanda sucked in a quick breath. It was not a good sign that the cops knew about Charley's gun. "Yes."

"Would you be willing to bring your gun in for us to test fire so we can eliminate a possible match to the bullet that killed your husband?"

"No," Brian said.

"Yes," Amanda said. They knew about the gun, and she knew it hadn't been used to kill anyone, was still in a

35

box in her apartment. Giving it to the cops would be the fastest way to get past that issue.

"Good." Daggett shuffled his notes. "What time did you last see Charley?"

"About five-thirty. I left his apartment, got on my bike and rode away. I didn't look back because I knew he'd be standing in his doorway, watching me." She shivered. "He always did that, went to the door and stood there and watched me, trying to look pitiful and make me feel bad. I'm sure one of those neighbors saw him after I left."

Daggett shook his head. "The neighbors say you ran out of the apartment, slammed the door, raced down the stairs and rode away as if the devil was chasing you, but Charley never opened the door or came out."

"Oh." Amanda bit back a brief, unexpected feeling of rejection. It was a good thing if he didn't come to the door and look longingly after her. No reason to feel rejected. "Okay, but what about the gunshot? Surely all those people who were fascinated with our fights would have heard a loud gunshot if I blew him away while I was there."

Daggett shook his head again. "Sofa cushion. Homemade silencer. Nobody heard the shot. Nobody saw Charley after you went inside his apartment."

Amanda bit her lip. Apparently her father and Brian hadn't been overreacting when they'd insisted on accompanying her or when they'd warned her to say nothing. This was starting to get scary. They might really arrest her. Put her in jail.

"Who found Charley?" she asked.

"One of the neighbors. Said he went over to borrow a cup of sugar."

Amanda snorted. "More like a can of beer or a baggie of marijuana."

Daggett lifted an eyebrow. "When Charley didn't answer the neighbor's knock, he tried the door. Said Charley often left it unlocked. It opened, and the neighbor walked in to see Charley's body. He went home and called us."

"I wonder if he got his *cup of sugar* first."

Daggett looked down at his notes but not before she saw the edges of his lips twitching upward. He'd like to smile, she thought, but he wasn't going to let her catch him at it.

"We'd really appreciate it if you'd bring in the gun and a list of anybody Charley had dealings with." He lifted his gaze to hers, his stern look restored. "Victims of scams, rejected girlfriends, buddies, anybody."

"I'll bring in my gun, you can compare it to bullet that killed Charley, and when it doesn't match, we'll be done, right?" Amanda moved to the edge of her chair, ready to rise, ready for this to be over.

The detective leaned back, ready to continue.

"How did you get along with Charley's family?"

That was an easy question. "Charley didn't have any family. He and his younger brothers were orphaned when Charley was ten, then his brother drowned a year later." There was, she thought, no need to go into the horrible details. None of Charley's life story was pertinent to the present situation.

The silence in the room reminded her of the silences she typically caused at family gatherings. It would seem she had expanded her silencing ability to police interviews.

Amanda stole a glance at her father. He was looking at his knees. That wasn't a good sign.

Brian appeared to be as puzzled as she at the reactions to her uncomplicated answer.

"Both your husband's parents are very much alive," the detective finally said, "as well as two brothers, three sisters, several aunts and uncles, nieces and nephews and too many cousins to count. Half the population of Silver Creek, Texas, is related to your deceased husband."

# Chapter Five

The walls of the room seemed to move closer, making it harder to breathe. Silence whirled around her, trapping the words inside her head where they bounced from one side to the other and back again, echoing over and over.

*"Both your husband's parents are very much alive, as well as two brothers, three sisters, several aunts and uncles, nieces and nephews and too many cousins to count. Half the population of Silver Creek, Texas, is related to your deceased husband."*

Her oft-repeated assertion that every word out of Charley's mouth had been a lie took on a new depth of meaning.

Charley had a family, a large family. She had in-laws she'd never met, never even known existed.

Charley had claimed to be an orphan from Waco, not Silver Creek, had told her in graphic detail how his father, a twice-convicted drug-dealer, had been shot by an aggrieved husband when he'd caught Charley's father with his wife in a local motel the night Charley was born. Then when he was ten, his mother, a prostitute, died in his arms of a drug overdose.

If his parents had any relatives, none stepped forward to claim Charley or his five-year old brother, Grady. Both had been sent to foster homes. Before a year was out, Grady drowned in the Brazos River, though Charley had taught him to be a strong swimmer. The couple had later been charged with physical abuse by another foster child, and Charley felt sure they killed his brother. As for Charley's experience, he lived in five different foster homes where he'd been used and abused and discarded, finally running away to Dallas when he was sixteen.

Amanda had cut him a lot of slack, excused much of his bad behavior, because of his troubled childhood.

All those lies had tipped the scales in her decision to marry him. When she'd been indecisive, he declaimed sadly that he didn't blame her for not wanting to marry someone who was the son of an adulterer and a prostitute, someone who'd never been a part of a family and would likely be a poor excuse for a husband and father.

She'd protested that her own family, while intact, was certainly no model for a '50s TV series, and to prove she didn't hold his unfortunate circumstances against him, she had, of course, agreed to marry him.

Lies, lies and more lies.

He'd manipulated her as surely as he'd manipulated all his other victims.

If he weren't already dead, she'd kill him. Rip his lying tongue out of his filthy mouth, cut off his arms and legs with a chain saw then shove his body in a wood chipper set on *slow.*

She glanced across the room to her father. He met her gaze briefly but couldn't maintain eye contact. Charley had a family, and her father had known it before today. A long time before today, she'd guess from his reluctance to face her.

Detective Jerk, on the other hand, was studying her intently. "You're saying you didn't know anything about your husband's family? He never took you home to meet his parents? No holiday dinners with the in-laws?"

Amanda glared at him. She'd just realized the enormity of her husband's deception, been confronted with the probability of her father's, and this creep wanted to twist the knife. She drew in a deep breath and leaned forward, returning the detective's gaze defiantly. "What part of *con artist* do you not understand? Charley conned me just like he conned everybody else."

"He married you."

"Con artists don't marry their victims? Give me a break. You hear about that on the news every day."

"When the victim is wealthy. You're not. Your parents are, but they're both in good health. You won't be inheriting money for a long time, and you've never made a lot at any of your short-lived jobs."

Amanda narrowed her gaze. "Thank you for pointing that out."

"So," the rude detective continued, "if it was all a scam, what was the scam? What did Charley Randolph expect to gain from marrying you?"

Amanda was pretty sure she knew the answer to that one, but she wasn't about to admit it to this creep. He seemed to know everything about her. He probably already knew the answer to that question.

How many times had her father bailed Charley out of trouble, used his influence to get the charges dropped or provided a lawyer who could keep Charley out of jail?

For a long time—maybe until this very minute when so many truths had been shoved in her face—she had believed that, in his own selfish way, Charley had loved her...that amidst all the deceit, that one element had been genuine.

He'd admitted that he lied when they met, when he came into the real estate office where she worked and said he wanted to buy a house. He had no money to rent a house, much less buy one. His excuse had been that he saw her entering the building and fell in love at first sight. He'd told "a little white lie" in order to meet her. Weeks later when she mentioned her father was a judge, he'd seemed surprised.

Had that been a lie too?

Had he pursued her because her father was a judge and could get him out of trouble?

"Mrs. Randolph?"

She rose from the wooden chair. "Apparently, Detective Daggett, you know more than I do about my ex-husband. Since I can tell you nothing else, I assume we're finished and I can go home."

"*Ex-husband*? Your divorce wasn't final, Mrs. Randolph."

"He's dead. I think that's about as *ex* as it can get."

The cop gave her a tight smile. "Go home. But don't plan any long trips."

She returned the pseudo-smile. "I'll send you a copy of my itinerary."

Brian took one arm and her father the other as they hustled her out of the interrogation room. She let them. She wanted to get out of there. She'd had enough of answering questions. She wanted to get her father alone and interrogate him. She wanted answers instead of questions. She doubted those answers would be anything she wanted to hear, but she needed to know the truth. There'd been little enough of that since she married Charley Randolph.

৵৵

That evening Amanda settled into her father's car for the drive home to her apartment. Finally she would have a chance to talk to him alone.

He backed out of the garage into the spring evening.

The neighborhood had a rich aura, cool and shady and prosperous. Mature trees lined both sides of the street, and the low sunlight touched the leaves, spinning the greens from light to dark as they fluttered in the gentle breeze. Though she couldn't hear birds from inside the well-insulated car, she knew the lilting songs of the robins and cardinals, the raucous summer calls of the blue jays and the ever-changing chorus of the mockingbirds.

The drive from her parents' house in Highland Park to her place off Harry Hines Boulevard was only a few miles, but the distance was more than spatial—it was a

42

journey from the upper crust to the lower, to an area where Amanda could operate her motorcycle shop, live above it and have relatively low mortgage payments.

"It's going to be all right," her father said, turning the corner and heading away from the quiet, tree-lined street. "The only evidence they have against you is circumstantial."

Amanda studied his profile, the strong nose, stubborn jaw and clear brown eyes. He had always been her hero, her best friend and her opponent. Her inheritance of his independence and his obstinacy guaranteed the two of them would butt heads, but he'd never lied to her. At the moment, however, he seemed to be making an effort to divert her from asking for the truth, from forcing him to either admit to something awful or to lie to her.

He wouldn't lie.

She couldn't believe he'd lie.

But he could refuse to tell her.

"How long have you known about Charley's family?"

For a couple of blocks they rode in silence.

Eventually, her father did not disappoint her. "I ran a complete background check on him as soon as you said you were thinking about marrying him."

"Why didn't you tell me?"

Another long silence. "Charley didn't want you to know."

Amanda's head snapped in her father's direction. "You hated Charley! Why would it matter what he wanted?"

Emerson slid smoothly into the traffic on I-35E. "Mandy, Charley is dead. Soon the police will find who killed him, or at least be certain you didn't, and everything—your marriage, the things he did—it will all be over. Charley is dead, and you need to put it behind you and get on with your life."

Amanda shook her head and laughed, angry and amused at the same time. "Stop that slippery lawyer talk! You know better than to think I'm going to let this go until you give me a straight answer."

Emerson's lips lifted in a faint smile. "You are definitely your father's daughter. You'd have made a good lawyer, you know." For a moment, his eyes gazed into the distance...to the possibilities for her life she'd thrown away? He gave a resigned sigh. "So what do you want to know about Charley's family? They're small town, hard-working but uneducated. Blue collar. Maybe he was ashamed of them. Charley always pretended to be somebody he wasn't."

"That's nuts. He'd make up a story about a drug dealer and a prostitute mother to cover the fact that his parents were blue collar? I don't think so. I think he'd have hidden his family no matter who they were. Charley was always pretending, always lying about who he was. Maybe he had to disconnect from everything and everybody real in his life so he could live the fiction he created."

"That's possible." Emerson pulled off the freeway, gaze focused on the road ahead. "Perhaps in order to become the persona or personas he became, he needed to block out the truth even from himself."

"Could be. I don't suppose we'll ever know the answer to that question, but that still leaves my original question which *can* be answered. Why didn't you tell me about Charley's family, my in-laws? They were my family too."

"I'm your family. Your mother, your sister and I. We're your family. If Charley chose not to share his family with you, that was his decision."

"Damn it, Dad, you're doing that lawyer thing again!"

Emerson turned down the driveway beside the large building that housed her shop, Amanda's Motorcycles and More. He pulled close to the outside staircase leading up to her apartment and stopped.

"You're my daughter. I'm your father. I love you beyond all reason, and my number one priority has always been your happiness, yours and your sister's. But I don't worry about Jenny like I do about you. She's easier. Her life flows smoothly along her pathways, no speed bumps. You came into the world screaming and waving your clenched fists, and you've been fighting ever since." He touched her cheek with the back of one hand. "You refuse to take advice. You refuse to learn from the experience of others. You're stubborn and willful and determined to make your own mistakes, and because I love you, I try to stop you. Maybe my advice isn't always right, but it isn't always wrong, and always my intentions are to spare you pain and make you happy."

Amanda gave a frustrated sigh. "You're not going to answer my question, are you?"

Her father leaned across the console and kissed her cheek. "I love you, Mandy." He opened his door and started to get out of the car.

Amanda placed a hand on his arm. "If you can't be honest with me, you can't walk me upstairs."

Emerson nodded gravely. "Very well. I'll wait here and watch until you get inside."

Amanda got out of the car. Her father could be very stubborn.

But so could her father's daughter.

She climbed the rickety wooden stairs of the old two story red brick building that housed her shop on the ground floor and her apartment on the second. When she reached the landing, she turned to wave to her father.

He waved back but showed no signs of leaving. Irritated as she was with him, she couldn't stop a slight smile at his protectiveness. Whatever his reason for withholding information about Charley's family, it probably sprang from some absurd notion of protecting her. She couldn't be truly angry with someone who loved her that much.

She grasped the door knob and inserted her key in the deadbolt. The door was unlocked. Had she been so upset she'd forgotten to lock it the day she left for that insane ride to Charley's?

No, she distinctly remembered locking it then testing to be sure since she planned to leave town.

Dawson had a spare key. Could he have come up for some reason then forgotten to lock when he left?

Not likely. Dawson was OCD to the *nth* degree. When he closed up the shop downstairs, he always checked the door, sometimes two or three times. If he'd gone into her apartment, he'd have locked, checked, relocked and rechecked.

Why was her door unlocked?

*He tried to kill you. He'll try again. You're in danger.*

Oh, for crying out loud! Why did she keep remembering that stupid warning from a pain-induced hallucination?

She turned the knob forcibly and shoved the door open so hard, it slammed back against the wall.

The place was dark, all the blinds down. That was creepy. The living room had great windows, and since this was the only two-story house on the block, she always kept the blinds open.

She licked her dry lips and told herself to stop being silly. Dawson could have closed up if he'd been in there. He preferred a cave atmosphere to a glass house. The two of them alternately and obsessively opened and closed the blinds over the small windows in the shop downstairs.

That had to be it. Dawson checked on her apartment and closed the blinds then inexplicably forgot to lock the door. Even Dawson couldn't be one hundred percent OCD.

She took a step inside, flicked on the light switch, heard her father's car drive away, and suddenly had to fight a rising, irrational panic at the thought of being alone.

She straightened her spine, closed the door behind her and turned the lock. She'd never been frightened to be alone, and she wasn't going to start now.

She was home. Home was a good place to be. She liked her home.

Immediately upon moving in, she'd freed the hardwood flooring from the sculptured green carpet that had protected it through the decades. Coffee table, lamp tables and a large bookcase—garage sale treasures of different wooden hues and textures—gave the place an air of genteel antiquity. Her sofa blazed with brilliant bursts of red, purple, yellow and green, adding a bright, eclectic note to the room.

Her home would never appear in Better Homes and Gardens, but the effect pleased her.

Tonight the familiar aura of comfort eluded her. Something didn't feel right even though nothing was wrong. Nothing was out of place.

Except the unlocked door and those blinds.

*Get over it!* she ordered herself. *Check the closets and under the bed then have a glass of wine and relax.*

Tomorrow she'd open the blinds again. Not tonight. Not because she was frightened of what she might see outside. There was no reason to open them tonight when it was dark out there.

She strode determinedly into the large kitchen with its white-painted cabinets and her old-fashioned enamel-topped table. Everything seemed in order there, except again the blinds were closed.

Had to be Dawson.

47

She took one of her mismatched crystal stem glasses from the cabinet, retrieved an open bottle of white wine from the refrigerator and poured a generous serving.

She started back to the living room but paused to slide a carving knife from the wooden block. Not that she was nervous, but, hey, you never knew when you might need to carve a roast.

This wasn't the best neighborhood in the city, but she'd never been frightened in the two years she'd lived there.

One night a couple of months ago two men had come to the door looking for Charley. They'd wakened her at one o'clock a.m. after she'd battled insomnia until midnight. When she told them Charley no longer lived there, they became belligerent. Rather than scaring her, they'd aroused her anger.

She'd grabbed the hammer she'd been using to hang a picture. Brandishing it above her head while shouting her opinion of rude people running around in the middle of the night disturbing women trying to sleep, she chased them down the stairs, into their car, and halfway around the block before she came to her senses and went back to bed.

She wasn't usually skittish.

Tonight something felt strange. Not scary, just wrong.

Good grief. One little tumble down a mountain and she lost her nerve.

She marched into the bedroom, flipped on the light and looked around.

No one there.

Of course not.

Maybe the head injury had scrambled her brains and made her paranoid.

She set her wine on the dresser, went over to the closet and yanked open the door, half-expecting to see a felon crouching inside.

Have to be a skinny midget felon, considering the crush of clothes and boxes in the small closet.

As long as she was in the vicinity of all those boxes, she might as well find that gun that damned Detective Daggett was so hot for. And once she found it, she could keep it on a night stand next to the knife. Surely this uneasy feeling would vanish when she was thus well-armed. She could even find the hammer that had put the fear of God and Woman in those rude men who'd wakened her in the middle of the night.

She tossed the knife onto the brightly colored quilt on her bed then dragged one of the cardboard boxes from the closet and frowned. Granted, she didn't pay much attention to the storage boxes, but she would have sworn the top box had been a computer paper carton containing sweaters instead of a sturdy liquor box marked *Christmas decorations*.

Prickles darted up her spine.

Some of the clothes Charley had left behind were in the middle of the rack rather than shoved to one side.

Her heart rate went up a notch.

She hauled out more boxes until she reached the one in the back of the closet...the one she knew contained the gun Charley gave her...and dumped the contents on the floor. A chipped crystal paperweight, some old CDs, a worn wallet, a tangle of ear buds and miscellaneous wires, USB ports, adaptors, a wide variety of paraphernalia, but no gun.

She was mistaken about which box she'd put it in.

No. The striped kitchen towel in which she'd wrapped it lay among the odds and ends.

"I know who took it."

Amanda shrieked and shot to her feet, heart pounding loudly in her ears, wishing she'd found the gun and a few bullets or at least hadn't tossed aside the kitchen knife.

For an instant, her brain refused to register what her eyes saw.

Charley stood on the far side of the room.

# Chapter Six

Amanda's immediate reaction was annoyance. Charley had managed to get into her apartment after she'd changed the locks.

But Charley was…dead.

*The accident. Head injury. Hallucinations.*

Amanda closed her eyes firmly then opened them again.

He was still there.

"Yeah, it's really me," he said.

He didn't sound dead. His voice was normal, a bit less arrogant than usual, but definitely not sepulchral.

She turned away and began tossing things back into the box. If she was going to have hallucinations, why couldn't it be George Clooney or an anonymous knight in shining armor? Even the Easter Bunny or Santa Claus would be preferable to Charley.

"It's no good ignoring me, Amanda," he said. "I'm not going anywhere. I can't."

Amanda tossed the last of the items into the box and closed it. But she couldn't put it back in the closet. Charley stood between her and the closet door.

"Damn it!" She dumped the contents of the box back on the floor then stood and confronted her hallucination. "Go away! Get out of my head! You're dead, and my mother's making plans to bury you!"

Charley's lips quirked in a grin she once found appealing. "That's just like your mother. I'll bet she wants to put me in one of those *nice navy blue suits* she's always going on about."

"Don't worry. I told her you wanted to be cremated, so I'm going to have you shoved—buck naked—into a blast furnace and reduced to ashes." Amanda lifted her hands to her face. "Omigawd! I'm talking to my hallucination!"

"Hallucination?" Charley looked shocked. "I'm not a hallucination. I'm your husband."

"No, you're not! You're dead. That ended the marriage deal."

"I might be dead, but I'm still right here, and you're still my wife."

She'd heard those last words way too many times. Suddenly everything seemed all too real. Somehow Charley had managed to cheat death. Not surprising. He'd cheated everybody else.

"Damn you, Charley Randolph! What kind of scam are you running now? Do you realize I'm being accused of killing you? And right now, that sounds like a damned good idea. Did you break in here? Did you take my gun? You did, didn't you? I wouldn't bring it to you, so you stole it. This time you've gone too far!" She reached for his collar, intending to choke him, but only until he turned blue.

Her fingers closed on air.

She looked at her hand then at Charley and frowned. "How did you do that? What kind of con are you up to now?"

"Okay, it's true. I'm dead. Sort of." His grin widened. "Depends on your definition of *dead*."

Amanda backed away. "Stop that! This is not the time for your tricks, and I'm the wrong person to try them on. I know you way too well."

"No tricks. Check this out." Charley disappeared into the wall then appeared again, smiling and spreading his arms. "Ta da!"

Amanda swung at his shoulder. Her fist slammed hard against the wall.

"Ouch! Damn you, damn you, damn you!" She rubbed her bruised knuckles. Slight-of-hand magic was one of Charley's specialties, but never anything fancy. *Pick a card. Look at this quarter I found behind your ear. Watch me get out of these handcuffs.* Nothing of the David Copperfield variety…until now. What was he up to? And how was he doing it?

A tiny wisp of suspicion niggled at the edges of her mind, a suspicion too absurd to be considered.

"Sweetheart, you need to sit down so we can talk," he said in his *I can explain the perfectly innocent reason I was kissing that woman* voice.

"Don't call me *sweetheart*, and I don't want to talk to you." She turned her back on him, trying to shut him out. She'd barely adjusted to his being dead, and now he was alive again. Typical Charley.

She sighed as she realized she'd have to go through with the divorce after all, figure out some way to get him to sign those papers.

"I know you don't want to talk to me." He sounded either a little abashed or a lot the con- artist. Amanda would put her money on the latter. "But you have to. I'm almost as confused about this thing as you are. Not having a body takes some getting used to. I could use your help."

Amanda spun back around to face him, ignoring everything he said except the last sentence, the only one that made sense, that sounded normal, sounded like Charley. "You want my help? Why should I help you?"

"Because you're a good person."

Amanda snorted, irritated, but a part of her was relieved. This was the Charley she knew, always working the angles. Simple con job. No fancy tricks. She didn't like this Charley, but she was comfortable with him, understood him.

She plopped into the wooden rocking chair in the corner of the room, leaned back and tented her fingers under her chin. "Start talking, creep, and if you say the right thing fast enough, maybe I won't call the cops and have you hauled in for stealing my gun and…and impersonating a dead person." She wasn't certain the latter was illegal, but it sounded like it might be, certainly ought to be.

Charley grinned. "I'd like to see them put me in handcuffs."

"Get to the point. What do you want to talk about, and how did you convince the police you're dead? Whose body was in your apartment?"

"Mine. It was my body. I'm dead."

"Fine. You're dead. What is it you want my help with? Getting rid of the body?" She sat bolt upright. "Did you kill somebody?"

"No! Of course not! But I know who did. The man who killed me is the same man who tried to kill you then broke into your apartment and stole your gun."

Amanda rocked back in the chair. "Let me see if I understand. You called me and told me if I'd bring you this gun in question that you'd sign the divorce papers. You didn't sign the papers, so I refused to give it to you. Now I come home to find that same object missing and you in my apartment with some crazy story about a man who killed you, tried to kill me and stole my gun because, of course, you had nothing to do with my gun going missing."

Charley looked uncomfortable, an expression she hadn't seen often on him. "That's about the size of it. He took the gun because he thought it was his, but it wasn't."

"It belonged to somebody else? You stole the gun you gave me? I've had a stolen weapon in my possession all this time? So that's why you took it. You couldn't have me turning it over the police if it was stolen." She slapped her hands on the chair arms. "I should have known!"

"No!" Charley protested. "I bought your gun. Totally legal. I can't believe you think I'd give you a stolen gift."

"Yeah, you're so morally upright, you'd never do anything like that. Why would this burglar think my gun was his if you didn't steal it from him?"

Charley looked down, refusing to meet her gaze. Totally unlike Charley. "I told him it was his. Then I tried to tell him the truth, that I never had his in the first place, but he didn't believe me." He shrugged. "So I told him you had it. I thought if I could get you to bring your gun to him, since it's the same kind as his, he'd take it and go away and not kill me."

Amanda shook her head. "Charley, Charley, Charley. With your talent for making up stories, you should have been a writer instead of a con-artist."

Charley looked up, his expression wounded. "I'm telling the truth."

"Okay, fine, you're telling the truth." There was no point in wasting her breath arguing with him. "So why did this mysterious burglar think you had his gun in the first place?"

"He's not a burglar, he's a murderer. Well, I guess he is a burglar now that he's stolen your property. But mostly he's a murderer. He killed a woman with the gun he thought I had."

"That's enough of your lies." She pointed a finger at him. "I am a murder suspect, and now you're somehow involved in the theft of the item that can prove my innocence. You need to tell me what's going on, and I don't want any of your evasions and bullshit."

"The guy, Kimball, he thought I had his gun, the one he used to murder a woman, and he wanted it back. But I didn't have it." Charley smiled and spread his hands, palms-up, as if that statement should clear up the whole matter.

"Kimball. So you gave this burglar a name," Amanda said. "Nice touch. Why did this Kimball, this murderer and burglar, think you had his gun?"

Charley's gaze locked on hers. She had once found that blue gaze riveting. Now she knew him too well. He was formulating a story.

"No! Do not lie to me, Charley Randolph!"

"Yeah, about that." He sighed and grinned ruefully. "I can't."

"You can't what?"

"Lie."

"Really? You can't lie? That's pretty amazing. We won't even discuss the times you lied to me about women and money. Let's just talk about your family, about the stories you told me about being an orphan. Your father was murdered. Your mother died in your arms from a drug overdose. Little brother murdered by his foster family. Poor orphan Charley. No family." She folded her arms. "Funniest damn thing, half the town of Silver Creek thinks you're family."

Charley gave her his big-blue-eyes innocent look. "That leaves a whole half of a town that's *not* my family."

Amanda leaned forward. "This is serious. I almost died in that motorcycle crash. There's a dead man in your apartment, and the police think I killed you. Him! Somebody! I'm in trouble, and the evidence that could clear me is gone. You claim you know who stole it. You need to tell me the truth for once in your worthless life."

"About your motorcycle accident—"

"Don't change the subject!"

"I was worried about you. I was afraid you wouldn't be able to make it back to the highway. I helped you. I saved your life. Doesn't that count for something?"

"So you *were* there. They told me you couldn't have been there because you were dead."

"Of course I was there. You needed me, and I was there." He looked pleased with himself.

"Oh, yeah, you're always there when I need you."

"Maybe I haven't been, but I will be now. I think maybe that's what this is all about, this hanging around after Kimball shot me. I'm here to take care of you."

Amanda closed her eyes and gritted her teeth. Getting something out of Charley when he didn't want to tell it was always painful and frequently futile.

She gave him her sternest glare. Probably not as effective as his riveting gaze, but it was the best she could do. "Charley, either you tell me something that makes sense about this whole thing—the gun your friend stole, why you aren't dead, what kind of scam you're up to this time—or I'm calling the cops right this minute to report a break-in and a stolen gun."

She rose, crossed the room, picked up her phone and punched in *9-1*.

"Last chance." When she looked up, Charley had left the room. Well, he couldn't have gone far. She hadn't heard the front door close. With a sigh, she punched the last *1*.

When two uniformed police officers arrived fifteen minutes later, she still could not locate her almost-ex, almost-deceased husband. He must have somehow slipped out without making any noise. It wouldn't be the first time.

"Come in," she invited. "The box where the missing gun was stored is in the bedroom."

The tall, lanky officer stepped into her living room and pulled a small notepad from his pocket while the other man studied her front door frame.

"Are you Amanda Randolph?"

"I am."

"You called 911?"

"I did."

"Can you tell us what happened, Ms. Randolph?"

"Someone broke in while I was gone and stole my gun," she said.

"No sign of forced entry." The second officer looked up from the door frame.

"It was unlocked," Amanda said.

"You left the door unlocked?"

"No, of course not." She glanced at the man's name badge. "Officer Penske, I've been away from home. In the hospital. When I came home this evening, the door was unlocked."

"Who has a key to your apartment?" the tall policeman asked. His badge identified him as *Officer Mark Robbins*.

"My assistant in the shop downstairs. That's the only person besides me. I changed my lock recently."

Robbins made a note. "Your assistant. What's his name?"

"Dawson Page."

"Do you have an address for this Dawson Page?"

"Yes. Why? I'm sure he didn't mean to leave my door unlocked. He's usually very conscientious."

"He left the door unlocked?"

"No. I don't know. Maybe. But I don't think so since my gun's missing."

"Did he know you owned this gun?"

"No! Are you implying Dawson would steal from me? No way! The thief's name was Kimball."

Both officers looked at her. "You know the thief's name?" Penske asked.

"My ex-husband...well, he's not my ex yet, but he will be. He's the one who told me someone named Kimball stole my gun."

"Is that the same ex-husband who was shot and killed?"

Amanda whirled to see Jake Daggett standing in the open doorway. His hair was still a mess and he still needed a shave. Tonight he wore faded blue jeans and a

Pink Floyd T-shirt and looked even less professional than he had at her interrogation.

"What are you doing here? I thought you were a homicide detective."

"You're a homicide suspect."

"At the moment, I'm the victim of a burglary."

"In which a suspected murder weapon was purportedly stolen."

Charley's words came back to her. *He killed a woman with the gun he thought I had, the one he thinks he stole from you.* "How do you know that?"

"You told the dispatcher when you called 911."

"Oh! You mean *my* gun. The one you think I used to kill Charley. Except he isn't dead, so that pretty much shoots down your theory."

"Hey, Jake," Officer Robbins said. "You got this case?"

"Yeah," he said. "Ongoing murder investigation."

Robbins nodded. "No sign of forced entry. Ms. Randolph claims the only person besides her with a key is her assistant—" he consulted his notes— "Dawson Page. We don't have an address yet."

"Thanks. I'll take it from here."

The two officers left, closing the door behind them.

Jake crossed his arms over his chest. "So," he said, "your husband's not dead."

"My estranged husband is very much alive."

Daggett raised one eyebrow. "Would this be the same estranged husband whose dead body we found in his apartment?"

"I don't know whose body that is, but it's not Charley's. He was just here, alive."

Daggett stared at her in silence for a long moment, searching her face as if trying to determine whether she was lying or just nuts. "Charley's fingerprints are in AFIS. We matched his prints to the dead man's prints."

She crossed her arms, mirroring his obstinate stance. "Maybe, maybe not. You don't know Charley very well if you seriously think he couldn't have somehow switched fingerprints in your system."

Daggett lifted both eyebrows this time. "Yeah, I seriously think Charley could not have switched fingerprints in our system. Trust me on this one. But even if you think he could have, Charley Randolph's mother identified his body."

"Some woman suddenly appears and claims to be his mother, and you believe her. Charley told me his parents are dead. Maybe they are. Maybe this woman isn't really his mother but somebody who has a hidden agenda. Maybe..." A sudden idea stopped Amanda in mid-sentence.

"Maybe?" Daggett encouraged.

Amanda swallowed. "Maybe my estranged husband's not Charley Randolph. Maybe he changed his name, stole someone's identity, the identity of that man who was killed in his apartment, the real Charley Randolph." *Maybe this was worse than not knowing she had a houseful of in-laws. Maybe she didn't even know who she was married to.*

Daggett dropped his arms to his sides, his dark eyes losing some of their sharpness. "Your father also identified the dead man as your husband, known to him as Charley Randolph. Your husband is dead."

Ice trickled down Amanda's spine. Her father would not, could not mistakenly identify Charley. He had kept Charley's family a secret from her. He hadn't told her everything. He had deceived her, but he hadn't lied.

She moved across the room and sank onto her brightly-patterned sofa.

Charley was dead?

Charley was dead.

Charley had not just been in her apartment.

But she'd seen him, talked to him.

No, she hadn't.

She'd been hallucinating.

Just like after her accident.

That explained the tricks and how he suddenly disappeared. He hadn't been there in the first place. She needed to get a grip. Hallucinating Charley was not a good thing.

"Mrs. Randolph? Are you all right?" *A soft, pitying tone.*

Amanda straightened her shoulders, lifted her chin. "I'm fine. Do you want to see the box where I stored my gun? Dust for fingerprints? Check for DNA?"

"What did you mean when you said Charley told you someone named Kimball stole your gun?"

She clenched her hands between her knees, focused her gaze across the room, and prepared to lie. "Oh, that." She cleared her throat. "Well. It was a dream. While I was in the hospital and they were giving me drugs. I dreamed about Charley." She stood. "Let me show you where the gun used to be."

"You dreamed about Charley, and he told you a man named Kimball had stolen your gun? Why didn't you tell me that during our interview down at the station?"

"I didn't remember until I got home and found the gun missing. What difference does it make? It was just a dream. You think it was maybe a psychic vision, somebody named Kimball actually did steal my gun? I suppose that's possible."

"Kimball—last name or first?"

"I don't know. Psychic visions. They can be so vague." She started toward the bedroom.

"You know anybody by that name?"

"Nope. Right over there. That box. The gun was wrapped in that striped towel last time I saw it."

61

Daggett surveyed the mess. "Is this the way you found your room? Have you touched anything?"

"Of course I touched things. Lots of things. The boxes were all in the closet, and this stuff was in that box. I pulled it out trying to find that blasted gun so I could bring it to you."

He looked at her, his left eyebrow shooting upward again. "So there was no evidence of a break-in when you got home?"

"The unlocked door."

"Other than that."

"My blinds were all closed."

"You don't normally close your blinds?"

"Not the blinds in the living room or kitchen. I hate being closed in. Claustrophobia."

The detective looked skeptical.

"And the boxes were in a different order than I left them," she continued.

"The boxes?"

She gestured toward the closet. "Those boxes. Someone took them out to get to my gun and didn't put them back the right way."

He nodded, his expression unchanged. He thought she was nuts. "When did you last see this gun?"

"A few weeks after Charley gave it to me. I packed it away." Probably not a good idea to tell him the reason she'd hidden it away was so she wouldn't be tempted to shoot Charley with it.

"And that would be...when?"

"A couple of years ago."

"And you haven't seen it since that time?"

"No."

"So you don't really know when it went missing."

"Yes, I do. I told you. The door was unlocked, the blinds were closed, the boxes were rearranged. Somebody was here while I was gone."

Daggett nodded, withdrew a pen and paper and wrote something. She could tell he didn't believe her.

At this point, she wasn't sure she believed herself.

"First of the evening?" Daggett indicated the half-empty glass of wine sitting on the dresser. "Second? Third?"

She sighed. "First." But it wouldn't be the last.

She couldn't really blame him for doubting her word when she'd been blithering about messages from her dead ex-husband.

After he left, she locked the door behind him, returned to the bedroom and retrieved her glass of wine. It was room temperature now, but she didn't care. She sank into the rocking chair, stared at the wall where she'd seen Charley, then took a big gulp.

"Kimball tried to kill you because he thinks I told you about him. He's going to try again. You're in danger. You need my help."

Charley. No more wine for her.

# **Chapter Seven**

She refused to look at him. "Go away. You're dead."

"Yeah, I am. But that's beside the point. Or maybe that is the point. I don't know. Believe me, I'm as confused as you are, but I think I'm here to save your life."

"I am not hearing voices. I am not hallucinating."

"That's true. You're not."

Amanda put her fingers in her ears.

Charley suddenly appeared, grinning, sitting cross-legged on the floor in her line of sight. "Hi."

Amanda shot out of the chair. "I need more wine." She sank back down. "Or less wine."

"Hey, I'm not thrilled about this either, but I'm stuck with it. That white light everybody sees when they die? It got yanked away from me before I could reach it, and next thing I know, I'm watching you go tumbling down that mountain. I took care of you, didn't I, got you back to the highway, saved your life? I thought maybe that would be it and I'd get to move on, but I'm still here. At least you can see me now. When I talked to you at your mother's house, you acted like you didn't hear me. Your mother never did like me."

"With good reason. Go away."

"I can't. I tried. I can go inside the dark like I did just now when those cops came, but other than that, I'm stuck with you."

Amanda rose, deliberately averting her eyes from the illusion of Charley. "I'm going to bed now, and when I wake up in the morning, I'm going to be completely normal again, no Charley, no little green men."

"You need to cut back on the wine, Amanda. There aren't any little green men here, just me. And I'll probably still be here when you wake up."

Amanda crossed the room and yanked open the bottom drawer of her dresser. She took out a nightshirt, clutched it to her chest, and turned around.

Charley's grin widened. "Go ahead. Change clothes. If I'm not really here, getting naked in front of me won't bother you."

Amanda hesitated, then, determined not to give in to her own delusions, laid the nightshirt on her bed and lifted the bottom of her T-shirt.

Charley whistled and clapped. "Take it off! Take it all off!"

Amanda spun around, turning her back to him. Charley's grinning image reflected in the beveled mirror of her antique dresser. Did hallucinations reflect in mirrors? Vampires didn't, but she wasn't sure about the protocol for hallucinations.

"Gotcha!" Charley exclaimed triumphantly. "If you didn't believe I'm here, you wouldn't be embarrassed to undress."

"I don't believe you're here. I believe I'm losing my mind, but I'm not going to undress in front of you anyway."

"Like I've never seen you—"

Amanda whirled on him. "That's enough! We're getting a divorce. You do not have the right to talk to me that way." She lifted her hand to her mouth. "I'm talking to my hallucination again."

"It's a start. Sit down. We've got a lot to talk about."

Amanda shook her head but followed his directions and sat in the rocking chair. "If I listen to you, will you go away?"

"Maybe." He sighed. "To tell you the truth—and I'm afraid that's all I can do anymore—I'm not sure. This

65

death thing, I don't have any experience with it. I don't really know what I'm supposed to do."

"So you're dead. You're a ghost."

Charley flinched. "You don't have to be rude."

"You're dead, but you're not a ghost?" If he was *her* hallucination, shouldn't he be more agreeable?

"*Ghost* just sounds so…hazy and insubstantial."

"Fine, you're dead, but you're not a ghost."

"I'm still Charley. I just don't have a body. At least, not the same kind of body I used to have. I'm not very solid anymore."

*Like a ghost,* she thought. But arguing with Charley had always been pointless. His hallucination wasn't likely to be any more open to logic.

"Whatever. It's late. I'm tired. What is it you want to talk about?"

"I guess we have to start with Kimball and that gun."

"Can you sit down? I don't feel comfortable having a conversation with someone who's standing while I'm sitting." *Standing and hovering a few inches off the floor.*

"Sure." He perched on the side of the bed—about an inch above the colorful spread.

Amanda motioned with her hand, indicating he should lower himself a little more.

"Huh?"

"You're floating. That doesn't make me feel comfortable."

Charley lowered half an inch into the bed.

"Up," Amanda instructed, and he rose. "That's good. You look like you're actually sitting."

Charley gave her a satisfied smile. "I'm getting better at this no body thing."

"Okay. Talk, then go away."

Charley drew in a deep breath. "Roland Kimball. Mayor of Silver Creek. Future Governor of Texas, if he and his family and his wife's family have anything to say about it, and, as much money as they've got, they probably do."

"The mayor of your home town, a rich man who could buy all the guns he wants, stole my gun. Do I have this right so far?"

"Sort of." Charley grimaced. "There's a little more to the story."

"Of course there is." There always was with Charley.

"Kimball thought I had the gun he used to kill his former girlfriend, and he wanted to get it back. But I didn't have it. But he didn't believe me. So he killed me, tried to kill you, searched my apartment, picked your lock, found your gun and thought it was his. He's going to try again because he thinks you know about him. Those anonymous calls Dawson told you about were him, calling here, trying to find you. He might have figured out the gun he took isn't his. If that happens, he's going to be really upset."

Perhaps this was Charley's ghost after all. Only Charley could tell such a nonsensical tale and sit there looking as if he'd just explained everything. "So this Kimball person killed you, tried to kill me, and the anonymous phone calls were from him, checking on my whereabouts so he can make another attempt?"

"Yeah. I didn't see him making those calls, and I didn't see him stealing your gun, but I know it happened like that. Now that I'm on the other side, I know things," he said smugly.

"Funny. You claimed to know everything when you were on this side."

"I might have been bragging then, but I'm telling the truth now."

"Got it. Kimball killed you, and now he wants to kill me. Why did he think you had the gun he used to kill his former girlfriend?"

"Because I told him I had it."

"Why did you tell him you had his gun?"

Charley lowered his head and mumbled.

"What?" she asked.

"Blackmail."

"*Blackmail*?" Amanda leaned forward. "You were blackmailing this Roland Kimball?"

"Yes."

"You told him you had his murder weapon?"

"Yes."

"But you didn't really have it?"

"That's right."

Amanda shook her head slowly. "I can't have a coherent conversation with you even after you're dead." And that statement itself was the ultimate in incoherence.

"I only did it to him twice."

Amanda's eyes widened. "Twice? You blackmailed him more than once?"

"Well, only once successfully. The second time I asked him for money..." He grinned and spread his hands. "He killed me."

Amanda massaged her temples, fighting the beginnings of a headache. "But this man once paid you money for a gun you didn't have? Why would he do that?"

Charley's grin turned cocky. "Because I'm damned good at what I do."

"You're dead. That isn't exactly a testimonial to your skills as a blackmailer."

"Yeah, but you have to admit, getting somebody to pay you, even once, for something you don't have is damned good."

"Tell me, Charley. Tell me how you did it." He was running on ego now. He'd tell her the story, though she'd have to figure out for herself how much of it was true.

"I was still living in Silver Creek. It's a small, hick town, and I wanted to get out of there, move to the big city. So one night I was in an alley when—"

"What were you doing in an alley?"

"Hanging out." He shifted, sinking into the mattress slightly. "Until my date's husband left the bar. Anyway, I was hidden in the shadows when I saw this big black Cadillac pull down the alley. Like I said, Silver Creek is small. Not many Cadillacs around. Kind of strange to see one in that part of town, going down a dark alley, so I kept still and watched."

Charley was getting into his story, his eyes sparkling, his voice exuberant, his body rising about an inch off the bed. Amanda tried to ignore that little oddity.

"My patience paid off. The car pulls up next to a trash bin, and His Honor, Mayor Kimball, opens the door and gets out holding a plastic bag like from a grocery store. He's not ten feet from me, so I can see he's got red spots on his white shirt." He paused and leaned forward. "Blood?" Another pause, and he leaned back. "So I stand there watching, not moving a muscle, knowing I'm about to see something important."

"Are we going to get to the point of this story before I die of old age and join you hovering over that bed?"

"That's very touching, Amanda, that you plan to join me in bed after you die."

Amanda scowled.

Charley lifted his hands, palms out. "Okay, okay! So Kimball tosses the bag into the dumpster, and it makes a nice solid *clunk* when it hits the side of the bin. Something small and heavy in that bag. Add that to the red spots on his shirt, and this story is getting real interesting. Kimball looks around, acting suspicious, then he jumps back in his car and speeds away. I figured whatever His Honor tossed into that dumpster, I needed to have it."

"Mr. Fastidious, climbing into a garbage container? Wish I could have seen that."

"It wasn't exactly my idea of fun on a Saturday night, but I had a hunch it might be worth it. I grabbed hold of the handle of the bin and hoisted myself up. Fortunately, it was almost full, so I was able to reach that little plastic bag by just leaning over. I pulled up, and *it* fell out."

Charley paused.

Amanda took her cue and supplied her line. "What fell out?"

"A gun. I reached to pick it up, when suddenly my date's husband comes charging out the back door of the bar, grabs my legs and yanks. He's a big man, but I fight him off. Had to run all the way through the town, though, and that kind of took my mind off His Honor's throwaway."

Charley had just told her the town was small, so *all the way* couldn't be very far. She let it go since he was in the zone of his storytelling.

He crossed his legs and dangled his arms over them. Casual, relaxed—floating several inches above the mattress.

"The next day, big story all over the news, murder in Silver Creek. Local woman, Dianne Carter. Looked like a carjacking. Happened in a secluded spot out by the lake. Her husband said she'd left to go to the grocery store about eight o'clock that evening and never made it back home. Word around town was that it was some druggie passing through, some guy who maybe saw her at the grocery store, forced her into her car, made her drive out to the lake, took the cash from her purse and shot her. But I wondered." Another pause.

Amanda obliged him. "Okay, I'll bite. How did you link the mayor in the alley with the lady at the lake?"

"It was obvious. Kimball's a few years older than me, but everybody knew him. He was the rich kid, class president, most likely to succeed, all that stuff. Dianne wasn't rich, but she was popular. Homecoming queen, head cheerleader, the girl next door that every guy wanted to be with. In her senior year, she started dating Kimball. They were the king and queen. Everybody thought they'd get married, but something happened when they were at college in Austin. They both came back, married other people and never spoke to each other again."

Amanda waited, knowing Charley would get to the point eventually. He loved being the center of attention and milked every opportunity.

"So after I saw the story in the newspaper, I got to thinking about Dianne's death and Kimball's visit to the alley right around the time she was killed. It would have been great if I could have got Kimball's gun, but when I went back, the trash had already been hauled off." He sighed. "Luck was not on my side. I didn't have anything except a theory. But, fortunately, I've always had the ability to make my own luck. I called Kimball. Couldn't get through to him, of course, not an important man like him. I left a message telling him I had something he'd dropped the night before. Anyway, long story short—"

"A little late for that, isn't it?"

Charley ignored her comment. "He met me in a bar, and I told him I had the gun he'd tossed into the trash, the gun he used to kill Dianne. I told him unless he paid me twenty-five thousand dollars, I was going to take that gun to the police. He paid me, but I couldn't give him the gun because I didn't have it, so I left town. Everything was fine until a couple of weeks ago." He drew in a deep sigh. "You left me and filed for divorce and I had to get my own apartment and pay a lawyer, so I needed money."

"My fault, of course."

"I didn't say that, but if you're feeling guilty—"

"I'm not."

"Anyway, I needed money. Kimball's getting ready to make a bid for governor, so I called and told him I wanted another payment."

Amanda groaned. "Oh, Charley! That was crazy."

"Yeah, I guess, but I was desperate. Kimball was pretty upset. He said he'd only give me more money if I gave him the gun first this time." Charley shrugged. "I couldn't very well give him what I didn't have. I thought I'd better just let that one go so I never called him again. A couple of weeks later, he slipped right past that lousy lock on my door and walked into my living room wearing motorcycle leathers and a helmet. He said my neighbors would think it was me, and he could get away with killing me. He wanted that gun. I told him I left it at your apartment. That's when he forced me to call you and tell you to bring the gun. And if you'd brought the gun like I asked you, I could have given it to him and I might still be alive."

Amanda sprang to her feet, hands on her hips. "You are *not* going to blame this one on me, Charley Randolph! If I'd showed up with that gun, he'd have killed you anyway. This whole thing is totally on you!"

Charley lifted his arms in a gesture of surrender. "Okay, okay! Anyway, you showed up without the gun. I tried to keep you out of my apartment. I was trying to protect you. But you shoved your way inside."

"I wanted to see what you had in there that you were so anxious to hide from me. And you know what I saw? Nothing! No mysterious stranger. No Kimball."

"He was behind the door. I got you out of there before he saw you and killed you. I saved your life, and here I am. End of story."

"This is not even close to the end of the story! The cops think I killed you. I could get sent to prison."

"Well, Amanda, it's not like you didn't threaten more than once to kill me."

"And you deserved to be murdered by me, but that didn't happen because somebody else beat me to it, and I shouldn't have to go to prison for something I didn't have the pleasure of doing."

Charley brightened. "Well, now I've told you the real story, you can tell the cops and they'll arrest Kimball. Then you'll be safe, thanks to *yours truly*. Presto, white light, angel wings and all that good stuff."

Amanda covered her face with her hands. Insane as it sounded, this must really be Charley's ghost. Surely her imagination couldn't create a conversation so totally *Charley*.

She took her hands from her eyes. "Did you not hear what happened this evening when I tried to tell that cop about somebody stealing my gun?"

"Yeah, I heard, but you were trying to tell him I wasn't dead. You have to admit, Amanda, you sounded a little crazy. I'm not surprised the man didn't believe you. You tell him the whole story, and everything will be just fine."

"Why, of course. All I have to do is tell the cops that the Mayor of Silver Creek, a respected man running for governor, killed his former girlfriend, then killed you and stole my gun because he thought it was the gun he used to kill his former girlfriend, but it isn't." She waved a hand through the air. "No problem making that story believable, especially if I tell him the ghost of my ex-husband swears it's true."

Charley grimaced, opened his mouth to speak, then closed it again. "Okay, maybe there are still a couple of things you'll have to work out, but I've done my part. I'm outta here." He looked around the room expectantly. "Yep. I did my good deed, redeemed myself. Time for me to move on, get my wings."

Amanda followed his gaze, half expecting to see a bright light of some sort, even if it came from a blazing fire accompanied by the smell of brimstone.

No light. Charley didn't vanish, didn't even fade.

His smile became a little strained. "I don't see any tunnel of light."

"And I don't see any less of you."

He shifted, sinking a couple of inches into the bed. "I don't know what else I'm supposed to do."

"Great! How am I ever supposed to get rid of you? I can't even threaten to kill you now because you're already dead."

Charley clutched his heart. "Amanda, you wound me. Here I am, staying around just to help you, and you don't appreciate it."

"You're staying around because you can't leave." She rose and strode across the room. "At least get out of my bedroom. This may be my last chance to sleep in my own bed for the next twenty-five years to life."

Charley walked dejectedly into the living room. His feet remained a few inches above the floor, but the motion of movement vaguely resembled walking.

Amanda turned away, making a conscious effort to also turn away from the insanity of the last few days.

Sleep was elusive, but finally she slipped into slumber. Her dream self was riding her Harley over amazingly smooth brick streets, dodging pop-up Charleys, when someone shouting in the next room brought her to full consciousness.

*Kimball? Come back to kill her?*

She grabbed her kitchen knife and dashed into the living room to find the television blaring with Charley sitting on the sofa, beaming happily. "I turned it on!" he said.

Amanda held her hands over her ears. "Turn it off!" She dashed across the room and hit the control button. Silence filled the room.

"I was bored," Charley said. "I tried to turn on the TV, but my hand just went right through the remote control, and I got so frustrated with this whole situation, I thought I was going to explode. I didn't, but the TV did. Pretty cool, huh?"

"No, it is not cool." Amanda turned to go back to bed.

"Hey, come on! At least turn it on low so I can have something to do."

"No!"

"I'll turn it on myself," he threatened.

Amanda grabbed the remote and turned on the television, adjusting the sound to low. Death with Charley wasn't going to be any easier than life had been.

☙❧

An insistent chiming woke Amanda to bright sunlight streaming through her bedroom window. She had somehow managed to get a few hours of sleep, but now her cell phone was pulling her back to reality.

She retrieved it from the night stand and checked the name. Her father. She felt a chill of anxiety. "Dad?"

"Good morning, Mandy."

"What's up?"

"I just talked to Brian."

Amanda's heart clenched. Last night she'd made a smart-mouthed crack about going to prison for twenty-five to life, but now it wasn't funny.

"What's going on?"

"I'm sorry, Mandy. The police found evidence that your bike had been tampered with. Your accident was no accident. Somebody almost killed you."

"I'll call you right back, Dad." She stabbed the button to disconnect the call. "Charley!"

# Chapter Eight

"I swear I didn't do it!" Charley came down the outside stairs behind Amanda, his movement a simulation of walking though producing no sound on the wooden steps.

Amanda continued her clattering descent from her apartment, on her way to meet with Brian Edwards to talk about this latest development. "I know, I know," she tossed over her shoulder. "It was Kimball. Kimball killed you. Kimball stole my gun. Kimball jacked up my bike. Kimball's responsible for global warming. Does Kimball even exist? I can't believe you'd really do something to my motorcycle. That's low, even for you, Charley Randolph, lowest of the low."

"It was Kimball!"

"And you know that because you have special knowledge now. It's a ghost thing. Fine. I'm going to Silver Creek to meet this Kimball and confront him and demand to know why he jacked with my bike."

"*No!*"

The genuine panic in Charley's voice stopped Amanda on the last step. She turned to look at him, a wry smile moving onto her lips. "So I was right. He doesn't exist." She shook her head. "You almost had me believing you last night."

"Amanda!" She whirled around to see a slim, dark-haired man standing in the open door at the side of her shop. "You're back." Dawson smiled up at her. The sunlight bounced off the lenses of his glasses and added to the impression of benign happiness her assistant exuded.

*You're back?* Was he talking about Charley's return?

Amanda cast a quick glance up the stairs behind her. Charley was nowhere to be seen. Dawson must be

76

referring to *her* return, not Charley's. His expression should have told her that. Dawson had never been fond of Charley. While he was too polite to say anything derogatory, he was too open to be able to mask his reactions. He wouldn't be smiling if he'd seen Charley.

"Dawson, hi. Yes, yes, I am. Back. Sort of. I'm sorry, I have to meet with my lawyer this morning, but I'll be at work this afternoon. I hate to ask you to keep holding down the fort, but would you mind just one more morning?"

"It's okay. I don't mind. But—well, can you spare just a few minutes? There's somebody here to see you."

"Somebody to see me?" Her heart triple-timed. The culpable Kimball? Did he exist after all? Had he come to finish her off, just as Charley warned?

A short, frumpy woman with a cap of silvery hair stepped out of the shop from behind Dawson. She wore a simple cotton dress of small white polka dots on a dark blue background. The style made her small, slightly-overweight frame look stocky, solid and capable. She clutched a square black purse in both hands, and her expression was even more joyous than Dawson's.

"You must be Amanda," she said with a wide smile.

"Let's go, Amanda." Amanda gasped at the sudden sound of Charley's voice in her ear. His tone held an edge of hysteria. "Appointment with your lawyer. Remember?"

Nobody seemed surprised to see him. Amanda looked from the woman to Dawson to Charley then back to Dawson.

"Let's go!" Charley urged. "Now!"

"No!"

Both Dawson and the woman looked confused.

"Yes, you are," Dawson said.

"I'm what?"

"You're Amanda. Are you all right?" Concern flickered across Dawson's guileless features.

77

"They can't see me," Charley said. "Let's go." Cold shivered through Amanda's arm as Charley tried to take it.

"You can't see…?" Amanda's question drifted off as she motioned vaguely behind her.

Dawson's concern increased, became more of a surge than a flicker. "Amanda, why don't you come inside and have a Coke? That always makes you feel better."

The frumpy woman rushed forward and took her hand. "It's all right, dear. Come inside and sit down for a few minutes. You've been through a lot."

Amanda looked into the woman's plain, kindly face.

Charley groaned.

"I'm your mother-in-law," the woman said. "Irene Randolph. Charley's mother." She took Amanda's arm on the opposite side from Charley and guided her toward the shop. Her touch was soft warmness rather than the cold chill Charley's had been. "I heard you were out of the hospital, and I wanted to meet you. I couldn't find your phone number, but I called your shop this morning, and your assistant said I should come on over. I wish we didn't have to meet like this, but it can't be helped."

Faced with a live mother-in-law on one side and a dead almost-ex-husband on the other, Amanda couldn't find the will to protest. Sitting down and having a Coke seemed like a really good idea, a sane, normal action.

"It's going to be okay," the woman said in a soothing voice as if she sensed Amanda's tension. "You lost your husband and you were in a terrible accident. You need some time to recover." The woman sensed the tension but didn't have a clue as to the cause of it.

Amanda let her mother-in-law lead her through the shop toward the small office at the back. Motorcycles and parts spread around the room were in a surprising semblance of order. In her absence, under Dawson's care, order had gained ground. Dawson's unrelenting determination to create structure everywhere was reassuring.

In the small, windowless office, Amanda sank onto one of the folding chairs. A clean camshaft lay at her feet.

She jumped at the sound of a *pop hiss*.

"Coke. Sorry." Dawson handed her a red can.

"Thanks." Amanda lifted the can and took a long swallow of the cold, bubbly liquid.

Charley's mother appeared on the other side, offering a rectangular plastic container.

Amanda blinked. "Cookies?" In the midst of Charley's murder, the appearance of his ghost, the sabotage of her motorcycle and her near death, this woman, her newly-discovered mother-in-law, was pushing cookies.

"They're delicious," Dawson assured her.

"They have nuts," the woman said, apparently misinterpreting Amanda's hesitation. "Are you allergic to nuts? Oh, dear, I hope you're not allergic to nuts." Her face wrinkled with concern.

"No. No, I love nuts." Amanda picked up a cookie. The whole world had gone insane. She might as well eat cookies. She took a bite. It was moist, chewy, rich, full of smooth chocolate chips and chunky nuts. "This is good. Very good."

The woman smiled. "I didn't know what kind of cookies you liked, but chocolate chip was Charley's favorite, so I thought you might like the same kind."

"You made these cookies for me?"

"Of course. I'm glad you like them."

"I love them." Amanda's throat felt oddly tight. To her surprise and consternation, tears brimmed in her eyes.

Mrs. Randolph fell to her knees beside Amanda and wrapped both arms around her, patting her gently. "It's okay to cry. I've cried an ocean over him. We both loved him, and now he's gone."

Amanda decided it wouldn't be a good idea to tell a grieving mother that she was crying because someone had made cookies for her, not because she'd loved the son in question who wasn't really gone anyway. "I didn't kill him." It was the only response she could think of.

Mrs. Randolph drew back. "Why, of course, you didn't! Why would you even say such a thing?"

Amanda wiped her eyes with the back of her hand and shrugged. "The cops. They've been questioning me."

Charley's mother patted her hand. "They questioned me too. Don't you worry. They'll catch whoever did this horrible thing." She straightened. "Bad enough you lose your husband. Those police shouldn't be making things worse. You've been through a lot. Herbert and I want you to come to Silver Creek and stay with us for a while, give yourself some time to heal and get to know your family."

"Herbert?" Amanda's brain didn't seem to be working that morning. Instead of thoughts flashing through her mind like mercury, they moved like sludge through murky quicksand. *Silver Creek. Family. Herbert?*

"Charley's daddy. Your father-in-law. He couldn't come today because he has to work. But we talked about it, and everybody wants you to come stay with us."

"Everybody?"

"Me and Herbert and the girls that are still at home—that's Paula and Penny, the twins. Charley has two brothers and two more sisters. Both boys and my oldest girl are married. You have four nieces and three nephews and one on the way. Then there's Herbert's kin. He had five sisters. Can you imagine being the only boy in that family? They all have husbands and kids. I have three brothers and one whole sister and one half sister. Anyway, point is, you have a big family you've never met that wants to be with you while we're all grieving for the same lost loved one."

Amanda lost count of poor orphan Charley's family members somewhere after the twins. "That's...uh...thank you." The manners her mother had drilled into her since birth kicked in to compensate for her total inability to process this overwhelming information. "I'd love to. But I can't leave right now. I have a business to run."

Mrs. Randolph smiled and waved a hand toward Dawson. "This nice young man says he can handle things here for as long as you want to stay with us. You can have Charley's old room at our house. There's a big cottonwood tree right outside his window that makes the prettiest sound when the wind blows. It's real peaceful."

His own room with a big cottonwood tree outside didn't quite coincide with Charley's tales of sleeping on a sofa with his little brother in a tiny living room while his prostitute mother turned tricks and took drugs in the only bedroom.

"That sounds wonderful." Amanda smiled, hoping the expression didn't look as forced as it felt. "I'll think about it after Charley's funeral and the police investigation are finished."

"I understand. I've got to get back home today, but I'll leave you our telephone number. I'll be up here to help you with the funeral all I can. I buried my momma and daddy and one baby. It's not easy."

"You're very kind."

"We're family."

"Mrs. Randolph..."

The older woman patted Amanda's hand. "Please, call me Irene. One day I hope we'll be close enough you'll call me Mom, but we'll give that some time."

"Uh, Irene, I have an appointment with my attorney this morning, but if you're still going to be here in a couple of hours, maybe we could grab some lunch." Even as she spoke the words, Amanda wasn't sure where they had come from. This woman was a stranger. She hadn't known her mother-in-law while she was married, and now she was no longer married. Yet there was something compelling about this woman who offered cookies and a big, loving family.

The happy smile on Irene's face relieved any misgivings Amanda had about her offer. "That'd be real nice. I'll just do some shopping while you're gone. They don't have stores like these in Silver Creek."

Amanda regarded her new-found mother-in-law with unexpected affection. How on earth had this gentle, compassionate woman produced Charley? "Let me give you my cell phone number," she offered. "I don't have a land line. That's why you couldn't find my listing." She scribbled on a piece of paper, tore it off the pad and handed it to Irene. She started out the door then turned back. "Charley mentioned one person from Silver Creek. Do you happen to know a man named Roland Kimball?"

Irene's lips tightened, and her expression looked as if she'd just tasted something bitter. "Everybody knows Roland Kimball. Big shot. Mayor of the town. Running for governor. Probably gonna win."

# Chapter Nine

"There's no doubt your motorcycle was deliberately sabotaged."

Amanda sat in the comfortable, soft blue client's chair in Brian Edwards' office, listening to the statement delivered in his matter-of-fact lawyer's voice. She understood the words, had even expected to hear them, but she was having trouble processing the meaning.

Somebody had damaged her motorcycle. Somebody had wanted her to have a wreck, be hurt, perhaps even die.

Charley denied tampering with her bike. Could she believe him?

Was it possible Charley's outrageous story about Kimball was true? Had the Mayor of Silver Creek tried to kill her to keep her quiet?

"Our expert tells me these things were done by someone who knows bikes, who knew you would have to ride several miles before your brakes failed and the rear wheel came loose. That person would presumably have also known you were going on a trip." Brian took off his glasses and laid them on his polished walnut desk beside a stack of papers, folded his hands and looked at her.

She felt that he wanted her to respond, to say something, but she couldn't think of anything to say.

"I'm sorry, Amanda, but the only conclusion we can reach is that Charley tried to kill you. He knows motorcycles, and he knew you were leaving on a long trip."

Amanda shook her head slowly. "I don't think Charley would do that." But hadn't she accused him or his ghost or her hallucination of doing just that? "Why would he try to kill me?"

Brian spread his hands. "The two of you were going through a bitter divorce. Perhaps he was angry. Perhaps he didn't want to be left with nothing, wanted to inherit your assets."

Amanda gave a snort of laughter. "That's not a whole lot more than nothing."

"People have killed for less."

"Well, he's the one who's dead." *I think.* "So what difference does it make if he tried to kill me?"

Brian replaced his glasses then took them off again. Amanda liked that he hadn't been a lawyer long enough to develop the air of supreme self-confidence and omniscience that seemed to come to all of them with age, experience and training. On the other hand, it didn't bode well for her that he seemed nervous.

"If you had reason to believe your life was in danger from Charley, it gives us a plea of self-defense."

A spear of cold shot through Amanda's chest and settled in her stomach. "I don't need a plea of self-defense. I didn't kill Charley." She almost added that Charley said Roland Kimball killed him but bit back the words. Brian would probably leap from self-defense straight to a plea of insanity if she started talking like that.

He pulled a yellow legal pad toward him and lifted a silver pen from its holder on his desk. "I need you to tell me everything you can remember about the day Charley was killed, especially your visit to his apartment and the gun he wanted you to bring to him."

The cold in Amanda's gut swirled upward, squeezing her heart. "It sounds like this is getting serious. Am I going to be arrested?"

"Don't worry," Brian reassured her. "If you should be arrested, we'll post bail and get you out immediately."

*We'll post bail and get you out.* Somehow, his words weren't reassuring.

સ્બ✧

Amanda met her mother-in-law (that concept still had her mind reeling) at a small restaurant next to an antique store. The place was run by a retired husband and wife who baked their own bread, cooked their own meats, and served sandwiches with homemade soup on antique china. She and Irene sat at a small round table, eating chicken salad sandwiches and drinking iced tea.

Irene took a bite of her sandwich, swallowed and nodded. "This is good."

"I like this place." Amanda sipped her tea. "I'm glad you do too. The chicken salad's one of my favorites." She bit into her sandwich, unsure how to make conversation with Charley's mother. Probably not a good idea to lead with his other women or his unscrupulous financial activities or her attorney's belief that he'd tried to kill Amanda. Those were not likely things a mother wanted to hear about her son.

"Charley was always different," Irene said. She didn't seem the least bit uncomfortable or at a loss for words.

"Yes." Amanda peeled off a bit of crust. "He was different."

"None of us were all that surprised when he disappeared. He always wanted to leave Silver Creek. He wanted bigger things from life, and he was smart enough to get them."

"Mmmm." Amanda took a large bite of her sandwich so she'd have an excuse not to talk.

"All my kids are special. Hank can build anything. Give him a piece of wood, and he'll make you the prettiest table or bookcase or carving you've ever seen. Travis, he's a horse whisperer. He can train those horses of his to sit up and talk. Carolyn has a voice like an angel, and Susie makes clothes like you find at Neiman Marcus. The twins, Paula and Penny, they make the best pies and cakes you've ever put in your mouth. Charley was the smart one." She sighed, took a bite of sandwich and chewed slowly, looking into the distance, as if at another time and place. "I wanted him to go to college, become a doctor or a lawyer. I told him we'd help him all we could. But Charley didn't want to go to school. He thought he could make it through life on his charm."

"He could be very charming."

"He loved you."

Amanda didn't respond. If this kindly woman wanted to think the best of her dead son, Amanda wasn't going to try to change that opinion.

"When he called, he always told us how happy you two were."

The bit of sandwich Amanda had just swallowed stuck in her throat. She coughed and swallowed again. "He called? While we were married?"

"Not often. He said he was in trouble and couldn't let anybody find out where he was, but he wanted us to know he was okay. Charley had a good heart. He called when he met you. Wanted us to know he'd met the woman he planned to marry."

"How sweet."

Irene missed the sarcasm. "Yes, he was a sweet boy. He called us when you married, and he called us when you decided to start a family. He was so happy."

Amanda choked, dropped her sandwich and went into a coughing fit.

Irene was immediately on her feet, came up behind Amanda and pounded on her back.

"I'm okay," Amanda managed to say, though she certainly was not. *Start a family?* Charley's cookie-baking mother was in for a lot of rude shocks. When she found out the truth, she wasn't going to be baking cookies or inviting her beloved son's estranged wife and suspected murderer to stay at the family home.

Amanda cleared her throat. "I need to tell you some things about Charley and me."

Irene gave her a gentle pat on one shoulder and returned to her seat. "I'm listening."

Amanda laid her napkin on the table, took a sip of her iced tea and drew in a deep breath. "Charley's and my marriage wasn't perfect."

Irene nodded knowingly. "Nobody's is. Herbert and I have had our problems, but we worked them out."

Amanda shook her head. "We were separated. We were getting a divorce."

"I know. The police told me. But I know how much you loved each other. You'd have worked things out if he'd lived."

"We weren't planning to start a family."

Irene's expression saddened, but she didn't appear surprised. "Charley's always been a dreamer. Sometimes he tells things the way he wants them to be instead of the way they actually are. He needed a family. It would have settled him down, made him grow up. He'd have been such a good father." She took a tissue from her purse and dabbed her eyes.

Amanda had her doubts about Charley's potential fathering abilities, but she elected to keep her opinion to herself just the one time.

At the end of the meal, Irene again extended an invitation to Amanda. "You're welcome at our place any time. You're family. We want to get to know you. Come when you can, leave when you have to, and every day in between will be a gift."

The invitation held an unexpected appeal, but Amanda knew she'd never do it. She wasn't really a part of Charley's family. If Charley hadn't died, they'd be divorced. It didn't seem right to establish a relationship with her former in-laws. She'd be accepting their hospitality under false pretenses.

❧

The next few days were surreal. Every time someone came into the shop, Amanda jumped for fear it would be a police officer come to arrest her. If that wasn't bad enough, Charley was underfoot all the time, listening to her phone calls, giving her instructions about motorcycle repairs, turning on the TV in the middle of the night, even more annoying than when he was alive.

And he was obsessed with Kimball.

"He put poison in the coffee," he told her one morning. "When he was going through your apartment, looking for the gun. He put poison in the coffee. Just in case you survived the wreck. I can feel it when I get near the coffee."

"Charley, I don't drink coffee. You left that container here. So long as he didn't put poison in my Cokes, I'm okay."

"But Kimball doesn't know that."

One morning a wooden step broke when Amanda trod on it, sending her thumping down the last three steps.

"Kimball did it," Charley declared.

"Actually," Amanda assured him, examining the step in question, "dry rot did it."

He woke her in the middle of the night to warn her that Kimball was approaching her apartment.

In spite of her certainty that Charley was being dramatic, she got up to look out and saw a man coming around her building toward the stairs leading up to her apartment.

"Call the police," Charley ordered.

"No way," Amanda said, though her heart was pounding so loudly she could barely hear Charley.

She watched the man move closer and weighed the terrors of dealing with an intruder or calling in the cops who might haul her away.

The intruder didn't seem very steady on his feet.

He stopped by the oak tree.

"Oh, good grief." She whirled away from the window and grabbed the hammer she'd been keeping close at hand.

"Don't go down there!" Charley called after her as she darted out the door.

"It's just some drunk from the bar down the street. Hey, you!" she shouted from the top step. "Yeah, you! This is not a public bathroom!"

The man ran away, zipping his pants and tossing a few curse words over his shoulder.

Charley was trying desperately to convince her that Mayor Kimball was out to get her. For the most part, he was just being annoying.

But one event did make her nervous. The anonymous caller phoned again the second day she was home. Dawson answered and handed the phone to her. The caller hung up as soon as she spoke.

Charley suddenly appeared beside her. "It was Kimball! He knows you're home. He's coming after you."

"Give it a rest," Amanda ordered. But she bought a deadbolt and chain for her front door.

Finally Brian called to tell her the police had released Charley's body.

She disconnected the call. "Now I have to decide what to do with you."

"I don't want to talk about this." Charley looked out the window, avoiding her gaze.

"I'd like to have you cremated and flush your ashes down the toilet, but you'd probably stop it up, and I'd have to pay a plumber."

"Amanda, you have a mean streak."

"Anyway, I can't do that to your mother." She found the piece of paper with Irene's phone number and called her.

Irene cried when Amanda told her the funeral would be in Silver Creek. "That's mighty nice of you to bring him home," she said.

*If you only knew,* Amanda thought. "It's what he would have wanted," she said.

Charley rolled his eyes and left the room.

"We've got a place for him in the family plot, and one beside him for you. Of course, you're young. You'll probably get married again. But if you want to rest beside him, we'll save it for you."

"Thank you. I'll keep it in mind."

"I got Charley's room all cleaned up and ready for you. When do you think you'll be getting here?"

"Oh," Amanda said, "I don't want you to go to any trouble. I'll just drive back and forth. It's only about an hour."

"It's no trouble," Irene said. "You do what you need to do, but you're always welcome at our house." She sounded disappointed.

"Well, I could come down a couple of days before the funeral." Amanda groaned inwardly when she heard the words come out of her mouth. Lying to this woman about her son's wishes was one thing, but agreeing to spend time with Charley's family was not a good idea. "If I can," she added, then began searching her mind for reasons she couldn't while a part of her didn't want to find those reasons. A part of her wanted to run away to the comfort of a mother-in-law who baked cookies for her, a town where she wouldn't flinch every time someone walked through the door, expecting to find Detective Daggett standing there with an arrest warrant. If she was in another jurisdiction, at least he'd have to go through her attorney to get to her.

Not surprisingly, Charley went ballistic when she told him her plans.

"You can't go down there! You're going into the lion's den! Kimball won't even have to leave town to kill you. I forbid you to go to Silver Creek."

Charley's reaction cinched it. "You forbid me? Excuse me? You didn't have the right to order me around when you were alive! You sure don't now that you're dead!"

Amanda was going to Silver Creek.

Later that day she met with her parents to discuss the funeral.

The three of them sat in their formal living room, her mother erect and dignified in a white, high-backed chair, her father relaxed but in control in a burgundy leather chair, and Amanda between them on the plush white sofa with burgundy pillows. That sofa was generation four, having succumbed on three previous occasions to Amanda's youthful escapades. Jenny, of course, had obeyed the rules and never destroyed furniture.

Amanda sat on the edge of the sofa, unable to banish a childish fear of somehow soiling the venerated sofa again. Why did people buy furniture if they didn't want it to be used? At the appearance of number three, she'd suggested her mother take a picture of the sofa, hang it on the wall, and let people sit on the floor beneath it. That hadn't gone over well.

"I'm going to let Charley's mom take him home to Silver Creek for the funeral. They've got a family plot where they can bury him."

Her mother folded her hands primly. "I think that's a good idea, dear. He should be back with his family."

"I'm going to go down a couple of days before the funeral to stay with the Randolphs so I can help."

Her mother and father exchanged shocked glances.

Her father leaned toward Amanda. "If you want Charley buried in his home town, we'll do whatever we can to help. I'll arrange to have the body shipped to his family and pay for all expenses at whatever funeral home they choose. You don't need to upset yourself by going down there and getting involved in all that. You shouldn't have to worry about anything except getting on with your life."

"Thanks, Dad. I appreciate your offer, but I need to go down there and help his family with the arrangements." She couldn't do something so impersonal to a woman who'd made cookies for her.

"If you insist on doing this," her mother said, "you're on your own. Your father and I will not participate in this mockery of a funeral."

*Thank goodness for small favors.*

Her father tented his fingers. He was getting ready to pronounce a verdict. Amanda sat straighter, ready to rebel. "You don't need to do that." His voice was soft, but she wasn't fooled. This was an order. "You've been through enough. We'll see that Charley and his family are taken care of. You can put all that behind you and move on."

Amanda rose, went over to her father and hugged him. "Thanks, Dad. I'll be fine. But if I get arrested for Charley's murder, I'm counting on you to bail me out in time for dinner."

The worried look on her father's face made her wonder if he knew something she didn't about the progress of the murder investigation.

☙❧

The next day, over Charley's continued protests, Amanda packed her saddlebags and prepared her ten-year old Harley Softail for the journey. The burgundy red bike wasn't as fast as the one she'd wrecked, but it would be a lot more comfortable.

The hour ride gave her plenty of time to mull over her parents' concerns about the trip as well as a growing trepidation about how she'd get through the next two days with strangers and a funeral. Irene had made all the arrangements. Tomorrow would be the "viewing and visitation," then the next day there'd be traditional funeral services at the Methodist Church, followed by a graveside service at the Silver Creek Cemetery.

The good part, the one that kept her going, was that she'd left Charley back in Dallas, running after her as she roared out of the parking lot, demanding she stay.

The Randolphs' big old farm house was a couple of miles outside of town, down a tree-lined, rutted dirt road that made Amanda glad she was on the softer-riding bike. Several pick-up trucks and a couple of older model sedans were scattered around the front yard among the trees that shaded the house.

She eased over the dirt and clumps of grass into a spot between the two cars, put down her kickstand and pulled off her helmet.

The screen door of the house burst open and two identical blond girls in cut-offs and pony tails rushed across the porch. Irene appeared behind them, wiping her hands on her apron and smiling.

The girls rushed up, surrounding her even though there were only two of them. "What a cool bike! I'm Paula!"

"I'm Penny. Can we ride?"

"You can't ride a motorcycle!"

"I gotta learn sometime!"

"We made pies!"

"Girls, girls! Let your sister get settled before you talk her to death." Irene walked up and hugged Amanda. "Come on in and meet the family. Paula, Penny, take Amanda's bags to her room." She indicated the saddlebags.

"I can do that," Amanda protested.

"No, let us!"

Amanda smiled and allowed Irene to lead her into the house. In that moment she knew she'd made the right decision in coming.

The old house was filled with food and relatives. Both continued to stream in until Amanda thought the house would burst from all the people, and the big wooden table would collapse from all the food. Irene had killed "a mean old rooster who's just been begging to get hisself into the pot" and made dumplings. That rooster might have been mean, but he certainly tasted good.

Herbert, Charley's father, a tall, quiet man who looked a little like Charley but acted nothing like him, contributed a platter of his specialty, venison sausage. "Killed that deer myself. That meat doesn't have any of those hormones and stuff you find at the grocery store."

The menu had no structure. Fried chicken sat next to pork chops. Pinto beans, baked beans and lima beans were all among the offerings. The food was served on platters, in bowls and in pans. Irene's china was comprised of at least five different patterns, some of it chipped. People heaped food onto their plates in delightful chaos and wandered around, eating and talking. It was totally wonderful. Her mother would have fainted had she been there.

Paula—or maybe it was Penny—had made a thick apple pie with lots of cinnamon and butter, and the other twin had created a buttermilk chess pie. The two animated blond girls watched and giggled as Amanda ate a piece of each pie then proclaimed that both were so good, she couldn't possibly say which was better.

Early on in the evening Amanda gave up trying to keep track of names and relationships. She smiled and ate, accepted condolences and well wishes, listened to general conversation about Charley, admired pictures of kids and grandkids, smiled when she was introduced as "Aunt

Amanda," and let herself pretend for the evening that she was part of this sprawling, boisterous family.

At the end of the evening, after everyone, including Amanda, pitched in to clean up, all the visitors finally left. Irene and the twins led Amanda upstairs to the third bedroom on the left. Charley's old room.

"There's a fan on the dresser if you get hot and a quilt in the closet if you get cold. Bathroom's at the end of the hall."

"We're right next door if you need anything," Paula assured her.

"And we won't be asleep for a long time." Penny giggled at her mother's stern glance.

After hugs from everybody, Amanda closed the door and looked around Charley's old room. It was the most comfortable room she'd ever seen, the complete opposite of the horrible stories Charley had told.

The iron bedframe, painted brown, was more ornate than the one she owned and had probably been in the family for generations rather than purchased at garage sale. The flowered bedspread had likely been added after Charley left. She couldn't see him choosing such a pattern. A small, scarred wooden desk and chair sat by the window. A place for Charley to do his school work. As Irene had said, a fan rested on the antique dresser, its cord dangling to the wooden floor.

She turned off the light and changed into her nightshirt then settled into Charley's old bed. The summer breeze coming through the open window brought the clean smells of trees and the sounds of crickets and night birds. This was the most relaxed she'd felt since Charley died. No fear of cops with arrest warrants, no drunks taking a leak on her property, no Charley freaking out about Kimball.

"Amanda, you shouldn't be here."

No! Charley couldn't be here.

Amanda squeezed her eyes tightly shut and pulled the sheet over her head.

"Stop doing that," he ordered. "Don't pretend you didn't hear me. Get up and talk to me."

Amanda rolled onto her back and threw the sheet away from her face. "What are you doing here? How did you get here?"

"On the back of your bike. You ride like a maniac. No wonder you get so many speeding tickets."

"You hitched a ride on the back of my bike and now you're complaining about the way I ride? Is there nowhere I can go to get away from you?"

"I don't think so. You need my help, so I'm going to be with you. We have to leave."

"It's too late. I already know about the lies you told me. *A sofa in the living room while your mother turned tricks and took drugs in the only bedroom?* Shame on you, Charley Randolph! You had a wonderful home life. Your family's wonderful. How could you make up all those lies about them?"

Charley, glowing luminescent and faintly transparent in the moonlight, flinched. "Okay, maybe I embellished a little."

Amanda sat upright in bed. "*Embellished a little?* You slandered these nice people who loved you and raised you. You lied. You said horrible things about them. Why did you do that? That served no purpose, even in your scams. Certainly it served no purpose in our relationship."

Charley looked out the window. "If you'd known about my family, you'd have wanted to meet them. You'd have wanted to come here."

"Duh!"

He shook his head. "You can't be here."

"What does it hurt if I'm with your family?"

An odd expression flashed across Charley's face, one she hadn't seen there before. It was gone so fast she

96

couldn't be certain, but it looked suspiciously like guilt and remorse.

Amanda groaned and fell back onto the bed. "Are you going to start on the Kimball thing again?"

Charley regarded her intently, and she thought for a moment he was going to say something important. But he only nodded. "Yes, you're in danger from Kimball. He killed that woman and he killed me. What's one more body when you're on a roll? At least in Dallas he had to make an effort to get to you, but now you've walked right into his hands. And by coming down here, it's like you're throwing it in his face that you know about him. You're in danger. He tried to kill you once. You want to end up like me? Dead?"

"No, I do not want to end up like you." If she died, would she have to travel around with Charley? Did they have divorce where Charley was? Would she be stuck with him through eternity? That was a far worse vision of hell than Dante's *Inferno*. "Go away, Charley."

"I've been left behind to take care of you. I'm sure of that now."

"You're nuts. You were nuts when you were alive, and dying hasn't improved your sanity. If you want to take care of me, disappear forever. Leave me alone. Let me enjoy your family, put your lying, cheating body in the ground and go back home."

"I can't disappear. You need me."

"Fine. Don't disappear. Go sit in the corner. Just shut up so I can sleep. And don't go downstairs and turn on the television. If you're bored, well, that's just too bad. It's your punishment for all the terrible things you did during your life. Karma."

She pulled the sheet over her head again.

Charley was quiet for a long moment. "Promise me you'll stay with my family the whole time you're here and go home immediately after the funeral."

"That's exactly what I plan to do, but I'm not promising you anything. Look what happened to the last promise—*love, honor and cherish.*"

Charley gave a big sigh but remained silent. Amanda didn't look, didn't want to see if he was still there.

However, the peaceful night she'd anticipated was ruined. She couldn't relax with Charley there.

And even though she thought he was probably lying about Kimball and the potential danger to her, she couldn't dismiss a niggling worry. Her motorcycle had been sabotaged, and she almost died. Somebody had tried to kill her. Was she now in close proximity to her would-be killer?

# Chapter Ten

Wrong, just wrong, Amanda thought as she squirmed uncomfortably on the first pew of the Methodist Church. Her mother-in-law sat beside her while her deceased husband lay in the coffin at the front of the church as well as stood beside it, peering in, criticizing what the undertaker had done with his body.

"Look at my hair. It's awful! I never wore my hair like that. And *make-up*? They put *make-up* on me? I hope you didn't pay these people to make me look like this, Amanda."

She glared at him, wishing she'd had him cremated. That would have solved the hair and make-up problems.

Things didn't improve as the pastor delivered the eulogy.

"Why'd he have to tell that schmaltzy story from when I was a kid? Makes it sound like pulling that cat out of that pond was the only good thing I ever did."

*Probably was.* Amanda made a note to tell Charley her thoughts later, including the cremation regret. For the time being, all she could do was scowl at him while Irene sobbed softly into a tissue. Herbert slipped a consoling arm about his wife's shoulder, his own eyes moist.

Finally the service ended. Amanda started out of the church with the family while Charley entertained himself by telling her all the "secrets" of the people around them.

"Big bald guy over there, Hayden Marshall, drinks a couple of beers every Sunday morning before he goes to the First Baptist Church with his wife. Can't blame him. Look at his wife. She never shuts up. That tall blond over there? She's not a natural blond. Want to know how I know?"

"Charley!" Amanda gasped involuntarily.

Irene slipped an arm around her waist. "I know, Amanda. I can't help calling to him myself sometimes. I keep expecting him to come around the corner, smiling, telling us it was all one of his practical jokes."

Amanda clenched her teeth and glowered at Charley.

"Hey, I was just going to tell you I dated her hairdresser. What did you think I was going to say, Amanda?" Charley's laughter died abruptly. "It's Kimball. He's here."

In spite of her certainty that all this Kimball stuff was nonsense, Amanda tensed at the genuine fear in Charley's voice.

A tall, dark man approached. "Herbert, Irene, I wanted to come by and pay my respects. I'm so sorry about your loss." He grasped each of their hands in turn.

"Thank you," Herbert mumbled.

The man was good-looking in a smooth, movie-star way, a way that would compel the attention of others from across the room. But up close, there was something disturbing in his eyes. They were large and brown and should have called up images of puppy dogs. Instead they sent a shiver down Amanda's spine. This man's gaze was not a warm brown. His eyes were cold and hard like a frozen pool in an underground cave where sunlight never had and never would touch.

The owner of those cold eyes reached for Amanda's hand. "And this must be Charley's widow. I'm Roland Kimball, mayor of our little town." She reflexively drew back. Not that she really believed this small town official had murdered Charley or was a threat to her. It was those eyes. If she touched him, she might be sucked into their frigid depths and never return.

"Yes." She forced a smile and tried to act as if she weren't deliberately ignoring his outstretched hand. "I'm Charley's widow."

"Be careful," Charley whispered.

100

"It's nice to meet you, Mrs. Randolph. How long will you be staying in our little town?" His voice and his smile were warm and compelling. Only his eyes gave him away, turning his words into a veiled threat.

"Tell him you're leaving tomorrow!" Charley ordered.

She wanted to leave right then, that very minute. Push through the crowd, get to her motorcycle and ride away from the man as fast as she could. "I'm not sure," she said defiantly. "I may stay several days with my…my husband's family. Get to know *everybody*." She emphasized the last word, returning his veiled threat—if, indeed, such a threat existed.

"She's going to be staying as long as we can keep her," Irene confirmed, smiling at Amanda.

"No!" Charley protested, waving his arms frantically. "You gotta get out of here! Go home! Buy a gun! Move in with the judge!"

"I hope to see you again while I'm here," Amanda said sweetly.

"I can't believe you said that!" Charley shrieked. "Are you nuts? Are you trying to get yourself killed?"

"I'm sure that can be arranged." For a fleeting instant, Amanda thought Kimball was responding to Charley's question about getting herself killed. Of course he had replied to her comment that she hoped to see him again. Nevertheless, his words chilled her. Perhaps the meaning was the same as if he had replied to Charley.

Kimball continued to smile. "Good day, Irene, Herbert, Mrs. Randolph." He turned away, offering condolences to other members of the family.

"That guy gives me the creeps," Irene said.

"Ah, you just don't like him cause he's rich," Herbert drawled.

"You don't like him either."

"No, I reckon I don't," Herbert said.

101

"Why?" Amanda asked.

Herbert shrugged.

"I won't gossip at my son's funeral," Irene said. "We'll talk later."

"Way to go, Amanda!" Charley exclaimed. "You want rid of me? You're never gonna get rid of me. I'm supposed to help you, but I can't help you when you won't listen to me. You're gonna die and be with me forever and we're both going to be stuck here. No white light. No forever after. What were you thinking, egging Kimball on like that, telling him you're staying here, that you'll see him again?"

Amanda wasn't sure of the answer to that question. Obstinacy, perhaps, thwarting Charley's orders. A determination to prove that Charley was lying. Or maybe that Charley was telling the truth.

Somebody had tried to kill her. Now that she'd seen the Kimball character in the flesh, she wasn't so certain Charley had made up the whole story.

"Amanda!"

She whirled at the note of increased stress in Charley's voice.

"I...uh...you need to..." He waved a hand vaguely toward the front of the church.

"Look, Herbert, there's Sunny and her mother," Irene said, and Amanda turned again, this time in the direction Irene was pointing.

Across the room, she met the wide gaze of a tall, slim woman with barely tamed red hair pulled back from a porcelain face. Beside her stood an older, slightly-stooped woman with short white hair who was also looking in Amanda's direction. The younger woman seemed vaguely familiar, but before Amanda could place her, she averted her gaze, spoke to the older woman, and both turned and walked out the door.

"That was nice of them to come," Herbert said.

"Who is she?" Amanda asked as the woman disappeared into the crowd outside. "The woman with red hair."

"Sunny Donovan. She's a lawyer. Nice lady. Takes care of her mother, helps a lot of people around town. Helped Charley when he got in some trouble a few years ago."

Behind her, Charley groaned.

"What kind of trouble?" she asked, more to make conversation than because she really cared about the answer. She was still trying to remember where she'd seen Sunny Donovan. Irene said the woman was a lawyer, so perhaps they'd met through her father. Or maybe, judging from Charley's apparent desire that she not see Ms. Donovan, she and Charley had been involved in more than her helping him with legal issues. That wouldn't be surprising either.

"Drugs," Irene said.

"It was just a little pot." Charley moved up beside Amanda. "No big deal. Let it go."

"He got in with a bad crowd," Irene continued.

Her husband snorted. "He started the bad crowd."

Charley grinned. "I always was a leader."

"Now, Herbert. Everybody does foolish things when they're young."

"Wasn't any younger than you and I were when we got married." Herbert's blue eyes twinkled as he spoke the words.

"And some would say that was a foolish thing." Irene took her husband's arm and gazing up at him fondly.

Amanda couldn't imagine her parents teasing each other or her mother gazing at her father with such an open, loving expression.

A tall man wearing an ill-fitting suit moved out of the crowd and draped a long arm around Irene's shoulders. Son Hank, the carpenter, a younger version of his father.

"We need to leave for the cemetery, Mama," he said softly.

Still clutching her husband's arm, Irene turned to her oldest son and nodded, her features crumbling at the reminder that they would soon be burying one of her children.

"The cemetery?" Charley exclaimed. "That place is creepy. I'm not going there."

Impulsively, Amanda stepped forward and took Irene's hand. "That's not Charley in that casket," she blurted. "He's still here." *Oh, great,* she thought as she realized what she was saying. *That'll comfort her a lot. Tell her Charley's a ghost and let her think her new-found daughter-in-law is nuts.* "I mean..."

Irene patted her hand. "I know what you mean. Charley will be with us in our hearts as long as we have his memory."

"Damn straight," Charley said. "I'm here and I'm not going anywhere anytime soon. Certainly not to that cemetery. Hey, what if I suffocate when they put my body under all that dirt? Come on, Amanda. Let's get out of here."

"I believe there's a tradition," Amanda said, "that someone close to the deceased drops the first bit of dirt onto the casket after they put it in the grave. If you don't mind, I'd like to have that honor."

"Of course you can." Irene smiled through her tears. "If Charley's watching from heaven, I'm sure he's real proud that you want to do that."

"I feel certain he's watching."

"That's low, Amanda," Charley said, "really low."

Amanda gave him a brief smirk as she joined the rest of the family, heading for the cemetery.

ॐ∽ॐ

Amanda piled fried chicken, fried okra, fried squash, Crowder peas, fried potatoes with onions, and a slice of

104

smoked ham onto a plate painted with purple flowers. She grabbed a fork with bent tines and a fruit jar filled with iced tea.

The after-funeral event packed the little house with more people and food than the first evening. They filled the house, the front porch and much of the yard.

She could get used to this. Perhaps it was a good thing Charley hadn't introduced her to his family. The thought of losing these wonderful people with their wonderful food would have made it a lot harder to divorce his sorry butt.

She pushed through the crowd to an unoccupied chair in a corner of the living room and sat down with her plate.

"Wish I could still eat." Charley sat cross legged on the floor. One of his knees passed through an elderly woman's stocking-clad leg.

"I wish you'd go away." Amanda bit into a crunchy drumstick, savoring the moist chicken.

"Mrs. Kemp probably killed that chicken this morning. Doesn't that bother you?"

"Might if that chicken's ghost was haunting me, but it's not." She took a bite of the okra. "Mmmm! This is so good!"

"You can be a cold woman, Amanda."

"I don't think the okra suffered."

"I'm talking about that huge clod of dirt you threw on my coffin. And you threw it with so much force. I'm surprised you didn't break the coffin."

"That was my intention. Break the coffin and throw the dirt in your face. Tell me about Sunny Donovan."

Charley's eyes widened, his face went distinctly pale, even for a ghost, and his gaze slid to the side. All those reactions belied his casual shrug. "Sunny does a lot of free legal work. You heard what my mother said. She got me out of a scrape once. A little pot. No big deal."

"You're lying to me, Charley."

His eyes lifted to meet her gaze. "I'm not! I told you I can't lie."

"You told me Kimball was outside my apartment, and it was just some drunk taking a leak. You told me he put poison in my coffee and broke my step."

"Okay, sometimes I may be mistaken, but I can't lie."

"And I'm supposed to believe that, why?"

"Ask me a question and I'll try to lie and you'll see."

Amanda realized Charley's assertion made absolutely no sense, but it was worth a shot just in case he might burst into flames or be sucked away into a void should he try to lie. "Did you sleep with Sunny Donovan?"

"No!" he responded indignantly. "I can't believe you'd even ask me something like that."

"She's beautiful."

"She's old."

"Did you try to sleep with her?"

Charley opened his mouth, and his face contorted as if the muscles were battling with each other. "N-n-n-yes." He drew in a deep breath and glared. "I hope you're happy now."

"There you are." Irene came up, and Charley moved away. "I've been looking for you. I see you got some food. If you haven't had dessert yet, you have got to have some of Dorothy Crawley's pecan pie. She's got a tree in her back yard and shelled the pecans herself this morning."

Amanda let Irene lead her across the room though she would have liked to question Charley further about Sunny Donovan. Being rejected by a woman didn't seem enough to explain the way Charley acted about her. That, added to the fact Amanda was certain she'd met the woman before, aroused her curiosity. Before she left Silver Creek, she was going to find some way to meet Sunny Donovan.

A shiver darted down her spine as she recalled the other person in Silver Creek she needed to find out about.

Mayor Kimball. If half of what Charley said about him was true, if he had stolen the gun that could prove her innocence, she would have to somehow get that gun back. After meeting the man and looking into his eyes, Charley's stories didn't seem so ridiculous.

"He's outside!" Charley hissed, as if reading her mind. She hoped that was not one of his special ghost abilities.

"Are you going to start that again?" Amanda whispered, turning her head toward Charley, away from Irene.

"I saw him. He's out there jacking with your motorcycle."

It was unlikely the distinguished mayor of Silver Creek would be outside in the dark, doing something to her motorcycle, but it wouldn't hurt to check.

"I'm going out for some fresh air," she said to Irene.

"You go right ahead. It is getting awful hot and crowded in here."

Amanda made her way to the front door and out on the porch. A man stood beside her motorcycle, looking down.

"I told you," Charley gloated.

She ran toward the man. "What are you doing?"

Kimball lifted his cold gaze to hers and smiled. "Nice bike."

She stopped in her tracks, a chill sliding over her in the warm night. It was him. Charley was right. Not some distant cousin admiring her motorcycle, not some vagrant thinking about stealing it or urinating on it. Next to her bike stood the man who, according to Charley, had tried to kill her by sabotaging her other motorcycle.

"Yes," she said. "It's a nice bike. What are you doing to it?"

He lifted his hands in a gesture of innocence and moved away from the bike, walking toward her. "Just looking at it. I ride a little."

She took an involuntary step backward, away from him. "Why are you here?"

"I came to pay my respects to the grieving family. Why are you here?"

"I'm a member of that grieving family. I have a right to be here."

"Oh? Two weeks ago you'd never met these people and now you're a family member? That's why you're here? That's the only reason?" He was no longer smiling, and his dark gaze held her as surely as if his hands gripped her. Suddenly the smile returned and he looked past her, over her shoulder. "Hello, Irene."

Amanda spun around to see her mother-in-law standing in the open doorway.

"Hello, Roland. How nice of you to drop by." Irene was saying the polite words, but she didn't sound as if she meant them. "Do come in. We have plenty of food and iced tea."

Kimball moved past Amanda, up the porch steps and into the house.

Irene remained on the porch. "Are you okay, Amanda?"

Amanda drew in a deep breath, steadying herself. "Yes. Fine. I'll be there in a couple of minutes."

But she wasn't fine. She was freaked out and a little frightened. *That's why you're here? That's the only reason?* What had he meant by that? Since a normal person would expect her to be at her ex-husband's funeral, was Kimball asking if she was there to expose him for his crimes?

She shivered then forced herself to walk over to her Harley. "What did that monster do to my bike?" she asked Charley.

"I don't know."

"What do you mean, you don't know? You said you saw him doing something."

"I saw him standing there. He'd already done it, or maybe he was thinking about doing it."

"So you didn't really see anything?"

Charley's amiable features became suddenly serious. "I saw the way he looked at you. I heard what he said to you. He thinks you're here because of him. He's scared of you, of what you know, and that makes him dangerous. You need to go back to Dallas tonight."

"Go back to Dallas? You think I'll be safe there? You didn't think so when you were finding poison in my coffee and attempted murder in my dry rot. Why are you so anxious to get me away from here?"

Charley looked down, avoiding her eyes. "You need to go back to Dallas. You need to trust me on this one." With that pronouncement, he disappeared. Into the house, into the dark, wherever he went when he wanted to avoid her.

Amanda couldn't inspect her bike properly until daylight. She went back inside. This would be a good opportunity to corner Kimball in the safe environment of so many people. She was going to demand some answers, though she wasn't sure what the questions were.

He eluded her all evening, moving through the crowd with a politician's practiced smoothness, then slipping away into the night.

# Chapter Eleven

Amanda checked her bike carefully that morning and found no evidence of tampering. Nevertheless, she rode more slowly than usual as she made her way to the downtown area to find Kimball.

The Silver Creek courthouse dominated the small town square. A venerable old building of red brick and limestone with wide steps and ornate columns of white marble, it was flanked on one side by a large live oak tree and the Silver Creek Police Department and City Jail, and on the other by a large live oak tree and the Silver Creek Fire department. All very symmetrical.

She passed the government buildings and went on to the end of the square, choosing a parking space in front of the First Baptist Church. She pulled off her helmet but remained astride her bike as she surveyed the quiet morning scene.

A young man polished a bright red fire truck that sat half in and half out the wide door of the fire department. Two men climbed the steps of the courthouse, one wearing a tailored, immaculate suit and carrying a briefcase, the other wearing a rumpled, ill-fitting suit and looking nervous. Easy to figure out their relationship. Lawyer and client. Probably guilty client.

Across the street from the Courthouse, Paw Paw's Cafe offered daytime fare while Billy Earl's Roadhouse promised evening entertainment. Small shops offered ice cream, candy and books. Manikins from the '50s wearing modern clothing posed in the windows of Hunt's Department Store. The Methodist Church where they'd attended Charley's funeral service yesterday sat at the far end of the square.

Small town serenity. On the surface.

She took the key from her bike and stood, peeling off her leather jacket in the growing warmth of the early morning sunshine. Helmet tucked under one arm and jacket tossed over her shoulder, she made her way to the white wrought iron bench under a magnolia tree on one side of the First Baptist Church lawn. The position provided her with a good view of the courthouse steps and the empty parking space reserved for the mayor. She'd be able to track Kimball's comings and goings, though she wasn't quite certain how that information was going to help her. The man wasn't likely to emerge, wielding her stolen gun and shouting a confession.

Hard to imagine the creepy Mayor Kimball inside this building that reeked of tradition and justice.

She sank onto the bench.

"What are you doing here?"

Amanda gasped, startled by the abrupt question. The familiar figure stood beside her, his feet not quite touching the grass.

"I might ask the same question of you. I thought dead people were supposed to leave this world." An elderly woman walking down the sidewalk eyed her curiously. "Good morning!" Amanda forced herself to smile. She'd met the woman at Charley's funeral but couldn't remember her name.

"Good morning, Miz Randolph," the woman replied, her tone and expression sympathetic.

"The whole town's going to think I'm nuts, talking to myself," Amanda muttered when the woman had passed.

"Grief-stricken over my death."

"Grief-stricken over your continued existence. Go away."

"You know I can't. I have to save you, and you're making it really hard, hanging around here. What are you trying to do? With me and the judge both telling you to go home, why are you still here?" Though she hadn't seen

111

Charley after his abrupt disappearance last night, obviously he'd been there when she'd called her father before going to bed.

"Dad told me to come home and you ordered me to go home. But your mother, your father, your sisters and about fifty other relatives asked me to stay *at least a week* or *until our barbeque next week* or even *until our big Independence Day celebration.* I think I'll go with the majority on this decision. Besides, if I go home now, they may put me in jail for killing you."

"You think you're some kind of a detective? You're going to prove Kimball murdered me?"

When Charley said it like that, the whole thing sounded absurd. "If I could just get my gun from him, at least I could prove I didn't do it. As for proving Kimball's guilt and seeing that he's punished for his crimes, who cares? If I find out for sure he murdered you, I'll give him a reward."

"Nice talk, Amanda."

A black Cadillac pulled into the mayor's parking space.

"There he is!" Amanda reached to grab Charley's arm, but her fingers slid through the chilly space. She shook her hand to rid it of the eerie sensation, but that same chill stuck in the middle of her chest, an area that hadn't even been close to Charley. She forced her gaze to remain focused on the car, forced herself to remain seated rather than follow her impulse to get on her bike and ride as fast as she could away from that car and the man she knew was driving it.

The driver's side door opened, and Roland Kimball emerged.

Amanda swallowed, trying to push down the lump that had somehow crept into her throat.

*Now what?*

Amanda drew in a deep breath and stood.

*Left foot forward.*

*Right foot forward.*

On shaky legs, she moved toward the courthouse.

"What are you doing? Where are you going?" Charley called from behind her.

The fear in his voice increased her determination and steadied her steps. Be damned if she'd let him know she was scared.

"Amanda, come back here!"

Her path intersected Kimball's just as he reached the bottom of the courthouse steps.

"Hi," she said, the sound more a croak than a word.

Sunglasses hid the man's demon eyes, but the rest of his face revealed enough to make Amanda cringe and wish she'd followed Charley's advice to go back. "Still here, Mrs. Randolph?"

He moved to go past her, and suddenly anger gave her courage. She hadn't come this far to be ignored. She moved with him, into his path.

"Could we...uh..." Okay, she hadn't thought this through. What was she going to ask him? *Could we get together for drinks, and oh, by the way, if you have my gun, would you please bring it along?*

"Is there something I can do for you?" The mayor stood his ground, seeming to grow in size, blocking the sun.

"Yes." She lifted her chin. "We need to talk. About a gun."

His jaw firmed, and his lips thinned. "We have nothing to talk about, and you have no reason to be here. Good day, Mrs. Randolph." He turned, dismissing her, and strode up the courthouse steps.

Amanda stood for a moment, blinking in the sunlight. The man had walked away and left her. Ignored her as if she were nobody. She wanted to call after him, to demand he talk to her, demand he confess to stealing her gun, to killing Charley, to trying to kill her, maybe even to killing Jimmy Hoffa.

She had accomplished one thing. Now she knew he had her gun. He hadn't flinched when she'd mentioned it. An innocent person would have been astonished at the accusation.

That gave credence to the possibility he had murdered Charley and tried to kill her.

She walked slowly across the square, back to the bench where Charley waited.

"That went well, Nancy Drew," Charley said.

"I found out for sure he's got my gun."

"I told you that already."

"Yeah, and you also told me your mother was a dead prostitute."

"That was when I was alive. It doesn't count."

Pointless to argue. She had more important things to think about than Charley, things like staying alive while she got her gun back so she could stay out of prison.

Amanda picked up her helmet and jacket. As she started toward her motorcycle, a gleam of bright fire drew her attention back to the courthouse steps. A familiar figure moved upward, the morning sunlight spinning her red hair into flames.

"There's that woman from the funeral, Sunny something or other."

"Sunny Donovan." Charley's voice sounded choked.

Amanda turned toward him. He looked as if someone was choking him.

"What is it with this woman?" Amanda demanded. "You said you didn't sleep with her."

"I didn't."

"Then why do you act so strange every time she comes around?"

Charley gazed into the distance, his lips tightly compressed.

114

"Come to think of it, you never acted the least bit guilty when you slept with some bimbo." She watched the tall, regal figure of Sunny Donovan disappear into the courthouse. "And that woman doesn't look like any of your other bimbos. She's dignified, not sleazy."

Charley said nothing. That meant something.

"You said you can't lie to me."

He looked at her, and this time she was certain she saw guilt and remorse in his gaze. "It's true. I can't lie."

*Guilt and remorse.* She would have sworn Charley couldn't spell either of those emotions, let alone feel them.

Had he hurt Sunny Donovan?

He'd hurt her—his wife—and never shown the slightest signs of guilt or remorse.

It was hard to imagine that elegant woman involved with Charley in any other capacity than as his lawyer, trying to keep his sorry ass out of jail.

But something was going on, something she needed to know.

"Then tell me the story about Sunny Donovan. Why do you freak out when she comes around? What's going on between you two? And where do I know her from?"

He said nothing.

"So you can't lie to me, but that's not the same thing as refusing to answer. Is that the deal?"

Charley shrugged, a remnant of his old, arrogant expression returning in his half-smile.

"Fine." She took a step forward. "I'll go ask her myself." After approaching Kimball, talking to this lady who seemed quite nice would be a snap.

"Wait!" A chill wind passed through Amanda's arm as Charley attempted to grab it and restrain her.

"Why should I wait?"

Charley opened his mouth as if to speak then closed it again. "You don't understand."

"My point exactly. I don't understand about Sunny Donovan, but I'm going to."

"No!"

She leaned forward, invading his space. He took a step backward. Oh, yeah. Something was going on. Charley never backed away.

"Then talk," she ordered. "Tell me why you don't want me to meet her. Tell me what's going on with that woman."

Charley drew in a deep breath and squared his shoulders as if prepared for battle. "If I help you get your gun back from Kimball so you can prove you didn't kill me with it, will you go home to Dallas, get out of Silver Creek?"

Amanda folded her arms and studied him. This was a completely unexpected turn of events. Mild curiosity about the woman had just turned into a puzzle she was determined to solve.

"Is that it?" she asked. "You help me get the gun, I go back to Dallas? That's all I have to do in exchange for your services?"

Charley's features contorted, his lips twisting as if they wanted to speak but he was trying to keep them shut.

"What else do you want from me, Charley? What's the rest of the deal?"

Charley opened his mouth then closed it. He rose a few inches off the sidewalk, straightened and met her gaze. "Forget about Sunny Donovan."

Wow. The Sunny Donovan story was big, so big Charley would do anything to keep her from finding out. "Okay, sure," she said.

Maybe Charley couldn't lie, but she could.

# Chapter Twelve

Only Irene and Amanda were home for lunch. The house was unusually but not uncomfortably quiet. All the windows stood open, and ceiling fans whirred in each room. A mockingbird chirped, tweeted, and trilled its diverse song from a nearby tree. Leaves on the dozens of large trees around the house stirred quietly in the faint breeze, their shade shielding the house from the midday heat. After her morning meeting with Kimball, Amanda had expected to feel stressed for at least the rest of her life, but Irene and this house had a calming effect.

"I thought we could have some ham sandwiches, if that's okay with you," Irene said, taking a large platter from the refrigerator. "Allan Middleton smokes his hams with mesquite instead of hickory. Some say he just does it because he has so much mesquite on his property. I say it's the best ham I ever ate so who cares why he does it."

"I agree," Amanda replied. There had been such a quantity of food the day before, she'd only eaten a few bites of the ham. However, those bites, unadorned with any of the fancy sauces her mother favored, had, indeed, been the best ham she'd ever eaten. "What can I do to help?"

"Why don't you look through the refrigerator and see if you can find that potato salad Alta Bernhart brought. And pick out anything else you see that looks good."

Amanda opened the refrigerator door and peered at the large quantity of food crammed inside. "It all looks good. If I stay here very long, I'll gain so much weight, I won't be able to get through the door of my shop."

"That's a big door. You'll have to eat a lot of ham and potato salad."

"I can do that." Amanda located the large glass bowl of potato salad and put it on the table.

"If you'll get the plates and silverware, I'll slice a tomato, pour some tea, and we'll be ready to eat."

Amanda set the table while Irene added tomato, lettuce and pickles to the tray of ham then cut slices from a loaf of homemade bread and poured the translucent amber tea into ice-filled glasses.

Finally they sat down at one end of the wooden table. Amanda built her sandwich, took a big bite and a drink of the cold, sweet tea.

"This is wonderful." She leaned back with a sigh. "Not just the food. You, your home, your family." This place and these people were one-hundred-eighty degrees different from her home and family, but Amanda felt more comfortable, more at home here than she'd ever felt in that mausoleum in which her mother held court.

Irene smiled, the lines around her eyes tilting upward. Beverly Caulfield would never have allowed those lines to appear on her face. Of course, her mother didn't smile often enough to cause them. "We're your family too," Irene said. "I can't tell you how much it means to me, to all of us, that you came down here, that we finally got to meet you and welcome you to the family." The smile remained, but her blue eyes misted. "You're all we have left of Charley."

*If you only knew.* Amanda's gaze searched the corners of the room to see if he was lurking. His mother would have been thrilled to see him again. Amanda would have been thrilled to *never* see him again.

For the moment, he was not in sight. She could relax and have a chat with this woman he'd kept hidden from her. "I don't understand why he told me..." She stopped herself before telling Irene the horrible stories he'd fabricated about his family. "Why he never told me about you all. I never even knew he talked to you."

118

"He was trying to protect you."

*Not likely. Protect himself, maybe.* "Protect me? From what?"

Irene sipped from her tea then set it on the table. "I don't know. He said he was in trouble, and all he could say was that we couldn't tell anybody where he was or who he was married to."

"So it was okay if people knew he was married, just as long as they didn't know my name?"

"That's right," Irene confirmed. "He told me your first name but not your last. He didn't intend to say that much, but he talked about you so often, it just came out."

If Charley admitted he was married, that probably ruled out Charley's hiding from an ex-girlfriend. Amanda chewed another bite of sandwich then decided to go for it. "How well did Charley know the mayor?"

Irene's gaze sharpened, and she frowned slightly. "Roland Kimball? Him and Charley didn't exactly travel in the same circles."

"Maybe not, but they had some sort of connection, didn't they?"

Irene shook her head. "No, but after Charley left, the mayor came by looking for him. Said he needed to talk to him about a business deal he thought Charley might be interested in."

"What kind of business deal?"

"He didn't say. I couldn't have told him anything even if I'd wanted to since Charley had left a few days before and hadn't told me where he was going. Roland seemed upset. Like the deal was important. Like he didn't believe me. When Charley finally called me, I told him about Roland's visit. He said he didn't know anything about a deal, and I shouldn't tell the mayor or anybody else where he was."

"Because he was in danger."

Irene nodded.

119

"From the mayor?"

"He never said that." Irene hesitated then continued. "I thought it probably had something to do with him. Otherwise, why would he have come around looking for Charley? I figured..." She bit her lip.

"You figured Charley had run some kind of a scam on the mayor."

Irene sighed. "Charley had a good heart. But the things he did weren't always good."

Amanda could attest to that. "He told you he was in Dallas?"

"Oh, no. I figure it was Dallas because that's where he'd always wanted to go. But I never told anybody what I thought. We didn't know where he was living or anything until the police came down here to talk to us after he..." Her voice wavered, she blinked a couple of times, then cleared her throat. "After he was killed."

Amanda ate a couple more bites of sandwich and some potato salad while she considered the ramifications of what Irene had told her. Adding her mother-in-law's information to what she'd learned about Kimball that morning, Charley's crazy stories were beginning to sound a lot less crazy. If Charley had blackmailed then double-crossed Kimball, he would need to hide, and a big city like Dallas was a good place to do that. But Dallas was only an hour's drive away. Silver Creek was practically a suburb of Dallas. It would have made more sense for him to go farther—Los Angeles, Chicago, Houston.

There were still a lot of unanswered questions, and Charley, for all his new-found honesty, probably wouldn't answer them. Perhaps she could verify the crime Charley claimed started all this mess.

"Was there a murder just before Charley left town, Dianne somebody?"

Irene nodded. "Why, yes. Dianne Carter. Charley told you about that? It was awful. They found her body in her car out by the lake. Shot and killed, her purse missing. Young mother, left a husband and two kids. Pecan pie?"

Amanda blinked in surprise at the abrupt change of subject, but this was the way of Irene's world. No matter what bad things happened, she kept her family fed. "Yes, please." Amanda accepted a piece and took a bite before she continued. "They ever catch the killer?"

"No. Had to be somebody passing through. She was the sweetest thing. Taught Sunday school at our church. Her and Greg—that's her husband—were always helping people, working with kids to keep them off drugs, delivering Christmas baskets to poor people. Greg's the coach at the high school. Penny and Paula have him for track, and they think he's wonderful."

"Sounds like Dianne was a regular saint." *Too good to be true?*

"Nobody ever had a bad word to say about her. Everybody loved her."

"Everybody? How about Mayor Kimball?"

Irene sat quietly for a few seconds, her blue gaze narrowed. Perhaps her mother-in-law wasn't quite as naïve as she seemed. "Funny you ask that. Dianne and Roland were sweethearts in high school. Everybody assumed they'd get married after they got out of college."

"But they didn't."

Irene wadded her paper napkin and put it on her empty plate. "People change. Nobody knows why they broke up, but they both came back and married different people."

"Did they stay friends? Or did they hate each other?"

"Dianne didn't hate anybody. But whatever happened with her and Roland, they kept their distance after that. Acted like strangers. Too bad. I think his mama and daddy were disappointed."

"They liked Dianne?"

"Everybody liked Dianne. Her family wasn't wealthy like the Kimballs. Her folks own a farm, raise soybeans, run a few head of cattle. But she was a good influence on Roland. He was pretty wild in high school. Son of the richest man in town. Privileged. Arrogant even then. Samuel Kimball, his daddy, doesn't want any taint on the family name. Mind you, that old man's not perfect, but he's always kept his sins under the table. He expected his only son to do the same. So when Roland started dating Dianne and settled down, Samuel was happy about it." She grinned a little sheepishly. "In a small town, we mind each other's business. It's better than daytime television."

"Did the police find Dianne's killer?"

Irene stood and began tidying the kitchen. "At first they thought it might be Claude Dobyns. Leastwise, they acted like they suspected him. I think they just wanted to look like they were doing something. Claude's different, so he gets picked on a lot."

"What do you mean, *different*?"

"He never was quite right in the head. His mama died when he was born. His daddy was too stingy to pay a doctor, had a neighbor woman come over, so Miz Dobyns died, and they say the baby didn't come out right." Irene ran water into one side of the sink and squirted in dishwashing liquid.

Amanda stood. "Where are your dishtowels?"

"Second drawer, over there."

Amanda pulled a snowy white dishtowel from the designated drawer. "That's sad," she said, "what happened to Claude."

"And it just got worse. His daddy raised him on their little farm a few miles from town, kept him out of school and made him work. Some say he beat him. I'd believe that of old man Dobyns."

The summer breezes coming through the window over the kitchen sink brought scents of magnolia blossoms

122

to mingle with the lemon scent of the dishwashing liquid. Irene set the glasses in the water and selected the first to wash.

"Anyway," she continued, "his daddy died a few years ago. Claude still stays at the farm, but I hear the place is bad run down. Claude drinks some, but that's not what's wrong with him. Mostly he's just not right. Thinks everybody's out to hurt him. Dianne used to take him food, and he tolerated her pretty good but then one day she brought out a doctor who wanted to put Claude on some medicine." She rinsed the glass, set it on the rack and began washing the next one.

"Schizophrenia meds? Bi-polar?" Amanda picked up the glass and wiped the moisture from it then set it in the cabinet.

"Don't know. But whatever that medicine was, Claude didn't take kindly to it. He threw an awful fit and run them both off his land. Threatened them with a shotgun."

"Does Claude live close to the lake where Dianne was killed?" she asked.

"Nope. Not close to the grocery store she went to either. The police couldn't find anything to say Claude did it. No trace of her purse or the money in it anywhere on his farm. They said he cried when he found out she was dead."

Amanda dried the final plate, a little disappointed the ritual was ended. It had been soothing and had established a connection between her and her mother-in-law, as if the two of them were bonded in some important activity. She'd never dried dishes with her own mother. She doubted her mother had ever washed a dish in her pampered life. Too bad.

"Did the police question Mayor Kimball about her death? I mean, since they used to date and broke up?"

Irene pulled a plug, and the soapy water gurgled as it rushed down the drain. "You mean just because he seems like a bad person?"

Irene's response surprised her. Amanda had expected her to think the question was totally out of line. "Something like that." *Because your son claims he was blackmailing Kimball for Dianne's murder.*

"No, the mayor was never a suspect."

As she watched Irene wipe off the counter and table top, Amanda reflected that the evidence was building to support Charley's claims. It was possible Kimball had killed his former girlfriend. She had no idea why and didn't suppose that really mattered. All that mattered was that she somehow get her gun back from the psycho mayor and prove she hadn't shot Charley.

A terrible thought hit her. What if he'd thrown her gun away like Charley said he did with the gun he used to murder Dianne? In that case, she had no choice but to forget about Kimball, go back to Dallas, and trust in the legal system.

After all her years of watching judges and lawyers in action, she knew she'd be better off trusting Charley than the legal system, and she'd be better off trusting the hangman than trusting Charley.

The jury might even deem it premeditated murder since she and Charley had been fighting so much, and, by her own admission, she'd had the gun in her possession before his murder.

Twenty-five to life.

When she got out of prison—if she got out of prison—would she still be able to ride a motorcycle? Would they still be making motorcycles or would everything be hovercraft?

Suddenly she wasn't feeling so good.

Maybe she'd better call her dad and see if they could work out some kind of a deal.

"Amanda, are you okay?" Irene asked. "You look kinda pale. Did that food not set well?"

"I'm fine. No, I'm not fine. I probably shouldn't have eaten that second piece of pie."

"You only had one piece of pie."

"I should have had two. If you'll excuse me, I think I'll go lie down for a few minutes."

Irene looked worried. "Holler if you need anything."

Amanda fled upstairs to Charley's old room. Before she could call her father, she saw Charley sitting on the window sill.

"Now do you believe me?" he asked.

"Were you eavesdropping?"

He shrugged. "I was listening."

"I didn't see you."

"I'm always there for you, whether you see me or not."

She moved toward him, pointing a threatening finger. "If I find out you've been spying on me in the shower or when I'm changing clothes, I'll..." She stopped. It was hard to threaten somebody who was already dead.

"Amanda, I'm shocked. I'm dead. I've risen above all that sort of thing."

"Ha!"

"What are you going to do now? I've got an idea. If you get me inside Kimball's house, I can look around and see if I can find that gun."

"Get you inside? Why don't you just zap yourself over there the way you do everywhere else?"

"Can't. I seem to be attached to you. I can only go where you go. Like when you rode down here, I didn't want to come with you, but I got yanked along."

Amanda groaned. "Are you saying you can't leave even if you want to? I can't get rid of you no matter what?"

"That sounds right. If you take me to Kimball's house, I can look around."

"Hey, no problem. I'll knock on the door and he'll invite me in for a glass of wine or maybe to stay for dinner because I'm his new best friend. What makes you think he's even still got the gun? You said he threw away the one he used to kill Dianne. The one you think he used to kill Dianne. *If* he killed her. Why would he kill her? They broke up years ago."

"I don't know. What difference does it make?"

"My gun's probably at the bottom of White Rock Lake or the Trinity River right now. Nobody's going to search the Trinity River. They'd die from the smell in the first five minutes."

"You got a better idea?"

Amanda sank onto the bed and covered her face with her hands. "Call my dad. Turn myself in. Throw myself on the mercy of the court."

"I asked if you had a better idea, not if you had an idea that was even dumber than mine."

"If you're here to help me, you're not doing a very good job of it. I don't think you're going to be earning your wings any time soon."

Amanda's cell phone chimed, announcing she had a text message. She pulled the phone from her pocket. The message was from Dawson.

*Cop came by today. Jake Daggett. Asked a lot of dumb questions. R u ok?*

Damn. Daggett again. She could feel the iron bars of prison closing around her.

*I'm fine*, she texted back, lying through her thumbs. *What kind of questions?*

*Do I have a key to ur apt. Did I go in and leave the door unlocked. All about ur fights with Charley.*

*What did—*

"Hey!" Charley appeared beside her on the bed, reaching for the cell phone, causing the letters she was laboriously typing on the small keypad to become gobbledygook. "That's it! The geek!"

"What? Stop that!"

"Dawson. He's a computer geek."

"He's an amazing artist and motorcycle repair assistant. He's smart and trustworthy and honest, unlike you."

"He does all that stuff on computers. He's a freaking genius on computers."

"Yeah, so?"

"Like on TV. He can run a check on Kimball and find out all kinds of stuff about him."

"Charley, there are limits to the information on the Internet. I don't think there's going to be a website dedicated to the exact location of my former gun."

"I've watched these crime shows. You can't imagine all the things they find. It'd scare you to death if you knew what's on the Internet about you."

"To death? Really?"

"Go with me on this. I got a feeling about it. Just ask him to do it. What have you got to lose?"

Amanda sighed. "Not much, I guess, since I'm already looking at spending the rest of my life behind bars." She texted Dawson with the request to find out anything he could about Roland Kimball. As an afterthought she added, *And Dianne Carter, especially their years at the University of Texas.*

"That last was a good idea," Charley said. "Asking about Dianne. I bet we find out all kinds of interesting things."

"Right. After Dawson discovers Roland Kimball has excellent credit because he's rich, and he has no outstanding warrants because he's rich, and he just bought his wife a ten thousand dollar ring for her birthday because he's rich, then I'll call my dad and turn myself in and throw myself on the mercy of the court."

"You can't do that. If you go to prison, I'll be in prison too."

Amanda slapped herself on the forehead. "Gee, Charley, I hadn't thought about that. Now that you've pointed it out, why, I guess I don't want to go to prison after all. I certainly wouldn't want you to be inconvenienced."

"I've got another idea." Charley moved across the room to the window, outside the window, then back in again, his face exultant. "This will work!"

Amanda stared at him. "What? If I go to prison, you'll be able to float out through the bars? That makes me feel a lot better."

"You don't have to get into Kimball's house. You just have to get close to it. I'll be close to you, and I can get inside his house. Go downstairs, go outside, and we'll see if I can be inside while you're outside."

"No," Amanda said. "I'm not going to do it. That's nuts. I'm not getting anywhere near Kimball's house. What good will it do if you find my gun inside? How will we get it out? You can't carry it."

"One thing at a time. First we find the gun then we figure out how to get it."

"No. Absolutely not."

A few minutes later she was standing in the yard, looking upward as Charley gleefully sailed in and out of the house several times.

What had she just been thinking about trusting Charley more than the legal system and the hangman more than Charley? No good had ever come of any of Charley's ideas. It was a measure of her desperation that she was considering this latest one.

# Chapter Thirteen

After lunch, Irene suggested a tour of downtown which consisted of the Town Square, Main Street and Grand Avenue. This activity would have taken less than thirty minutes except for the fact that Irene knew everybody. They all greeted her, offered their sympathy on Charley's death, were introduced to Amanda, then chatted about their kids, their grandkids, the weather, the state of the union, and sometimes their bunions. Rachel in Wood's Drugstore had pictures of her new granddaughter, and Joe in McAllen's Feed and Seed had pictures of his new pig.

It was, Amanda reflected, not a bad way to spend an afternoon. If nothing else, it kept her from thinking about going to prison for the rest of her life, skulking around Roland Kimball's house in the middle of the night, and any number of other unpleasant activities that could be a part of her immediate future.

"Here we are," Irene announced as they approached her ancient faded blue Ford where it sat in a parking space in front of Miss Emily's Ice Cream Parlor. "Want to go in for one of Miss Emily's famous chocolate malts?"

"No," Amanda declined, "I'm saving myself for some more of that pecan pie."

The windows of Irene's car were rolled down and the doors unlocked. Apparently they hadn't heard of crime in Silver Creek. Not that it didn't exist, Amanda thought grimly as she slid into the passenger seat. Silver Creek had its secrets.

"You know," she said, "there's someone I'd hoped to meet today, but we didn't see her."

Irene twisted the key back and forth a few times, and eventually the car choked to life. "Who's that?"

"Sunny Donovan, that lawyer we saw at Charley's funeral, the one you said helped him."

"No!" Charley suddenly appeared, hovering between her and his mother in the front seat. Had he been following her all afternoon, or had he just popped in at the mention of Sunny Donovan's name?

"Sunny's office is a few blocks out of downtown," Irene said. "I'm not sure if she'll be there right now, but we can stop by. I know she'd love to meet you."

Whatever secret Charley was hiding about Sunny Donovan was his alone. Irene didn't seem to see any reason Amanda shouldn't meet her.

"That would be great. I'd like to thank her for helping Charley."

"You would?" Charley asked in surprise.

Amanda smiled.

"I don't believe you," Charley said. "You're just being nosy. You need to trust me on this one. Stay away from her."

"Is she from Silver Creek?" Amanda asked.

"Born and raised," Irene said. "Her daddy died when she was three. Hunting accident. Margaret—that's her mama—raised her alone, and she did a fine job of it. Worked two jobs most of the time, but she made sure that girl got a good education. Sunny got a scholarship to the university down there in Austin. Went to law school. Margaret said with her grades, she could have practiced law anywhere. She got an offer from a big firm in Dallas, lots of money. But she came back here. Margaret's always been kind of frail, and her health got worse the harder she worked. Sunny takes care of her mama. There's Sunny's place now."

She pulled over to the curb in front of an older home that sat between a service station and the Silver Creek Library.

Amanda and Irene strode along the cracked sidewalk with Charley bringing up the rear.

"You can't stay long," he insisted. "We have to figure out our plan for tonight."

"She likes to keep her rent low," Irene explained, "because she does so much work for people who don't have any money." She sighed. "Like Charley."

"Why would you want to see a woman who knows what a scum your husband is?" Charley persisted. "This is going to look bad on you."

"Herbert and I told her we'd pay for Charley's defense, but she wouldn't take a penny from us. Made Charley pay what he could. He didn't have much money. That's why he was trying to sell those drugs in the first place."

"It was a terrible time in my life," Charley said. "Don't go in there and make me relive it."

They climbed the two wooden steps to the porch, and Irene knocked on the door then pushed it open. "Martha?" The small room they entered had once been a front parlor in someone's home. Now it held two file cabinets, two green utilitarian chairs and a wooden desk cluttered with file folders, stacks of papers, a computer and a desk phone.

"Hi, Irene. Y'all come on in. This must be Charley's widow." A short, plump woman with a pleasant face rose from behind the desk. "I'm so sorry about your loss." She looked as if she really meant those words. "Y'all have a seat. Can I get you a cup of coffee or a Coca-Cola?"

"Thank you, Martha," Irene said, "but we can't stay. I know y'all are busy. I've just been showing Amanda around town, and she wanted to meet Sunny, thank her for helping Charley."

Martha smiled. "She'd like that. Let me just tell her you're here." She went over to a door at one side of the room, knocked and peeked inside. "Sunny, have you got a

131

minute? Irene's brought her daughter-in-law from Dallas to meet you."

"I'm leaving," Charley said, but he made no move to go.

After a long moment of silence, a quiet voice from inside the other room said, "I'll be right there." The words sounded tight, not open and friendly like the other people Amanda had met that day.

Martha closed the door and turned back to Amanda and Irene. "She'll be right out. Y'all have a seat. Sure I can't get you something to drink?"

Irene shook her head. "No, thanks. Like I said, we can't stay but a few minutes."

The door opened again, and the woman who had stirred Amanda's curiosity for the last two days walked out. She still wore the same blue suit she'd worn earlier when Amanda had seen her on the courthouse steps, but her red hair had been released from any form of restraint and fell in loopy curls about her shoulders. Up close the woman looked older than she'd first thought, perhaps mid to late forties. Threads of white wove through her hair, and her smiling expression was a little pinched.

Up close, she looked even more familiar. Amanda knew she'd seen her before, and she sensed that Sunny knew it too.

"Irene, it's so good to see you." She hugged the older woman.

"That was real nice of you to come to Charley's funeral."

Sunny stepped back, nodded, then moved her gaze— reluctantly, it seemed—to Amanda. "And you must be Charley's widow." She extended a hand.

Amanda shook the stiff, proffered hand and was surprised when, after a perfunctory, lackluster shake, Sunny squeezed her hand firmly and immediately released it.

"Yes," Amanda said, studying Sunny's shuttered expression. No clues there. "I'm Amanda Caulfield." She immediately realized her mistake and added, for Irene's benefit, "Randolph. Charley's widow. Charley told me so much about you."

"I did not!" Charley protested.

Sunny's porcelain face seemed to become even paler, her smile more forced, her expression more distant. "Did he?"

Not exactly an eloquent speaker. Surely she did better than that in front of a jury. So what was this huge secret that could render almost speechless someone accustomed to arguing for her client's life in front of a judge, jury and courtroom spectators?

"Yes," Amanda replied. "He did. He was very grateful to you for helping him with his...uh...problem."

"I'm glad I could be of assistance. Sometimes people make mistakes. I try to get them a second chance." She paused, looking confused...trapped. "Let me know if I can do anything else to help." She took a step backward toward her open office door. "It was nice to meet you, Amanda." The tone of her voice, a sudden warmth in her green eyes, made Amanda feel she really meant the throwaway line in spite of her odd behavior. "Irene, always good to see you. I hope you'll excuse me. I've got a deadline for a brief I'm working on."

"Don't let us keep you," Irene said. "If you have time, we'd love for you to come by after church next Sunday. I'll kill another one of those pullets. They sure do fry up good."

Sunny regarded them for a brief moment, and her expression seemed a little wistful. Or maybe it was a trick of the afternoon sunlight coming through the wavy glass of the old windows. "Thank you. I'm not sure. I'll let you know." She spun around and strode rapidly back into her office, closing the door behind her.

Whatever the big mystery was, Irene didn't know it, but Charley and Sunny certainly did.

"That brief must be really important," Irene said as they walked back to the car. "Sunny wasn't herself today. She's usually real friendly."

"I hope you're happy, Amanda," Charley said, "interfering with that woman's work. Maybe now you'll leave her alone."

*Not a chance,* Amanda thought as she fastened her seat belt.

"We have more important things to do," Charley continued, "like keeping you out of prison."

He had a point. Discovering Charley's relationship with Sunny Donovan became far less important when put in perspective by her potential future behind bars.

Even so, she had a feeling, especially after Sunny's reaction to meeting her, that the secret Charley and Sunny shared must be important, something way beyond a brief fling between the two of them. The secret, she felt sure, somehow involved her. She and Sunny Donovan had met before. Why couldn't she remember where and when?

☙❧

The fear of a future life behind bars with Charley flitting in and out while she sat trapped inside drove Amanda from the house after dark with the excuse of a "moonlight motorcycle ride." Following Charley's directions to Kimball's house, she pulled off the road. It was a perfect night for a ride, but a lousy night for skulking around someone's house. The moon was full in a cloudless sky. Fortunately trees surrounded the Kimballs' house...large, graceful oaks, elms, magnolias, cottonwoods and other varieties. The gnarled native mesquite trees were conspicuously absent from the lush setting.

A large fence with a gated entrance surrounded the property.

Amanda opened the face plate of her helmet. "Had I known I'd have to leap over a six foot fence, I'd have worn the shoes with springs instead of these heavy boots." She was actually relieved that they wouldn't be able to get in. Charley had probably done this sort of thing many times, but she was terrified at the thought of sneaking around someone's house—especially if that *someone* was a murderer.

"Hide your bike in the bushes. I think I can deal with this gate. It's electronic. Should be sort of like turning on the TV."

"This bike weighs over seven hundred pounds. I'm not putting it in the bushes. How do you think I'll get it out? Are you going to help lift it?"

"All right, all right. Get it as far off the road as you can and let me concentrate on opening this gate."

Amanda moved her bike to the side of the road but did not pull off her helmet, gloves or jacket. She waited, ready to roll, heart pounding, adrenalin pumping, terrified that Kimball would emerge from behind her at any moment or a police car would pull up beside her, lights flashing, siren blaring, ready to haul her in.

*What are you doing here, ma'am?*

*Oh, just waiting for my ex-husband to jimmy the lock on this gate so I can get in to spy on your mayor.*

*Your ex-husband? There's nobody here but you.*

*Well, yeah, you see, he's dead.*

*Please raise your hands and step away from the bike.*

Jail or the loony bin? Where would they take her?

"I did it!" The gate was sliding open so quietly, she wouldn't have noticed if not for Charley's exultant yell.

Great. He'd never been able to get the lid off a jar of pickles when he was alive, but now that he was dead, he could open security gates.

"Come on," he urged when she sat unmoving.

"Charley, I don't think this is a good idea."

"Do you want to stay out of prison or not? I'm trying to help. I'm the one who's going to do all the work. You can stay hidden in the trees and bushes. All you have to do is get me close to the house."

With a sigh, Amanda climbed off her bike, removed her helmet, gloves and jacket and forced her unwilling legs to walk through the open gate, following Charley. *No good could come of this. No good ever came of taking Charley's advice.* But she was fresh out of ideas on how to get herself out of this mess Charley had got her into by blackmailing Kimball and getting himself killed.

"Could you walk a little quieter?" Charley asked as they moved off the driveway and into the undergrowth.

"No, I can't," she whispered. "I'm wearing motorcycle boots, and I'm still flesh and blood. If you had real feet, you'd be making noise too."

"There's an art to stealth."

"Oh? And just why would a man of your high moral standards need to acquire that art?"

Charley didn't answer but kept moving toward the large brick house where the driveway curved in a circle. Amanda followed as quietly as she could, the pounding of her heart sounding louder than her footsteps.

Finally they reached a spot only a few feet from the side of the house. The drapes were closed, but light shone around the edges of a large downstairs window.

"This is it," Amanda whispered, so terrified she couldn't have spoken aloud if she'd wanted to. "I'm not getting any closer."

"Let me see if you're close enough that I can get in."

He disappeared, and Amanda stood alone, perspiring in the moonlight in the middle of Roland Kimball's yard in the middle of the night.

She twisted around at the sound of rustling in the darkness behind her.

A small animal? A bird? A serial killer?

Cricket song burst forth as if sounding an alarm.

Who knew there were so many noises in the night? How did the animals ever sleep?

She wrapped her arms around herself, backed deeper into the shadows, and bumped into a solid object. She spun around, ready to defend herself. Ready to die.

A tree trunk.

She took a deep breath and told herself to relax.

Not likely.

A dark shape swept across the moonlit sky. Amanda's heart went into triple-time.

Breeze blowing the trees around.

Or a ghost.

She almost laughed at that idea. Now that she'd met one, ghosts didn't have quite such a scary reputation. Not nearly as scary as the man who lived in that house.

A mosquito buzzed near her ear, and she slapped futilely at the sound.

When she got out of there—if she got out of there alive—she might reconsider the idea of spending the rest of her life in prison. It couldn't be worse than this.

Finally Charley returned. "Got in," he announced, sounding pleased.

"Great! What did you find?"

"Saw him and his wife sitting in the living room. They didn't even have the television on."

"That's really helpful. An obvious sign of guilt. I'm out here putting my life in danger and getting bitten by mosquitos and who knows what other creatures so you can watch Kimball and his wife sitting in the living room in front of a dead television."

"That's not all I did. I looked through their closets and cabinets and everywhere I could reach."

"How did you do that? You can't open doors or drawers, can you?"

"No, but I can go inside things."

137

"So there's no privacy when you're around."

"Yep." He grinned as if pleased with himself.

"Stay out of my underwear drawer."

Charley agreed so readily she was certain he'd already checked out her underwear drawer and anything else of hers he could find.

"Did you see a gun?"

"No gun."

Amanda heaved a deep sigh. "That's it then. This was a complete waste of time. Let's get out of here."

"No! We're not done. I need to get upstairs, into the bedrooms, the attic, all the places in this big house where he could hide stuff. I need you to move closer."

"I don't want to move closer. I want to leave. Now."

"I don't think we can do that." Charley's gaze moved past her, over her shoulder, toward the driveway where they'd entered.

Over the thundering of her heart as it tried to beat out of her chest, the sound of her blood rushing past her ears, crickets chirping and mosquitos buzzing, Amanda noticed another sound. An engine and tires on pavement.

She turned in horror to see a police car coming down the driveway. A spotlight flashed through the trees then burst across her face.

"Put your hands on your head and move into the open," said an electronically magnified voice.

"You are so screwed," Charley said, helpful as always.

# Chapter Fourteen

Amanda lifted her arms above her head and ordered her feet to move forward, to carry her within reach of the police. Images of prison bars flashed before her eyes. Why had she ever listened to Charley?

Two uniformed officers got out of the patrol car, guns drawn and aimed at her.

"Stop right there!" the taller one ordered.

She stopped.

"Who are you?" the shorter one demanded.

Amanda opened her mouth to tell them her name, but discovered it was so dry, she couldn't speak.

"Put your hands behind your back," the second officer ordered, holstering his gun and approaching her with a pair of handcuffs.

Amanda lowered her arms, and the man slapped the cuffs onto her wrists. They were heavy and cold. Though only her hands were trapped, she felt as if the metal encased her entire body, making it impossible to move, hard to breathe.

The front door of Kimball's house opened, and the mayor himself stepped out onto the wide porch. "Well, well," Kimball said. "I do believe that's Charley Randolph's widow come to visit." He walked down the steps toward her.

"You know her?" the officer standing beside the car, gun still drawn, asked.

"I met her at the funeral yesterday. Charley Randolph's funeral. You remember Charley, don't you?" Damned man looked even more evil in his casual slacks and knit shirt. Every hair was in place, and his eyes were darker and more threatening than the night she'd just been hiding in.

139

"I remember," the officer said. "Always in some kind of trouble. Left town a couple of years ago. Wasn't surprised somebody finally killed him. Probably a jealous husband. Beg pardon, ma'am."

"He hasn't got any room to talk," Charley protested. "Smoked my first joint with that guy back in the seventh grade. I could tell you some things about him."

Amanda would have told him to shut up if her throat hadn't been constricted from fear.

"What are you doing at the mayor's house in the middle of the night?" demanded the cop standing beside her, the one who'd so eagerly slapped the handcuffs on her.

"Tell them you were taking a walk," Charley ordered.

"What?" she gasped. Great. The first word she was able to speak would make her sound like an idiot, talking to someone who wasn't there.

"The officer asked what you were doing at my house in the middle of the night," Kimball said. His expression as he approached told her he had a pretty good idea what she was doing there.

"Taking a walk," she blurted.

He lifted both eyebrows in disbelief.

"Is that your motorcycle parked just outside the gate?" he asked.

So much for the *taking a walk* story. For an accomplished liar, Charley wasn't coming up with a very credible tale to keep her out of jail. He'd do a lot better if it was his butt on the line. "Yes," she choked out. "My motorcycle."

"You were riding in the moonlight and saw the gate. The open gate," Charley continued easily.

"I was riding in the moonlight and saw the gate, the open gate," she parroted. It wasn't a great story, but it was better than anything she could come up with.

"You wanted to see where the driveway led."

"I wanted to see where the driveway led."

"Then you saw the house."

"Then you saw—I saw the house."

"So you stopped to spy on me?" Kimball asked.

"You twisted your ankle," Charley said, "and you were resting for a few minutes. Stepped in a hole. He'd better be careful you don't sue him." Charley was getting better, more fluent with his story. Maybe he couldn't tell lies anymore, but apparently there was nothing to stop him from making up lies for someone else to tell.

"I...stepped in a hole and twisted my ankle. I was just resting for a few minutes."

Kimball studied her, his sinister gaze raking her from perspiration-covered brow to uninjured ankles safely encased in motorcycle boots. He smiled, and his smile, full of control and power and absolutely no scruples, was the scariest thing she'd seen all night. "Your ankle seems to have healed quite nicely."

"Yes," she said. "It's better. Much better."

"It's okay, officers," he said, never taking his eyes off her. "You can remove the handcuffs. Mrs. Randolph was taking a stroll to escape the depression of losing her husband. I'm not going to press charges. Thank you for coming out."

"You sure, Mayor?" the officer with the gun asked. "Maybe we ought to take her down to the station." He sounded disappointed, cheated out of what was probably the only arrest he'd had a chance at all week. Maybe all year.

"I'm sure, Ted. Mrs. Randolph, why don't you come inside, and my wife will get you something for your ankle."

Even as the steel shackles fall away from Amanda's wrists, she felt tighter, heavier, invisible ones wrap around her chest. Go inside his house? Let his wife get something for her ankle? A knife, maybe? Or a chainsaw? Hiding in the dark had been scary enough. She wasn't about to go inside that house.

"All right, Mayor. But if you have any more problems, just give us a call. Be sure and close that gate behind us. You don't want any more trespassers tonight."

The officers got back in their car and continued around the circle drive, eventually heading away from the house.

Amanda shivered. Suddenly she wanted to call them back. She'd be better off going to jail than stuck there alone with Roland Kimball.

"Now, Mrs. Randolph," he said, any pretense of a smile disappearing from his shadowed face, "let's talk about what really happened tonight. So you say the gate was open when you happened by?"

She nodded, the movement jerky and uncertain.

"That's very interesting. The alarm on that gate went off about ten minutes ago, and when I looked at the video from the gate camera, I saw you walking through."

"Damn!" Charley exclaimed. "An alarm and a video camera! I should have thought of that."

"Yes, you should have," she said.

"What?" Kimball asked, taken aback at her response.

Amanda shook her head.

"You're confused. The pain," Charley suggested. "The pain of that twisted ankle is awful. It's making you crazy, and it was his hole you stepped in. This could be a lawsuit. Tell him that."

"Sorry I bothered you. Bye." She turned to leave, but Kimball placed a hand on her shoulder. Amanda halted in mid-step. His hand felt as heavy and metallic as those cuffs had a few minutes ago. Was she going to be murdered there in the mayor's front yard? Or would he haul her inside and let his wife help him? A bonding activity for their marriage?

"You're leaving so soon?" he asked, his voice low, sleek, and dangerous. "But you just got here. Oh, that's right, you were standing around outside for about ten minutes, weren't you? Still, that's not long. And you couldn't have seen anything because I pulled the drapes as soon as the alarm went off. So why don't you stay awhile and let's have that talk you asked for this morning."

"Run, Amanda!" Charley ordered.

Great advice. If only Kimball's hand on her shoulder wasn't holding her firmly in place.

Slowly she turned toward him.

He dropped his hand and smiled again, aware he was in control.

"What...?" The word came out a whisper. She cleared her throat and tried again. "What do you want to talk about?"

"You're the one who wanted to meet with me and talk. You're the one who approached me at the courthouse and then came to my house. Why don't you tell me what you want to talk about?"

The tall front door of his house opened a few inches. "Is everything all right, Roland?" came a quiet female voice. In the moonlight Amanda could see a small, blond woman.

"Everything's fine, Catherine. Charley Randolph's widow was out walking and got lost. I'll be inside in a few minutes."

The woman disappeared back into the house, closing the door behind her. It seemed Kimball had his wife under control too.

At least it appeared Amanda wasn't expected to go inside that house. And surely he wasn't going to murder her if he had told his wife she was there. Maybe she had a chance to make it out of this alive.

"It's been great, having this little chat with you," she said. "But I've really got to go. The Randolphs are expecting me back soon."

"That's good," Charley said. "Let him know there's somebody out there who'll be suspicious if you don't come back."

*If you don't come back?* She swallowed. "They'll probably be looking for me by now."

"Then I guess we'll have to cut our little chat short. Amanda—may I call you *Amanda* since we know each other so well that you would pay me an unexpected visit in the middle of the night?"

Amanda didn't want to hear her name come out of his oily mouth, didn't want the closeness a first-name basis implied. On the other hand, she didn't want to hear anybody call her *Mrs. Randolph.* "Of course you can call me Amanda, *Roland.*" She put her feeling of complete disgust into his name.

"Very good, Amanda. Since it's getting late and you need to go, let me just cut straight to the heart of the matter and say that I have nothing you would be interested in. If I once had the object of your interest, it's long gone now."

"You threw away the gun you took from my apartment." The words escaped from her lips in little more than a whisper. Even though she'd known that was a possibility, had told Charley it was, actually hearing it from Kimball was a cold slap in the face. This man had destroyed her only chance of vindication.

"I hope you don't intend to tell anyone that outrageous story your husband told you. You'd only be making a fool of yourself and risking a lawsuit for slander since you have no proof."

"That gun—"

"Let's get out of here, Amanda," Charley said.

144

She moved her gaze from Kimball to Charley and back again—the two men whose crimes had put her in danger of losing her freedom. She'd married Charley, and he'd brought Kimball into her life. At least Charley looked somewhat abashed, but Kimball looked complacent, in control, certain he'd won. Damn both of them, but especially that smug, arrogant jerk looking so self-satisfied and pleased with himself, so sure he'd beaten her.

She took a step toward him. "That gun you stole from my apartment and disposed of, it wasn't your gun. It was mine. Charley gave me that gun when we got married."

Kimball's arrogant smile widened. "I have no idea what gun you're talking about, Amanda, but if Charley gave it to you, you can bet it was stolen. Our discussion is over. It's getting late. I think you should leave before I call Ted and his partner to come back and take you to jail for trespassing." Kimball turned and started up the steps to his house.

"Hey!" Charley protested. "I didn't steal that gun! I bought it for you because I was afraid this jerk would find me after I took his money and ran. I was trying to take care of you, Amanda."

"Good job," Amanda snapped, her hands clenching into fists as she watched Kimball's back moving up the steps, walking away from his crimes, returning to his world of wealth and power where he always got his way.

"You made a mistake, *Roland*," she shouted after him. "That gun you stole from me was not the one you used to kill Dianne."

He paused then continued, turning the knob, opening his front door.

Damn him! She had to do something. She couldn't let him get away with messing up her life so easily. "I wouldn't leave valuable evidence like that lying around the house. The gun you used to kill Dianne is hidden away somewhere that's safe from you."

145

He didn't go inside. Slowly he closed the door and turned back to her. He was still wearing the arrogant, confident expression, but she had his attention.

"It's in a safe deposit box," she improvised, trying to come up with the most secure place she could think of. "And also in that safe deposit box is a document with the whole story of how Charley saw you throw that gun into the trash behind that bar, how you had blood on your shirt, and how he fished the gun out of the garbage bin. It's all written in Charley's handwriting." She hoped Kimball wouldn't know that Charley's handwriting was completely illegible.

Kimball did a good job of maintaining a stoic expression, but she thought his face paled a little, enough to notice even in the moonlight.

"My dad," she continued, emboldened by his lack of reaction and her own rising anger, "he's a judge, you know. He has a key to the safe deposit box, and if anything happens to me, he'll open it and they'll match the bullet to the one that killed Dianne, and, poof!" She threw her hands in the air. "No more Governor of Texas."

"You go, girl!" Charley encouraged. "Tell him you know the details of how he killed me."

"Shut up!" Amanda snapped at Charley then returned her attention to Kimball. "You killed Dianne, and you killed Charley. You wore motorcycle gear so you wouldn't be recognized going into his apartment, and then you made him call me, asking for the gun you used to kill Dianne, the one he used to blackmail you, but I'm not stupid. I didn't bring it. You hid behind the door, and when I left, you killed him, and you thought you'd killed me too, so you strolled through my apartment and took the first gun you found—the wrong gun."

Kimball glared at her. Even in the low light she could see storms roiling in the midnight depths of his eyes. Apparently he hadn't noticed that Charley's duplicate gun wasn't the one he'd tossed into the garbage after killing Dianne. "I advise you not to go around town telling lies like that." Kimball still spoke with authority, but his voice had lost some of its self-assurance.

Amanda moved closer to the porch and put one foot on the bottom step as if she might go after him. "You tampered with my bike and caused it to be destroyed, and you're going to pay for that. I loved that bike."

"It's not a good idea to threaten people, Amanda, especially people with a lot more power than you have."

She jutted her chin forward defiantly. "You think you have power? You have no idea the power I have. I need that gun you stole from me to prove I didn't use it to kill Charley. Whatever you did with it, you need to find it and return it to me. If you don't—" she moved back from the steps and leveled her gaze on him— "I'll have to take Charley's story to the cops along with Dianne's murder weapon."

She spun around and stomped back down Roland Kimball's driveway before he could recover his arrogance, call her bluff and kill her on his porch, in front of God, his wife, Charley and all the creatures hiding in the trees and bushes.

"You need to be careful, Amanda." His words were heavy and dark and carried well on the still night air.

Amanda glanced back, trying to put a smug smirk on her face. "No, Roland, you need to be careful."

"That was awesome," Charley declared, strolling happily beside her. "I couldn't have done better myself."

"Go away." The adrenalin of righteous anger was leaving, and fear was returning.

"I'm so proud of you, the way you stood up to him! Stroke of genius, telling him we had his gun hidden away in a safe place."

"Are you insane? Well, yes, you are. And so am I, going along with a madman's...a mad ghost's plan.

Almost getting arrested. What would your mother think if she had to come bail me out of jail? And then on top of that, I stand there like a crazy woman, baiting a murderer!"

"So you finally believe me, that Kimball's a murderer, that he killed Dianne and he killed me?"

Amanda turned back to see the murderer in question still standing on his porch, watching them. In the moonlight his tall silhouette seemed to glow with an unholy light. "Yes, I believe you." She increased her pace toward the end of the driveway. "I believe he's an egotistical, self-centered monster who thinks he has the right to take the lives of commoners, and I believe I just tweaked his tail. I never should have listened to you."

"But we had to do something. We can't let him get away with killing me."

"Yes, we can. If he could do away with your ghost too, I'd give him a medal. All I wanted to do was find evidence to prove I didn't kill you, but I think all we accomplished tonight was to set me up as his next victim."

"Nah. You warned him that your dad would get that gun and my story if anything happened to you."

Amanda snorted. "Even if he believed me, what would it prove? He studied law. He knows we can't connect the gun to him without your eye witness testimony, and you're dead. He'll feel a lot better when I'm dead too."

Charley was quiet for a few moments as if considering that possibility. "He already tried to kill you once, and that didn't work."

Amanda walked through the gate which closed quietly behind her. Creepy. Obviously the jerk was watching her on video. She tried to shake off the feeling that he'd be watching her no matter where she went or what she did. "What if he succeeds this time?"

Again Charley was quiet.

Amanda wanted to shake him or punch him or somehow inflict physical pain, but that was now impossible, thanks to His Honor, the Mayor of Silver Creek. "What if he succeeds in killing me this time?" she demanded.

"It's not so bad," he finally said, "being dead."

Amanda glared at him then shoved her motorcycle helmet onto her head. "Thank you for sharing that information. I feel so much better now."

# Chapter Fifteen

Amanda did not feel safe until she was back at the house with the door closed and locked behind her. Even then she stared out the window of Charley's old bedroom, half expecting to see Kimball standing among the trees, looking up at her, that self-satisfied smirk on his face, murder in his eyes.

"You're safe here," Charley assured her. "Dad's a hunter, and he's got this old shotgun—"

Amanda whirled from the window to face him. "Shut up! I don't want to hear about any more freaking guns. That's what started this whole thing in the first place, Kimball's gun in the trash. I wish you'd never seen it, and you wouldn't have if you hadn't been hanging out with another man's wife." She plopped down on the edge of Charley's old desk chair. "After tonight, I believe he killed Dianne, but why? The man has everything. Why murder someone like Dianne, his former girlfriend, the town saint? They hadn't had any contact since college."

Charley shrugged. "Maybe they still had something going. Maybe she threatened to tell his wife."

Amanda shook her head in disgust. "Of course you'd come up with something sordid and stereotypical, something you could relate to."

"Hey! That kind of thing happens all the time. That's what makes it a stereotype."

"Fine. Whatever." Amanda stood. "I'm going to bed. You need to leave."

"What if I don't leave?"

"Then I sleep in my clothes."

"I've seen you without your clothes." Charley smiled smugly.

"*Seen* being the operative word. Past tense. Not present, not future."

"You gotta admit, we made a good team tonight. We've got Kimball on the run." He looked pleased with himself.

"Excuse me? *On the run?* We stirred up a hornet's nest! Yeah, we're a great team. Between the two of us, we're going to get me killed."

"Relax, Amanda. I know how to read people. You've got him on the defensive. He'll mess up, and we'll catch him."

"Stuff it, Charley! This is all totally, completely, one hundred percent your fault. Even dead, you continue to cause problems."

"You're getting all worked up. That's not good for you."

She flopped across the bed and pulled a pillow over her head.

Charley gave a deep sigh. "Fine. I'm leaving. I'll go outside and stand guard for you. Let you know if I see anything threatening. I'll take care of you, Amanda."

She rolled over, tossing aside the pillow so she could glare at him. "Great. At the rate you're taking care of me, I'll be joining you soon."

&#x6002;&#x6002;

After a night of tossing and turning, dreaming of Kimball shooting her, choking her, dismembering her and in other ways disposing of her, Amanda dreaded the thought of breakfast, of being polite and shoving food into her knotted stomach.

But then she came downstairs to the smells and the people.

Breakfast in the Randolph home was a rushed, frantic, completely wonderful affair. That morning Irene made biscuits, sausage, fried eggs and hash browns. Yesterday they'd had scrambled eggs and bacon.

151

Cholesterol heaven. Amanda's mother would have had a heart attack just looking at the food.

"How do you want your eggs?" Irene stood at the stove, tending a skillet. "Over easy? Over medium? Please tell me you don't like them just dipped in hot grease and still all slimy on top like some people." She arched an eyebrow in Herbert's direction.

"Eggs sushi." In his faded denim work shirt and blue jeans, Herbert sat at the table already eating some of the maligned eggs, dipping pieces of biscuit in the yolk and grinning.

Penny—or maybe it was Paula—stood at the counter making ham sandwiches for the girls' lunches. The other twin cut two pieces of apple pie and put them in plastic containers.

"Over medium," Amanda replied. "Can I do something to help?" She stood behind a chair at the place setting with a can of cold Coke instead of the coffee or orange juice at the other places.

"Not a thing. You just sit down and relax. Penny, Paula, here's your eggs. Come to the table and eat." She slid eggs onto two of the plates then returned the skillet to the stove.

"Mom, we gotta hurry today. We have debate practice before school."

"All the more reason to eat a good breakfast." Irene cracked four more eggs into the hot grease. Apparently everyone got two eggs, no need to specify. None of this, *I'll have one poached egg, a croissant and fruit.*

Amanda sat and helped herself to a hot biscuit, breaking it open and spreading with butter. Real butter. She smiled as she imagined the shock on her mother's face if she were at the table. Would her oft-touted manners require her to eat of the commoners' fare, or would she politely request a poached egg and fruit? If she did, Amanda had no doubt Irene would prepare it for her.

The twins moved to the table and sat down. The one sitting closest to Amanda added hash browns, a biscuit and sausage to her plate then leaned over close to Amanda to whisper. "I heard you talking to Charley last night."

Amanda almost choked on a bite of light, fluffy biscuit. "You...you heard?" Could Charley's sister hear him too? Could she see him? How could she be so calm about it?

"I wasn't eavesdropping," the girl continued. "Our room's right next to yours, and we were up late reading. It's okay. I sometimes talk to my cat that died last year. At first I was really mad at my cat for dying just like you're mad at Charley. It's a stage. It'll get better." She patted Amanda's hand then returned to her breakfast.

Amanda felt small and guilty, taking this girl's sympathy under false pretenses. She was involved with the whole family under false pretenses. They had loved Charley. They missed him.

In her defense, she'd loved him once. And she might miss him if he'd ever go away.

Nevertheless, she was enjoying being a member of this family way too much. She wasn't entitled to their caring, their concern, the total acceptance they gave her. She should cut this visit short, leave that day. Go back to her apartment, her work at the motorcycle shop, her life with her own family.

Irene slid two perfect fried eggs onto Amanda's plate, the other two onto her own, then sat down beside her husband.

"Your eggs okay?" Irene asked, and Amanda realized she was sitting with a cooling biscuit in one hand, staring into space.

"They're delicious." She returned her attention to the food cooked by her newly-discovered family.

Maybe she'd leave tomorrow. What difference would one more day make?

꙰

That afternoon Irene gave Amanda a lesson in preparing homemade bread.

"Just pretend the dough is somebody you're really mad at and whack the living daylights out of it." She demonstrated by slamming a fist into the mound of dough.

Amanda laughed. "That's a pretty good punch you've got there. Remind me not to make you mad."

Irene smiled, then her face became serious. "Never you, sweetheart. Right now, I'm punching the face of the monster that killed my son and your husband."

That ruined Amanda's plan to pretend the dough was Charley's face.

As if summoned from her thoughts, Charley appeared at her elbow. "Dawson's calling on your cell phone. He must have information. Hurry!"

"Excuse me," Amanda said, "I've got to answer my phone. I'll be right back."

"You sure do have good ears," Irene said. "I don't hear a thing."

Amanda dashed upstairs where she'd left her phone on the charger. "Hello? Dawson?"

"Hi. You okay? You sound out of breath."

"Ran up the stairs. I'm fine." *For the moment.* Until Kimball decided how to do away with her. "Did you find out anything about Roland Kimball?"

"Lots, but most of it's public information, probably stuff you already know."

"Let's hear it anyway." She sank onto the bed. Charley joined her, leaning close to hear what Dawson had to say.

"Mayor of Silver Creek. Comes from money. His grandfather started out with a sawmill. Family owns most of the county now. Dad's a bigwig in Silver Creek and has a lot of friends in high places in Dallas and Fort Worth.

Mayor's making noises about being the next governor of Texas."

"That's a scary thought," Amanda said. "He's not a very nice person."

"No," Dawson agreed, "he's not. And Daddy knows it. All is not well in Camelot."

"That's what I want to hear. Tell me more."

"Dad's a megalomaniac, but he's hard line when it comes to morals and ethics. Son got a little wild when he went to college and out of Daddy's sphere of control."

"Wild, like how?"

"The usual. Drinking, drugs, women. When he was in high school, he dated that woman you asked me to check on, Dianne Carter. Her name was Dianne Ferguson at that time. Sounds like she was a nice person. Dad approved of her even though she didn't come from wealth. Her family went to his church, and she had a good influence on Roland. He was running with a pretty rough crowd in high school until he started dating Dianne. All was well for a while. Looked like Roland and Dianne would get married and live happily ever after. But during their junior year in college, they broke up. After that, Roland got in so much trouble, he almost failed to graduate."

"I knew it!" Charley exclaimed.

"Did not," Amanda said.

"Yes," Dawson said, his tone puzzled, "he did."

"Sorry. Just clearing my throat. Tell me about the trouble he got into."

"Received a couple of DUIs that Daddy got him out of, missed a lot of classes, got in a few fights, that sort of thing. Things Daddy could buy him out of, but a couple were pretty expensive like his senior year when a girl almost died from some kinky sex activities."

Amanda gulped. "Kinky sex activities?" *Was she in danger of more than just a straight murder?*

"They take a rope—"

Amanda shuddered. "Never mind. I don't want details. *Kinky* tells me all I need to know."

"Anyway, that near-miss with the justice system seemed to get Roland's attention. He straightened up, graduated, went to law school, returned to Silver Creek and married Catherine Montgomery, the daughter of a buddy of his dad. Combined the family fortunes."

"What's she like, Mrs. Roland?" The woman she'd glimpsed last night didn't seem the type to play kinky sex games, but Amanda wasn't sure she knew what type would.

"She seems to be the perfect politician's wife, quiet, submissive, always gracious, content to live in her husband's shadow."

"That sounds like an interesting match."

"Almost like a medieval marriage of alliance between ruling monarchs. Catherine Montgomery and Roland Kimball. Two powerful families combined to rule Texas. They got married two months after he came home from law school. Wasn't a long courtship."

*Two powerful families combined to rule Texas.* The future governor of Texas could be a murderer and a sexual pervert. Nice.

"How about Dianne Carter? Did you find out anything else about her after she came back to Silver Creek?"

"A year after she came back, she married Gregory Carter. They had two kids, both boys. She was a grade school teacher, he's a high school athletics coach. Both were active in the church and charity organizations." Dawson continued with the same information Irene had already given her.

Amanda sighed. Dawson had uncovered some things about Kimball she hadn't known, but nothing that would help her.

Another call popped up on her cell phone. "I need to go. My dad's calling. Thanks, Dawson."

She answered the incoming call. "Hi, Dad."

"What in the devil were you doing trespassing at Roland Kimball's house last night?"

Amanda sat upright, stunned. "How did you find out about that?"

"Amanda, what have you got yourself into?"

"It was…a mistake."

"Yes, it was. Your trip to that town was a mistake. You need to come home. Brian is working on a defense for you with regard to Charley's death, and he needs your assistance."

"Have they…" Amanda gulped. "Have they decided for sure to arrest me?"

"Not yet. You're my daughter. They're going to be very careful before they make their move."

Amanda shivered. "But you think they will make that move eventually."

Her father was silent for a long moment. "I think you need to come home and help us put together a good defense just in case."

*Just in case.* The casual way her father tossed out that phrase told her it was pretty close to a certainty. A chill crept down her spine, and she suddenly found it difficult to breathe.

"Dad, I can't come home right now." For a moment she considered telling him what was going on. She'd always been able to count on him when she needed help. He was her rock.

But if he found out she was taunting a murderer, he'd come down and physically carry her home.

"Why can't you come home right now?" he demanded, his tone strangely sharp.

"I…uh…Charley's mother. She likes me. I think having me here comforts her." She wasn't lying, just not

157

telling everything she knew, an old trick she'd learned from Charley.

"How much longer do you plan to stay there?" Again her father's voice held a note of stress.

"Two weeks." That should get her a week.

"Three days."

*Three days?* "Dad! I'm an adult. You can't just order me around."

Judge Caulfield chuckled. "Sweetheart," he said, sounding more like his normal, in-control self, "I couldn't order you around when you were a child. Please come home in three days. Is that better?"

"One week."

"One week. If you promise no more prowling around in the middle of night. Stay at the Randolphs' house. Don't go anywhere."

Her father's admonition to remain at the Randolphs' house was oddly reminiscent of Charley's. *Promise me you'll stay with my family the whole time you're here.* The two of them were rarely in accord. "One week." She agreed to the time element only.

"Do I have your promise?"

"I promise to come home in one week."

Her father sighed. "All right. Please don't do anything crazy."

She couldn't agree to that either. "I love you, Dad."

"I love you too, Mandy."

She disconnected the call. "Something's going on with my dad."

Charley laughed—nervously, she thought. "Why do you say that?"

Amanda shook her head. "I don't know. He just sounded funny."

"Your dad's fine. I gotta go." Charley disappeared.

Amanda stared at the empty space. Did Charley know something about her father that she didn't? The two men didn't even like each other. Her father had adamantly opposed her marriage to Charley.

Yet he'd known about Charley's very-much-alive family and had kept the knowledge a secret from her when that might have persuaded her not to marry Charley.

And he'd bailed Charley out of jail more than once, used his influence to rescue her husband from a number of scrapes. In fact, she'd come to wish he'd stay out of things and let Charley deal with the consequences of his petty crimes, but Judge Caulfield insisted on upholding the family name.

Tonight her father gave her the same instructions Charley had given her the first night she was there, to remain within the confines of this house.

Charley, who could no longer lie, had chosen to disappear rather than talk about her father.

A ridiculous idea floated through her brain.

She dismissed the thought immediately. No way was it possible that Charley had been blackmailing her dad into getting him out of trouble. She could believe that of Charley, but her dad was the most morally upright man she'd ever known. Stodgily so. He could never have done anything to be blackmailed for, nor would he have given in to a blackmailer.

Her whole world had been turned upside down. Some of the changes were good, like meeting Charley's family. But she was having doubts about her father and fears for her life.

That reminded her she had not yet checked her motorcycle after her run-in with Kimball last night. She hurried downstairs and out into the yard. Her bike was still parked where she'd left it. It seemed to be intact, but a cursory inspection before her ride into the mountains had not revealed the things Kimball had done to her bike.

She moved up close, ready to do a complete check of everything.

She didn't need to. Someone had made three yellow chalk marks on her back tire, the kind police left on automobile tires to determine if they stayed in a parking zone too long. But the marks hadn't been there the night before. They were fresh, not driven over. And if there should be any doubt as to who was responsible, someone had written a capital letter *K* in the dust on her gas tank.

Kimball was sending her a message. Nothing she could take to the police, just a warning that he could get to her any time he wanted.

Amanda rose slowly, her gaze glued to her bike. Kimball wanted to frighten her. He'd succeeded. The extent of his power, the fact that he could get to her so easily was terrifying.

But he'd also roused her anger. How dare he sneak around in the middle of the night, intruding on Irene and Herbert's property and touching her motorcycle? He'd already ruined her favorite bike. Now he'd touched this one, and that felt creepy beyond words. She'd have to check it for problems and wash it thoroughly before she rode it again.

Killing Charley was one thing. She could hardly blame him for that. She'd thought about it often enough herself. But breaking into her apartment, stealing her gun and putting her at risk of going to prison, causing her to wreck one motorcycle and leaving his evil presence on another...the jerk had to be stopped.

# Chapter Sixteen

That afternoon Amanda made a thorough inspection of her bike followed by a thorough washing before she rode to the high school football stadium to talk to the coach, Dianne's widower. If she could figure out why Kimball killed Dianne, that might give her a lever in dealing with him.

Charley, of course, came with her. When he was alive, he'd spent a lot of time away, working on scams, having affairs, a night or two in jail. Now, when he should be gone forever, she couldn't get rid of him.

The two of them stood at the rail around the football field and cheered for Paula and Penny as the girls ran laps. When they finished their track practice, they came over, smiling and mopping perspiration from their faces.

"Hi, Amanda!" Paula greeted. They had their names on their shirts so Amanda could tell which twin was which. Unless they'd switched shirts. "Did you ride your bike? Can I ride back with you?"

"No, let me!" Penny protested.

"Tell them both they can't," Charley said. "I don't want my sisters riding with somebody who goes so fast, my life flashes before me."

"I have one spare helmet. I could take one of you home and then come back for the other."

The sisters looked at each other and nodded. "We'll be right back as soon as we shower and change clothes."

"Before you go, is that Greg Carter?" She indicated the man in a baseball cap holding a clipboard and talking to another sweaty girl.

"Yeah, that's Coach," Paula replied.

"Can you introduce me?"

161

"Sure." Paula trotted over to Greg Carter, said something to him, pointed to Amanda, and the two walked back to where she stood.

"Amanda, this is our coach, Mr. Carter."

The man was tall and muscular as expected of a football coach, but his broad face and warm brown eyes gave him a mellow appearance. Amanda extended a hand, and Greg took it in a firm but gentle grip. "You're Charley's widow?"

"Yes. If you have a minute, I'd like to talk to you."

"Sure."

Penny and Paula took this as permission to leave. "We'll meet you back here after we get cleaned up."

"They're good kids," Greg observed, watching them go.

"The whole family's great."

Greg turned to her. "You want to talk about Charley? I didn't know him very well. He never went out for sports."

That figured. Even in those days he probably had no time for something as clean-cut as sports. "Actually, I want to talk about Dianne."

Pain flashed across Greg's face, and he looked down for a moment, composing himself before he met her gaze again. "I could talk about Dianne all day, but she didn't know Charley very well either."

"I realize that. It's just that they came from the same town, and they both died violent deaths."

Greg shifted his clipboard from one hand to the other and studied her for a long moment. "Two years apart, in different towns."

"Both were shot with a thirty-eight caliber hand gun. I know I'm probably reaching, but I'd really appreciate it if you could answer a few questions."

Greg pushed his baseball cap toward the back of his head and drew in a deep breath. "It's hard to get past something like that. The boys and I still miss her every day. But I guess I don't have to tell you what it feels like when your life partner is gone."

Amanda wished she knew what that felt like.

"Do you know why Dianne and Roland Kimball broke up?"

Greg blinked a couple of times as if startled by the question. "I…no, that was before we started dating."

"I know. I just thought she might have told you."

"She never talked much about that time in her life."

"Did she stay in touch with him after they came back from college? Did they remain friends or at least friendly?"

Greg shook his head. "She had no contact with him, and she never brought up his name."

"So the breakup must have been a bad one."

Greg drew in a deep breath. "My wife is dead. All I have left is her memory. Why do you want to dredge up things from her past that are better off forgotten?"

"I'm sorry. I don't mean to upset you. Her killer was never brought to justice, and Charley said he thought her death might be connected to what happened in college." That wasn't a lie. She just didn't specify if Charley told her before or after he was killed.

Greg gripped the rail and leaned closer. "You think that bastard Kimball had something to do with what happened to Dianne?"

Amanda hadn't expected that reaction. For all his money and prominent position in the community, Kimball didn't seem likely to be voted Mr. Popularity. "I don't know. That's why I'm asking questions."

Greg leaned back. "She was different when she came home from college. In high school she was the girl everybody loved. A cheerleader, smart, funny, bubbly, adventurous. Always right there when somebody wanted to do something silly. One time she and her friends put

163

pink flamingos in the biology teacher's yard. Another time they blew up hundreds of balloons and filled the boys' bathroom with them. Never anything bad, just high-spirited. About the worst thing she ever did was smoke a cigarette in the cafeteria on a dare."

"She doesn't sound like the kind of girl who'd date Roland Kimball."

"He was rich and good looking, she was beautiful and popular. Nobody was surprised when they started dating. After they went off to college together, everybody thought they'd get married." Greg was silent for several seconds, his gaze focused on the ground.

"But they didn't," Amanda supplied.

He slowly lifted his head. His eyes were damp, but he smiled. "No, they didn't. She came home and married me. She never looked at me in high school, but when she came back, she was quiet, subdued, ready to settle down. We had a good life."

"She never mentioned Kimball? Never even something like, *gee, I wish I'd never met that creep?*"

Greg shook his head. "Never. Not even when somebody else brought up his name. She never talked about him, and she went out of her way to avoid him, like if he was speaking to a group or visiting the school or something public like that. Yes, I thought that was suspicious. I thought he'd probably hurt her, but I didn't see any reason to bring up bad memories, so I never pushed her." He hesitated, holding his clipboard against his chest. "She had nightmares. Sometimes she'd wake up crying, sobbing as if her heart was broken."

"Did she say what the nightmares were about?"

"No. She always claimed she didn't remember. The nightmares got worse just before she was killed." He hesitated then seemed to make up his mind. "Sometimes I'd catch a word here and there in all the crying. She'd mumble things like, *forgive* and *blood*. She was very religious, obsessed with never being good enough. So that seemed normal, forgiveness and the blood of Christ. But sometimes she begged somebody to stop." He swallowed. "Sometimes she talked about *death* and *murder*."

A cold chill shot down Amanda's spine. "Death and murder? Did you ask her what she meant?"

Again Greg shook his head. "She always claimed she didn't remember the dreams."

"Coach Carter, can you come see if I'm doing this right?" Another young girl in track gear came up behind him.

"Sure, Julie. Be right there." He looked at Amanda, smiled weakly and spread his hands. "I'm sorry I can't tell you anything more."

"Thanks," she said. "You helped." While the information that Dianne had nightmares and talked in her sleep about murder seemed ominous enough, she had no idea what to do with that information, where to go from there. Feeling a little frustrated, she started to leave, find the twins and head home.

"Mrs. Randolph?"

"Yes?" She turned back to Greg Carter.

"You might talk to Sandy Lawson. Dianne and Sandy were friends, and they roomed together in college. When Kimball walked into Dianne's funeral, Sandy got upset. Said he had no right to be there. Going to funerals is part of being the mayor, but Sandy said, *after what happened between him and Dianne*, he shouldn't have come."

"Do you have her phone number?"

"It's in the phone book. Her husband's name is Don. She still lives here in town."

"Thank you."

"Now we're getting somewhere," Charley said as Coach Carter walked away.

"We?"

Paula and Penny ran up, clean and ready to roll. As the three of them—four if you counted Charley—headed for the gate, Amanda noticed a man a few feet away duck his head and turn from them. He looked ordinary enough, and there was no reason he shouldn't be hanging around the high school stadium, but why was he trying to hide his face?

The girls didn't seem to notice anything, but she glanced at Charley and saw him watching the man too.

A pervert scoping out the kids, or one of Kimball's flunkies keeping an eye on her?

She didn't much care for either possibility.

৵৶

As soon as Amanda ferried Penny and Paula home, she looked up Sandy Lawson's number and called her. The woman was more than ready to talk about Dianne and Kimball.

"But not on the phone. Can you drop by after dinner?"

"Absolutely!"

When Amanda announced she was going for another moonlight motorcycle ride, Irene looked at her skeptically but said nothing.

She climbed on her bike, and Charley climbed on behind. "I thought you didn't like riding with me."

Charley shrugged. "Not gonna hurt me. I'm already dead. I was just worried about my sisters."

"Be sure and put on a helmet." Amanda laughed at her own humor.

Charley sighed. "I wish I could."

Ten minutes later she arrived at a small brick house with a wide front porch. The place was neat and well-kept, bushes trimmed and grass mowed.

A tall woman with short blond hair came to the door. "Come in," she invited. "You must be Amanda. I'm Sandy. Can I get you something to drink?"

166

"Iced tea would be great." Amanda was stuffed from dinner, but conversations in Texas were always smoother when accompanied by drinks.

Amanda removed her helmet and jacket and sat down on the sofa. Sandy's living room, like her yard, was neat and tidy, the furnishings subdued and tasteful.

Charley plopped down on the recliner. Actually, he sank a couple of inches into it, but Amanda had become accustomed to that sort of thing. "Give me a hand," he requested. "I can't make this thing go back. I like recliners. How come we never had one?"

Sandy returned with two glasses of iced tea and set them on coasters on the coffee table. "Don took our little girl to get ice cream," she said, taking a seat beside Amanda. "I told him we needed some alone time."

Amanda's spirits lifted. That sounded encouraging. A little scary but encouraging as far as information she could use against Kimball.

"Thank you for talking to me. You were Dianne's roommate when she broke up with Kimball?"

"Yes. We were best friends from grade school on. We told each other everything." She grimaced. "Until that night."

Amanda's spirits took a nose dive. Dianne hadn't told her what happened? "That would be the night they broke up?"

Sandy nodded, reached for her tea and took a long drink. "It was her birthday, and she went out with Kimball for a celebration. She came in late, upset, pale and shaking. She had something that looked like mud splatters all over her dress."

"It *looked* like mud splatters?" Amanda repeated. She glanced at Charley. He'd caught the implication too and was leaning forward. Dianne had mentioned *blood* during her nightmares.

"She had on a yellow sundress, and I thought maybe she'd fallen and got mud on it and was upset about it." She wrapped both hands around her glass of tea, clutching it tightly. "I asked her what happened, if she was hurt, but she wouldn't talk to me. Not one word. She went straight to the bathroom and turned on the shower." Sandy's gaze drifted across the room, her gray eyes unfocused, as if she were looking into the past. "I followed her into the bathroom. She was in the shower, crying. I didn't know what to do. I started to walk out and give her some privacy, but then I saw her clothes on the floor."

"The yellow sundress? With the mud splatters?"

"Yes," she said softly. "The dorm bathrooms were tiny. You couldn't get in the shower without splashing water all over everything. Dianne had tossed her clothes on the floor, and some of those spots got wet." She paused "It wasn't mud."

"I knew it!" Charley shouted.

"It was blood, wasn't it?" Amanda encouraged when Sandy went silent.

"I think so. Where her dress was wet, the stains ran red, not brown."

"Was it her blood? Was she hurt? Did Kimball hit her?"

Sandy shook her head. "No, I don't think it was her blood. She didn't seem to be injured."

"Do you think he raped her?"

"I don't know. I waited until she came out of the shower, then I tried to talk to her. She sat on the edge of her bed and started to cry, completely hysterical. I asked her if she and Kimball had been doing drugs. I knew the two of them had tried marijuana. Most of us had. I didn't consider that any big deal. It wouldn't have caused her behavior that night, but another kind of drug might."

Amanda realized she was holding her breath, waiting to hear about Dianne. "What did she say? Was she on drugs?"

"She admitted they'd tried something early in the evening that made her really high, but she swore she was completely sober by then. I believed her. She was out of it, but she didn't seem to be stoned. I asked her if Roland hurt her. She shook her head and kept crying. Said she never wanted to see him again as long as she lived. That was strong, coming from her. Dianne wasn't one of those girls who had big break up scenes. If she and Kimball had an argument, she'd shrug it off, say it'd be okay, and it always was. She never said they were breaking up until that night. I knew it was serious." Sandy drained her tea and set the empty glass back on the coffee table.

"But she never said why they were breaking up?"

"Never. When I pushed her on it, she asked me to pray with her. Dianne had never been super-religious. She went to church once in a while, but in all the years I'd known her, she never asked me to pray with her until that night."

"What did she pray about?"

"Forgiveness. She begged God to forgive her, then she cried some more and said she knew He never would."

"Forgive *her?*"

"Whatever happened that night, she felt guilty about it. She finally calmed down enough to go to bed, but she got up in the middle of the night, took the yellow sundress down to the common room and burned it in the fireplace."

"Wow." Amanda realized she was sitting on the edge of the sofa, gripping her glass of tea as if trying to crush it. She took a sip, set it on the coffee table, and leaned back.

"Yeah," Sandy said, "that was my reaction. She never talked about it again, but from then on, she went to church every time the doors opened, and she had bad dreams.

169

Cried in her sleep almost every night, and sometimes she talked in her sleep."

"Yes?" Amanda leaned forward, anticipating the words—*death, murder*. "What did she say?"

"Dianne was a good person. Whatever happened, she had nothing to do with it. That man is the devil incarnate." Sandy straightened, set her jaw. "In her sleep, over and over, she begged somebody to stop. One night, I'll never forget, she sat bolt upright in bed and shouted, *He's dead! You killed him!*"

Amanda shivered and looked at Charley.

He shrugged. "So Dianne wasn't his first murder. Doesn't surprise me."

Amanda supposed it shouldn't surprise her, but somehow it did. How many people had the mayor of Silver Creek killed?

"Did you tell the police about this after Dianne was shot?" she asked.

Sandy shook her head. "No. I didn't see any point in telling a story that would put Dianne in a bad light— drugs, blood on her dress. It didn't seem important since they said she was killed by a transient."

"But now you're not sure?"

Sandy bit her lip and again shook her head. "I don't know. Greg called before you got here and said you thought maybe Kimball had something to do with her death."

Amanda shifted uncomfortably on the comfortable sofa. Even though Kimball had all but admitted to Dianne's murder, she felt uneasy at the thought of coming right out and saying he'd done it.

"Tell her!" Charley ordered. "Sandy, he killed her!"

"Do you know of any reason Kimball would want to get rid of Dianne?" she asked.

"Maybe."

That got Amanda's attention. "Really? What?"

"After that night in college, Dianne went to church regularly, and she helped a lot of people. I think she was trying to atone for whatever happened. Then just before she died, she started talking about how one could never be forgiven for their sins if they didn't confess." She paused, drew in a deep breath. "I think she was going to confess about that night, maybe about Kimball murdering somebody. I think he killed her to keep her quiet."

ॐॐ

Amanda set some new speed records as she rode home from Sandy's house. Every headlight coming toward her could be driven by Kimball or the creepy man at the high school. Every tree along the roadside could hide someone aiming a gun at her.

Dianne and Kimball had taken drugs that night in college, and someone had died, likely been murdered by Kimball while Dianne watched and begged him to stop. She'd been close enough to get blood all over her yellow sundress, close enough to see the entire incident, and Kimball had killed her to keep her quiet about it.

That knowledge emphasized his threat to her, made very real the possibility that he could and would kill her. Not like she'd be his first victim. He had experience at the murder thing.

It was dark when she got back to the Randolphs' house. The family sat in the living room, reading and studying. Amanda waved to let them know she was home then went straight to her room.

"Did you see anybody following me?" she asked Charley.

"No," he said. "Was I supposed to be looking for somebody?"

"You keep saying you're here to help me. Warning me if somebody's trying to kill me would be a good start." She went over to the window and stared out into the darkness. The first evening she'd been there, the night was

171

soothing with its soft breezes and relaxing sounds. Now it was frightening with the darkness cloaking secrets, emitting sounds she couldn't identify. In the warm, cozy bedroom, she shivered.

"Whose blood was on that yellow sundress?" she asked the darkness.

"Whoever Kimball murdered that night."

Couldn't even talk to herself anymore. Never a moment's privacy.

"The man's evil," Charley continued. "He deserved to be blackmailed."

Amanda scowled and started to berate Charley, but a movement of shadows among the trees caught her attention. She pressed closer to the window but saw nothing more. Had she really seen movement, or was she being paranoid? Was she so worried that Kimball was coming after her she was seeing threats in an innocent man hanging around the school yard and shadows in the trees?

She could ask Charley to flit outside and look around. But then she'd have to admit she was scared.

She turned away from the window, away from the view of the moonlit trees outside, and sat in the wooden chair of Charley's old desk.

What was the matter with her? She wasn't going to let some control-freak, power-hungry tyrant creep her out. Nor was she going to let him murder her, not when there were still Cokes to be drunk and motorcycles to be ridden.

"I think we have enough information to talk to that obnoxious Detective Daggett again," she said. "Tell him what we learned about Dianne and the incident in college. He can check the records for unsolved murders on that night."

"Really? Would that be the same detective who thought you were nuts when you told him I wasn't dead?

All of a sudden, you want to talk to that jerk? Why? You scared, Amanda?"

"Absolutely not!" That was a lie, and both of them knew it. "I just think I'm not very good at this do-it-yourself murder investigation stuff. I need a little help."

"No! We're making progress. This is no time to wimp out."

"That's easy for you to say. You're already dead. You have nothing to lose."

"What if I'm stuck here until I help you solve my murder? This in-between business isn't a lot of fun. Sure, it's nice to be able to fly and go through walls, and my knee doesn't hurt anymore. But I can't eat, I can't sleep, I can't ride motorcycles, I have to wear the same clothes every day. Don't you care if I make it to the other side?"

"Not really." Except she did want him to go away from her. "What else can I do if I don't talk to the cops? We kind of know what happened, but I don't know where to go from here. I'm fresh out of ideas."

"Fortunately, I'm not. We can set a trap. You told Kimball we've got his murder weapon in a safe deposit box. So we buy an unregistered gun from one of my old buddies then tell Kimball we're going to give him back his gun. You meet him wearing a wire, hand him the fake gun, and we get him to confess."

Amanda's eyes widened. "Buy an unregistered gun? Wear a wire? That's insane!"

"I know some guys—"

"I have no doubt you know some guys who could fix me right up with an illegal weapon, but I really don't think I want to go there."

"You got a better idea?"

"Yeah. You leave so I can go to bed. Let me sleep on this."

Charley shrugged and disappeared. Knowing him, he was probably still watching. She flipped off the light before changing clothes and felt compelled to look out the window one more time. With the room dark, she'd be able to see outside better, assure herself that no one was out there.

The hairs on the back of her neck stood up, and a cold chill skittered down her spine. The shadowy shape of a man was walking among the trees, moving away from the house.

"Charley!"

He appeared so quickly, she wondered how far away he'd been, but the possibility of his spying on her while she undressed was the least of her worries at the moment.

"Go outside and see if there's somebody in the yard." She pointed toward the shadow. "Hurry! He's leaving."

Charley darted through the window.

Fingers clutching the sill, heart pounding double-time, Amanda watched as he disappeared through the trees. *Please come back and tell me I'm being silly. Come back and laugh at me.* Any of that was preferable to thinking someone was really out there spying on her. Seeing the man at the high school football field was creepy, but it was daylight then and he could be an innocent pervert. This was scary.

After what seemed like an eternity, Charley returned.

Amanda held her breath.

"I couldn't get close enough to see who it was, but there was a man out there."

"Lost," Amanda whispered hopefully. "Maybe he was wandering around lost. Did he look lost?"

"Yeah, like we were lost when Kimball caught us. He's watching you. You're in big trouble. We need to go tomorrow and get that gun for you."

At that moment, Amanda didn't feel like getting a gun. She felt like running away and hiding. "Tomorrow we go home and talk to the cops. I'll tell that damned Detective Daggett what I found out about Dianne, and I'll tell him somebody's following me. Surely that will get his attention."

"You better hope he doesn't decide to arrest you as long as you're there."

"You better hope that too. If I go to jail, you go to jail." As soon as she spoke the words, Amanda realized that was a double-edged threat. Going to prison would be bad enough. Being trapped in prison with Charley would be even worse. "Maybe just in case, you might be thinking about who would sell us a gun."

# Chapter Seventeen

"You've been drying that same plate for a good five minutes," Irene said.

"Oh." Amanda put the plate into the cabinet and reached for a wet one. Herbert had left for work, Paula and Penny had gone to school, and Amanda stood in the sunny kitchen, drying the breakfast dishes while Irene washed. However, her mind was far away, formulating what she could say to Jake Daggett to make him believe her and help her.

She'd phoned him immediately upon waking and scheduled a meeting for that afternoon. He'd seemed a little surprised to hear from her, and she couldn't decide if that meant he was surprised she was willing to put herself in a position to be arrested so easily or if it meant Charley's murder was a cold case and he was surprised she'd bring it up again. Neither possibility made her eager for the meeting, but she could think of no alternatives.

Sandy's story of what happened with Dianne brought home to her how dangerous Kimball was, and the man outside her window convinced her she could be next on his list of dead people. Between the two events, she'd had terrible dreams all night.

"Everything okay?" Irene asked. "You've been a little preoccupied the last couple of days."

A part of Amanda wanted to do something she'd never done in her life—tell this kind woman everything, dump all her problems on Irene's comfortable shoulders, accept the sympathy and caring she knew would be forthcoming.

She would not, of course, do that. Irene would worry about her, and she didn't want to upset her mother-in-law.

"Everything's fine."

"Paula told me you've been talking to Charley at night. That's a good thing, a healing thing. We all have to cope with grief in our own way."

Grief? Terror and anger more closely described her feelings, though she would certainly be grief-stricken if she got sent to prison for killing Charley or if Kimball murdered her.

"I have a surprise for you that should put a smile on your face." Irene beamed, her pale eyes twinkling. The sunlight streaming through the window over the sink sparkled on her silver curls. That image alone put the promised smile on Amanda's face.

"More pecan pie?"

Irene laughed. "We can do that. But my surprise is that your mama's coming for lunch."

The handful of flatware Amanda was drying slipped from her fingers and clattered to the floor. "What?" She leaned over and hastily retrieved knives, forks and spoons. "My mother? Here? How? Why?"

"She's worried about you, so I invited her down for lunch." Irene took the flatware from Amanda's paralyzed hands and tossed it all back into the soapy dishwater.

"You called my mother?" Though calling her visiting daughter-in-law's mother was probably a perfectly normal thing to do, Amanda felt betrayed.

Irene's brow wrinkled. "Your mother called me this morning."

"Oh. I...I'm just a little surprised. My mother...well, she doesn't usually worry about me." *And she was pretty adamant that she didn't want to come to Silver Creek.* Amanda could not see her uptight mother having lunch in the comfortable old farm house, eating ham sandwiches and pecan pie, drinking sweet tea from a fruit jar.

Irene reached over to give her a quick, one-armed hug. "Of course your mother worries about you. She may not say it, but mothers always worry about their kids. You'll understand one day when you're a mother."

Not bad enough she had to worry about being murdered by Kimball or arrested by Daggett, now she had to deal with her mother. What was the woman up to? Surely her father hadn't told her mother about the trespassing incident. Usually she could count on her father to keep her more erratic behavior from her mother in the interest of not upsetting her.

Amanda could only hope her mother wasn't going to make a scene and say something unintentionally cruel to Irene. Beverly Caulfield had impeccable manners and would never do something like that deliberately. But she had always lived in a rarefied atmosphere, out of touch with the rest of the world.

At least Amanda wouldn't have long to wait and worry and stress about the upcoming event.

৵৽

Beverly Caulfield arrived just before noon, parking her white Mercedes on the dirt between Amanda's bike and Irene's car.

From the living room window, Amanda watched in delight as her mother, every hair in place, wearing a beige silk blouse, tan linen slacks and beige heels with red soles, teetered across the patches of dirt and scruffy grass in the yard. Her lips were tightly clenched, but she came gamely up the wooden steps and across the porch.

Amanda stepped in front of the screen door and pushed it open before her mother could search in vain for the doorbell. "Come in, Mother. Irene's putting the finishing touches on lunch."

Beverly patted her immaculate hair and smiled tightly, her gaze taking in Amanda's jeans and T-shirt. "Hello, Amanda. You're looking…relaxed."

*Relaxed* was not a word Amanda would use to describe herself at the moment, but she knew her mother

178

was only referring to her style of clothing, nothing below the surface. "I hope you're hungry," she said. "Irene's been cooking all morning."

"It smells wonderful."

Irene came through the door from the kitchen, pulling off her apron. "This must be Amanda's mother." She crossed the room, beaming, in her flour-smudged blue cotton dress, and took Beverly Caulfield's hand between both of hers. "It's so nice to finally meet you. Amanda's told me so much about you. Come in and sit down. I'll bet you're hot after that drive. Let me get you a nice cold glass of iced tea."

"Thank you. That would be lovely." Beverly sank onto the worn sofa, sitting primly on one of the faded cabbage roses.

Amanda sat next to her mother, one careful cushion away. "Hello, Mother."

"How are you doing, dear?" Beverly asked.

"I'm doing fine." *If you don't count spending time with Charley's ghost and worrying about being murdered or going to jail.*

"You don't look fine. You look like you're not sleeping well. You have dark circles under your eyes."

"Thank you. That makes me feel so much better."

Beverly gave a small, exasperated sigh. "Your father and I are worried about you. He said you plan to stay here another week, and we don't think that's a good idea."

Irene arrived with three glasses of iced tea enabling Amanda to ignore her mother's comment.

❧

Amanda should have known her mother's ubiquitous manners would see her through any situation, even lunch at the Randolphs'.

Beverly tackled the crispy fried chicken, creamy mashed potatoes with gravy, green beans flavored with bacon, and fried green tomatoes as if she ate such fare every day. From earliest memory, her mother had taught Amanda that only sandwiches should be eaten with fingers. Watching her mother eat a drumstick held daintily in greasy fingers was definitely one of the high points of Amanda's day.

"This is delicious," Beverly assured Irene, patting her lips with the paper napkin. "I must get your recipe for mashed potatoes."

Irene beamed. "Plenty of butter, a little sour cream and half a block of cream cheese."

Amanda munched contentedly on her chicken breast as she imagined her mother's arteries clenching at the thought of all that fat. Wait until she found out Irene made her gravy with bacon grease and real cream.

Though Beverly refused second helpings, she did justice to the food, including Irene's pecan pie which she pronounced, "Wonderful, and your crust is so flaky."

Amanda debated telling her that was likely due to Irene's usage of lard instead of oil but decided to save it for later.

When all three dessert plates sat empty and both Amanda and Beverly had refused a second piece of pie, Irene stood and began gathering up the dishes. Amanda rose to help, but Irene stopped her. "I'll take care of this. You and your mama go sit in the living room and visit."

"No, I'll help," Amanda insisted, carrying her plate and her mother's to the sink. In the scheme of things she wanted to do, cleaning up the kitchen was miles ahead of visiting with her mother.

"No," Irene said firmly, donning her apron. "My kitchen, my rules. Pour your mama some more tea, and the two of you get out of my kitchen. Go on, now." She smiled while giving Amanda a gentle push toward the living room.

"I don't need any more tea, thank you." Beverly rose from her chair.

This was beginning to feel like a setup, Amanda thought grimly. The pecan pie and fried chicken began turning somersaults in her stomach.

This time Beverly chose the upholstered chair where she perched regally, feet crossed at her ankles.

Amanda sank onto the sofa, folding her arms across her chest, ready to defend herself.

"Charley's mother seems nice."

"She is. The whole family is."

"It was kind of them to invite you to stay with them after the funeral. It's given all of you a chance to get to know each other and to grieve together."

Amanda nodded, waiting impatiently for her mother to finish with the BS and get to the point.

Beverly smiled. "Your sister's having a baby."

Though that announcement didn't seem to justify the drama of this trip, it did get Amanda's attention. "Omigawd! What will she do when she's no longer the baby?"

Her mother's smile tightened to a straight line. "You're going to be an aunt."

"I'm already an aunt to Charley's nieces and nephews."

"I'm sure they're all wonderful children, but this will be your sister's child, your own flesh and blood."

"Are you sure Jenny and I are related? Are you absolutely positive you didn't find me on the doorstep?" Amanda knew she shouldn't antagonize her mother, but sometimes she couldn't help herself.

Beverly sucked in a sharp breath. "Amanda, I wish you wouldn't talk like that. It's not amusing. Of course Jenny's your sister. We're your family." She paused, clasped her hands in her lap, and lifted her chin. "The Randolphs are lovely people, but they're Charley's family. Your father, Jenny and I would like for you to come home to your family."

181

"I'm coming home in a week. I already told Dad."

Her mother's stiff posture stiffened even more. "You don't want to wear out your welcome with the Randolphs."

"I've only been here a few days. They've invited me to stay all summer." Amanda's words were true, but suddenly she felt unsure. Charley's family had insisted she stay. They all went out of their way to make her feel welcome. But were they now ready for her to leave? Had Irene and her mother talked about this? "Did Irene say something to you?"

Beverly looked aghast. "No, of course not." She straightened. "It's up to you to be a courteous guest and leave before you put a strain on your relationship with Charley's family."

Amanda had felt so comfortable, so welcome there. She'd felt she was a part of the family. Now her mother had squelched those warm feelings. "Fine. I'll move to a motel."

Her mother blinked several times. "A motel? Why on earth would you do that?"

Amanda had the satisfaction of seeing her mother disconcerted, but it was a hollow victory compared to her sick feeling of being an imposition on people she'd come to care about, of having lost a family.

"You want me to leave the Randolphs' house. Okay. But I'm not leaving Silver Creek right now."

"Why not? Your home and family are in Dallas. We want you back with us."

Amanda studied her mother curiously. What was up with her parents? First her dad and now her mother demanding she come home? It wasn't like she lived at home or even visited on a regular basis. Was this the purpose of her mother's visit, to drag her home? Why? She knew they hadn't liked Charley and hadn't wanted her to associate with his relatives, hadn't wanted her to come to Silver Creek, but even her mother had admitted Irene was "nice."

Whatever her parents' problem, she wasn't ready to leave. She had to get proof that Kimball, not she, had killed Charley.

"I'm not coming home just yet. I have something I need to do down here, some information I'm trying to find." That should make it sound business-like, official, make her parents back off.

Instead of relenting, her mother's face sagged, the color draining from it.

What had Amanda said wrong now?

Her mother licked her lips. "What sort of information?" Her voice was low, barely audible. Could she somehow know about the situation with the mayor, the danger Amanda was in? Had her dad told her mother about the trespassing issue?

"I'll be fine. I'll be home in a few days. You have no reason to worry." That last part could be true if her visit with Daggett went well.

Beverly shook her head slowly. "You've always been stubborn," she said quietly. "If you'd listened to your father and me and not married Charley, you could have saved yourself a lot of heartache."

Amanda glared at her mother. What she said was true, but it was big-time wrong to say it after eating a meal prepared by Charley's mother, with Charley's mother only a few feet away in the kitchen, doing dishes from that meal.

Her mother leaned forward, one hand extended, as if she were begging. Nah. Beverly Caulfield never begged. "Listen to your family this time and come home. Today. Now."

"Mom, this is ridiculous. Give it up. I'll be home in a few days."

Her mother leaned back in the chair, one hand on the side of her face as if she had developed a sudden headache.

Irene chose that moment to appear in the doorway between the kitchen and living room. "Anybody want some iced tea or a Coke?"

"No, thank you," Beverly said.

"I would love a Coke," Amanda said.

Her mother left shortly thereafter, giving Amanda an unaccustomed hug at the door. What on earth was going on?

While Amanda stood watching the white Mercedes drive away, Irene came to stand beside her.

"Your mama loves you an awful lot," she said.

Amanda thought that was not an accurate statement, but she didn't argue.

"And we do too," Irene continued. "We want you here for as long as you want to stay." She wrapped an arm around Amanda's waist. "You're at least a year or two away from wearing out your welcome."

Amanda turned to look at her. "You heard?"

Irene's face went pink. "Not on purpose. I was trying real hard not to eavesdrop, but there's no door between the kitchen and the living room."

Amanda chuckled. "No, there's not. Well, I apologize for anything rude my mother said. She's...different."

"Not really. She's worried about her daughter. That's normal. She doesn't want to lose you to another family."

Amanda laughed out loud. "You think...? I don't really know what's up with my parents, but fear of losing me to you all is not their worry. We're not what a closely knit family. More like loose weave."

Irene considered that for a moment. "I'll invite both of them down for dinner. Your sister and her husband too. Then we can show them we just want to be one big family. We'd never try to steal you from them. We just want to share you."

"Oh, let's don't do that." Seeing Irene's hurt expression, she added, "Not just yet. I'm sorting through some stuff."

Irene nodded. "Whenever you're ready."

"Soon." That was a nice generic time indicator. *The Triassic period was* soon *followed by the Jurassic.*

Irene moved back into the living room and sat on the sofa. "I guess now we know why they didn't come to Charley's funeral with you," she said. "They didn't want you to marry Charley."

Amanda walked over to the sofa and sat down beside Charley's mother. "No," she admitted, "they didn't want me to marry Charley."

"They didn't like him?"

"Not really."

Irene nodded. "Charley had his faults."

Amanda couldn't disagree with that, but she felt reluctant to agree. She said nothing.

"He loved you."

"I loved him." *Past tense. Very, very past.*

"You told your mother there was something you need to do down here, some information you need to find."

Amanda hesitated, but she couldn't lie to this woman. "Yes, there is."

"Does this have something to do with those night-time motorcycle rides you've been taking?"

"Well, yes."

"Can you tell me what it is? Maybe I can help. I know a lot of things about this town."

"I can't give you any details right now, but it would be great if I could get back to you later with some questions."

Irene smiled. "Any time. I'll be here."

"Thank you. I appreciate that. Right now I need to run over to Dallas. I may not be back in time for dinner."

"There'll be plenty of leftovers in the refrigerator."

Irene didn't ask what she was going to do or when she'd be back. She offered to help and promised food when Amanda returned.

❧

Amanda sat in the same room where Daggett had originally grilled her. She'd been waiting for three hours or fifteen minutes, depending on whether she measured time by her watch or her nerves.

"The judge is going to come unglued when he finds out you talked to the cops without an attorney present," Charley said.

"I don't plan to tell him, and I'd like to see you try."

"If Daggett arrests you and the judge has to post bail, he's going to figure it out, and you're going to be in big trouble."

"I'm already in big trouble. I can't get rid of you."

"Talking to yourself?"

Amanda turned to see Daggett standing in the doorway. He hadn't slammed the door to announce his arrival this time.

"Uh, yeah. It's what I do. Sometimes. When I'm stressed. Talk to myself. Try to get things clear in my own mind."

Daggett took a seat across the table from her. He still hadn't got a haircut, but he had shaved. "Everything clear in your mind now?"

"Not really."

"You need a little more time alone? I can leave."

Amanda considered her response. She'd like to tell this rude man to stuff it, then get up and walk away. But she needed his help. "I've got some information for you about the man who murdered my ex-husband."

"I'm not your ex!" Charley shouted.

Daggett lifted a dubious eyebrow. That eyebrow must have some powerful muscles as often as he lifted it. Or maybe it was just when she was around. "Tell me your information," he said, setting a notebook and pen on the table.

Amanda drew in a deep breath. "Roland Kimball, mayor of Silver Creek. He killed Charley because Charley was blackmailing him." She told him the entire story, including her conversations with Greg and Sandy.

Daggett listened without expression or comment. As she talked, Amanda realized she was speaking faster and faster, and the temperature in the room seemed to be rising with each word. Finally she finished her story and clenched her hands on the table top in a gesture that mimicked the way her stomach felt and waited.

"Is this the same *Kimball* you told me about the night your apartment was allegedly broken into?"

She had hoped he'd forgotten that conversation. "Yes."

"The same *Kimball* that your deceased husband told you about?"

She swallowed but kept her voice firm. "Yes."

"The same night you thought your deceased husband came by for a visit?"

Obviously he had not forgotten anything.

"Yes. I was...confused that night." She clenched her jaw and forced herself to tell the outrageous lie she'd concocted in anticipation of this situation. "I was under a lot of stress. I'd just lost my husband, and I had a head injury."

Charley gave her a thumbs-up.

The heat in the room intensified.

"But you're okay now?"

"Yes."

"Head injury healed?"

"Yes."

187

"Recovered from the loss of your husband?"

"Yes." She would be if she could just lose him.

"No more psychic visions from your husband?"

Did the man have a photographic memory?

"No."

Daggett leaned back in the wooden chair and tapped his pen on the table, his gaze never leaving hers. "So where did you get this information about Mayor Kimball if it wasn't from a psychic vision?"

Time for another lie. "Charley told me about the blackmail before he died. I, uh, guess I had a slight case of amnesia due to the head injury and forgot most of the story. It came back to me in bits and pieces." She was becoming as good a liar as Charley. Not an ability she was particularly proud of or one she intended to cultivate when this was over. Unless, of course, she ended up in prison. Then it might be an ability that would come in handy.

"He told you he was committing a crime, blackmail, and you didn't report it?"

"He only told me the morning he was killed. He was worried. After he tried it a second time, Kimball threatened him." *Oh, what a tangled web we weave...*

"Good job, Amanda," Charley encouraged.

"He called you that morning?" Daggett asked.

"Yes."

"And we'll find that call on your phone records?"

Amanda could feel sweat forming on her brow. This lying business wasn't easy. "I meant he called *on* me. Came over to talk to me. Personal conversation." She could only hope they wouldn't have records of Charley's comings and goings on that morning.

"I see. And then he called you on the phone after Kimball came to his apartment?"

"Yes." Damned man wasn't taking notes. He didn't believe a word she was saying. Or maybe he just relied on his memory. That seemed to work pretty well.

"Asked you to bring a gun which he planned to substitute for the murder weapon he didn't have, had never had."

"That's right."

"How did you know Kimball was there when Charley called? Surely he didn't dare tell you what was going on if this man was threatening his life."

A bead of sweat rolled down the side of her face. She wanted to swipe it away, but that would call attention to it. "Charley used special code words we'd worked out that morning in case he needed to let me know he was in danger from Kimball."

"So why didn't you take the gun to his apartment, do what you could to save your husband's life?"

"I didn't believe him."

"Amanda," Charley said, "you're letting that cop take control of the conversation. It's time to go on the offensive. Attack him. Ask him if he's going to help you or let you get killed."

Amanda sat straighter. Much as she hated to admit it, Charley was right. She floundered worse with each successive lie. "Are you going to check up on this man or let him kill me? I risked my life by going to his house to get evidence on him. When I told him I had the gun he used to kill Dianne, he threatened me. If he kills me, my death is on your hands."

"What did he threaten to do?"

"Kill me."

"He said those words, *I'm going to kill you*?"

Amanda shifted and looked away. "Not exactly. He said it wasn't a good idea for me to threaten someone who has as much power as he does."

"*You* threatened *him*?"

"No! I just told him he was going to pay for jacking with my bike."

"I see."

"And then I told him if he didn't give me back the gun he stole from my apartment so I could prove I didn't kill Charley, I was going to take the gun he used to kill Dianne Carter to the cops, and that's when he said I needed to be careful."

"He threatened you by telling you to be careful?"

"You had to be there. Trust me, it was a threat. The next day he left yellow chalk marks on my motorcycle tires and wrote the letter *K* in the dust on my bike." That sounded lame. "He was sending a message to let me know he can get to me anytime he wants. And last night when I came home from talking to Sandy, somebody was outside, watching me."

"Was it Kimball?"

"I don't know. It was dark."

"I see."

"You're losing," Charley admonished her. "Do the guilt thing again about your death being on his hands. That was good."

"If you check on unsolved homicides in Austin on the date when Kimball and Dianne broke up, her birthday their junior year, you'll have him."

That eyebrow shot up again. "What will I have?"

"Well, proof that he killed somebody in Austin, and Dianne was going to confess so he killed her."

Daggett nodded. "Is that all?"

"Yes." Against her will, she slumped slightly. "That's the whole story. Are you going to do something about Kimball?"

"I can't discuss an ongoing investigation."

"Not even with someone whose life depends on that investigation?" Maybe her story had a few flaws, but she'd given him some solid stuff.

He stood. "Thank you for providing us with this information. If there's nothing else...?"

She shot up from the chair. "No, there's nothing else. I just wanted to let you know who killed Charley and who's going to kill me so when I turn up dead, you'll be able to do a better job of investigating my murder than you've done with investigating Charley's. That's all. Nothing else."

She picked up her helmet and stalked out.

"Total waste of time," she said when she was outside the station. "He doesn't believe me. So much for the cops. So much for *protect and serve*. We're on our own."

Charley smiled. "Don't worry. *We* can handle it. I'm glad you're finally including me in your plans."

Amanda groaned, realizing what she'd said. "It looks like I'm stuck with you for the time being. Thanks to you, nobody else believes me."

"Not a problem. We'll show them. Tonight we'll go buy a gun from one of my friends, and then we'll use it to trap Kimball."

Amanda bit back a protest. She wasn't sure about the *trap* part, but she would feel safer if she had some sort of protection. This situation recalled the old joke, *I carry a gun because a cop's too heavy*. The cop she knew wasn't going to provide any protection for her.

"Fine," she said. "We'll buy an illegal weapon. Just for the record, this is not my idea of a good time, but at this point, I'll do anything to save my life and to get you on your way. I'm not sure which is more important."

# Chapter Eighteen

"It's Friday night. All my friends will be in bars. Won't be any trouble to find one of them," Charley had assured Amanda.

That was three bars ago. They were running out of bars, and Amanda was running out of patience.

She waited impatiently outside the Shade Tree Inn. Sitting astride her bike, sweating in her leather jacket, tapping her motorcycle boot on the dirt, her irritation grew. Charley had been inside the bar for what seemed like an hour, though it was probably only a few minutes. That time distortion thing again. How long did it take to determine if any of his low-life "friends" were inside? Charley was probably trying to figure out a way to drink a beer.

All around her, older model trucks, cars and motorcycles were parked erratically on the packed dirt lot. A couple in a car were making out. On one side of the dilapidated wooden building with peeling paint, a man leaned over, retching. It really wasn't the kind of place where Amanda wanted to hang out.

The door opened, spilling raucous laughter and country music into the night. A large man wearing a sleeveless denim vest exposing thick arms covered with tattoos stumbled out. Amanda straightened and pushed her gloved fingers around the edges of her helmet, tucking any stray hairs out of sight so the man wouldn't see she was only a biker chick instead of a macho biker dude he didn't want to mess with.

"Nice bike," the man growled as he passed her.

"Thanks," Amanda said, lowering her voice several octaves.

"Amanda!" Charley. Finally. "My friend Dub is in there." He floated outside the bar, motioning her to come in. "He'll be able to help us."

Amanda yanked off her gloves and helmet then climbed off the bike.

"Hey! You're a chick!" The voice came from behind her.

Damn. She'd forgotten about tattoo man. She strode toward the bar, ignoring him.

"Pretty lady like you don't want to drink alone." He appeared at her elbow. "I wouldn't mind a couple more beers."

Oh, good grief. "Actually, yes, I do want to drink alone." She kept walking.

He took her arm, and she whirled on him, her irritation finding a target. "Back off, buddy, or I'll beat your brains out."

The man released her arm and stepped back. "Sorry," he mumbled.

"Way to go, Amanda!" Charley applauded.

"I'd beat your brains out if you had anything but air in your head."

"Hey!" the drunk behind her protested. "No call for talking like that. You got a mouth on you, lady!"

Amanda started to protest, but tattoo guy glared at her and revved his motorcycle engine. She shook her head and followed Charley into the bar, except he went straight in and she had to go through the mundane process of opening the door. She needed to talk to him about acting a little more like a flesh and blood person. She wasn't comfortable with seeing him do *ghost* things like going through walls or floating a few feet above the ground.

The scent of stale beer and cigarette smoke greeted her. An old country song played on the juke box. The dozen or so men and a few women sitting at the bar and scattered at various tables turned to see who the newcomer was then went back to their drinks and conversation when they didn't recognize her.

"You always did hang out in the best places," she said through gritted teeth. "Where's your friend? Let's get this over with."

"Over there. That's Dub." Charley pointed to the far end of the bar where a small, sharp-featured man sat hunched over an almost empty beer. Greasy brown hair straggled just past the neckline of his Budweiser T-shirt.

Amanda sucked in a deep breath and moved across the room, settled on the bar stool next to Dub and placed her helmet and gloves on the bar. "Hi," she said. "I'm Charley's widow. Amanda."

Dub lifted his gaze to her face. His bored, unenthusiastic expression didn't change. "Hi."

The buxom blond bartender appeared in front of her. "What can I get you?"

"A Coke, and another beer for this gentleman."

"A Coke?" Charley questioned, taking a seat on the bar between Amanda and Dub.

"A Coke?" Dub echoed. "You came in here for a Coke?"

"I'm riding." She lifted her motorcycle key. "And I didn't come in here for a drink. I came in here to talk to you."

Suspicion clenched Dub's features. "Me? Why?"

The bartender chose that moment to return with their drinks. Amanda pulled bills from her pocket and paid, then waited for the woman to leave before continuing her conversation.

"Charley said you could sell me a gun," she whispered.

Dub reached for the package of cigarettes lying in front of him on the counter, shook one out, flicked a disposable lighter and drew in the smoke then blew it out, straight through Charley. Finally he turned back to Amanda. "Say what?"

"A gun. Charley said you could get me a gun. A Smith and Wesson .38."

"Lady, I thank you for the beer, but I don't know any Charley, I don't know you, and I don't know what you're talking about."

Amanda glared at Charley and lifted a questioning eyebrow. Was this one of his scams? Did he not know this man?

"How would you feel if a stranger came up to you at a bar and asked to buy a gun? You gotta convince him you know me. Ask him if he remembers the time we broke into our sixty year old tenth-grade math teacher's house and stole her red thong then flew it from the school flagpole."

Amanda drew in a deep breath. If Charley was lying...no, Charley couldn't lie.

Unless that assertion itself was a lie.

"Charley told me about something you two did in high school that involved your math teacher's red thong and the school flagpole."

A wide grin spread over Dub's thin face. "That was pretty funny when everybody put their hands over their hearts and started to pledge allegiance to Miss Dunigan's panties." He chuckled and turned his stool to face Amanda. "Those were good times. So you were married to Charley."

"Yes, for two years."

"Funny. I never pictured crazy Charley settling down with a wife and family. You have any kids? His obit didn't mention any."

"No."

Dub drew on his cigarette and considerately blew the smoke away from Amanda. "I got two boys, but I don't get to see them much. Ex got married again and moved to Corpus."

"I'm sorry."

Dub shrugged and ground his cigarette out in an already full ashtray. "Too bad about Charley. Somebody shot him, huh?"

"Yes. And I really need that gun because now somebody wants to shoot me."

Dub's eyes widened. "No shit?"

"No shit."

"Who?"

"Tell him," Charley encouraged. "You can trust him."

"I don't have any evidence, so I'd rather not say," Amanda replied cautiously.

"That's cool. About that gun, you know how to shoot?"

Amanda sipped her Coke and smiled. "I'm from Texas, aren't I?"

Dub laughed. "I reckon you are."

"I've got a Right to Carry permit. My dad taught me to shoot when I was a little girl, and Charley took me to some classes when he gave me a gun."

"Charley gave you a gun? Why do you need another one?"

"Kimball...somebody stole it." Damn! She was so obsessed with the man, his name had slipped out.

A knowing expression settled on Dub's face. "Kimball. That the SOB that shot Charley?"

She shook her head, then changed the motion to affirmative. "I can't prove it, but I know he did. I confronted him, and he didn't deny it. He threatened me if I told anybody."

Dub picked up his beer and took a long swig from it then wiped his mouth with the back of his hand. "He's slime. My brother went to school with him. Said he was sneaky. Me and Charley, we did a lot of stuff we probably shouldn't have, but if we got caught, we took the blame. Roland Kimball, he'd always manage to put the blame on somebody else when he got caught, like after he started dating Dianne Carter and he slashed Jerry Stewart's tires. That's her old boyfriend. Everybody knew he did it, but his old man slipped Jerry's family some money, and—" Dub waved a hand— "everything went away."

"So he didn't really clean up his act when he started dating Dianne."

"Nah. He just got sneakier. Dianne was a classy lady. She deserved better than him." Suddenly he sat straighter. "You think he killed her too?"

Amanda lifted both hands, palms out. "I can't say."

Dub's eyes narrowed. "He did, didn't he? That sorry son of a bitch. Why'd he do it? Why would anybody kill Dianne? I can see why he might have had reason to kill Charley—"

"Hey!" Charley protested.

"—but Dianne," Dub continued, unaware of his friend's protest, "she never hurt nobody. Never did anything bad."

Amazing how easily this man accepted that the town mayor was a killer. At Charley's funeral, Irene had said Kimball gave her the creeps. Greg Carter hadn't been surprised at the idea that Kimball had been involved in his wife's death. Apparently those who knew the man well knew his evil nature. "Yes, Charley did something to Kimball that caused him to want Charley dead. I don't know why he killed Dianne, but I'm certain he did."

Dub lit another cigarette and puffed quietly for a couple of minutes.

Charley waved irritably but ineffectually at the smoke as it floated lazily through him. "That's a bad habit you've got there, Dub," he said. "It's going to kill you if

197

you don't quit, and this death thing isn't all it's cracked up to be."

"That tight-ass wife of his," Dub said, ignoring Charley's admonition, tapping his ash into the overflowing ashtray.

"What?"

"Probably made him do it because she was jealous."

Amanda thought of the meek-looking blond woman she'd seen at Kimball's house. "Catherine? Short blonde? That wife?"

"You know her?"

"I've seen her once. She seemed pretty subdued, even a little subservient to her husband."

Dub snorted. "You bought into that Miss Priss act? She's a cold one, that woman. Her daddy's got more money than Bill Gates. Him and old man Kimball set up that marriage so they could keep Roland under control. He's a loose cannon. Gets in too much trouble on his own. You be careful. Between his daddy and his wife, Roland Kimball's got a lot of money on his side, and money is power."

"So you can see why I need that gun. Will you get it for me?"

"Least I can do for Charley's widow. Meet me back here tomorrow night. I'll get you a good one."

"Smith and Wesson .38 Chiefs Special, blue."

Dub frowned. "I can get you a gun easy enough, but if it has to be a certain one, this may take longer. There's other guns out there that kill just as good as a Smith and Wesson."

"I realize that, and I hate to be picky, but it has to be a Smith and Wesson .38 Chiefs Special, blue." She hesitated then continued. "It's for more than protection. It's part of my plan to expose Kimball."

"*Our* plan," Charley corrected.

"May take more than a day or two."

"I need it as soon as you can get it."

"I'll do my best."

She wrote her phone number on a napkin, thanked Dub, chugged her Coke, and left.

The night air smelled incredibly fresh after being in the smoky bar.

"You said we could get a gun tonight," she accused Charley.

Charley shrugged. "Well, since it's a special order, it takes longer. But don't worry. He'll get it fast. Dub's a good guy."

Amanda reached her bike and shoved her helmet onto her head. "Let's just hope he gets it before Kimball gets me." She tugged her chin strap tight and snapped it in place then climbed onto her Harley. The roar of the bike's engine in the still night air gave her a sense of security in a world where nothing seemed secure anymore.

She rode through the warm summer night, constantly searching the roadside shadows and trying to distinguish the faces in oncoming cars. She was not being paranoid. Someone had been outside last night.

Charley appeared to be making an effort to look out for her. At least, that's what she assumed he was doing, darting back and forth in front of her, obstructing her view.

When she pulled into the Randolphs' yard and parked her bike, he stood directly in front of her, waving his arms frantically. She yanked off her helmet. "What is up with you? Do you have any idea how annoying that was, not to mention dangerous? I need to be able to see where I'm going."

"I've been trying to tell you, somebody followed you!"

Amanda's stomach clenched, and suddenly she felt cold even wearing a leather jacket in the summer heat. "Who?"

"I don't know." Charley glared at her. "He stayed far enough back, I couldn't see him up close, and you wouldn't stop so I could get closer."

"Are you positive he was following me and not just going the same way?"

"Yeah, coincidentally somebody that was parked in the trees at the Shade Tree left right behind you and headed directly for my parents' house but decided to pull off the road and park a couple of hundred yards back."

Amanda swallowed around the huge lump in her throat. "He...parked?"

"Just down the road. Probably so he can sneak through the trees and spy on you again tonight."

"Thank you for being so comforting," she snapped.

"If you would have stopped when I tried to get you to stop, we could have confronted him."

"And then what? Shoot him with the gun I don't have? Or maybe you could have punched him in the nose."

"Don't you think it might be important to know who's following you?"

"You don't think it was Kimball?"

"Not his Cadillac. This car's an old Pontiac."

Had Kimball hired somebody to follow her? She found that easier to believe than the possibility that His Arrogance, the mayor, would want to be seen driving an older, inexpensive car.

She drew in a deep breath and straightened her shoulders. "Then let's go see who's in that car."

"Let's go," Charley agreed. "And don't worry. I've got your back."

"That's so reassuring." She swung off her bike, stuffed her gloves in her helmet and secured it on the handlebars. "Think your folks have got a hammer somewhere close?"

"Probably one in the shed behind the house. Why?"

"I'd feel a lot better if I had a weapon of some sort."

The shed was unlocked, and Amanda selected the sturdiest hammer she could find.

This wasn't exactly her idea of partying on a Friday night, Amanda thought as she walked across the moonlit yard toward the side of the road, clutching her hammer. After last night, the cops weren't going to help her. She had to take care of herself, and that meant confronting her stalker.

Keeping as close as possible to the shelter of trees, Amanda made her way down the side of the road.

Charley darted ahead then came back. "I see the car. Right around that curve."

"Can you see who's in it?"

"Nobody. He must be circling around to the house to look in your window."

Amanda let out a long breath and tried to talk the knot in her stomach into relaxing. Knowing she wasn't going to confront her stalker in the next few minutes made her feel a little safer. On the other hand, knowing he was out there somewhere, maybe watching her window for her appearance, maybe watching her right now as she tried to sneak up on his car, ramped up the feeling of danger.

She rounded the curve in the road and saw the car.

The sight of the older model, two-tone blue Pontiac made it all frighteningly real. The car was parked off the road, under a tree, partially hidden. It appeared to be, as Charley had said, unoccupied. Nevertheless, she studied the area carefully, looking for any sign of movement.

"What are you doing?"

Amanda gasped and jumped at the sound of Charley's voice. "I'm checking things out before I get any closer. The driver could still be lurking."

"He's not. I've already looked around. Didn't I just tell you he's not here? Come on."

Even with Charley's reassurances, Amanda felt exposed and vulnerable as she approached the vehicle. Her steps crushing the leaves and twigs underfoot sounded like gunshots. The moonlight created eerie shadows as it glowed through the trees. An owl hooted a spooky call, and Amanda let out an involuntary shriek.

"Shhhh!" Charley cautioned. "I said the man was gone, I didn't say he was in the next county."

On the positive side, Charley's annoying behavior focused her anger on him and kept her fear somewhat at bay.

She made a mental note of the license plate number then approached the car and peered through the passenger's side window. Soda cans, cigarette packages and fast food wrappers littered the seat and floor, but the item that caught Amanda's attention was the picture that lay on top of the mess in the seat—a picture of her on her recently-deceased motorcycle, a picture taken at least a couple of weeks ago before all this started.

# Chapter Nineteen

As soon as breakfast was over the next morning, Amanda rushed upstairs and placed a phone call to Jake Daggett.

"Detective Daggett is not in the office at the moment. Can someone else help you?"

"No." Amanda leaned back in Charley's desk chair with a frustrated sigh. "Can you give him a message? This is Amanda Randolph, and I have the license plate number of the man who's stalking me." She repeated the number she'd memorized the previous night. "Please tell him—oh, just have him call me when he gets in."

She disconnected the call and looked at Charley where he perched casually on the windowsill as if basking in the sunshine.

"He was there," Charley said smugly. "He's just ignoring you because he thinks you killed me and you're just trying to blow smoke up his, uh, ear."

"For once, I think you're probably right." She let the hand holding her phone hang limply at her side. "He was there and didn't want to talk to me. I can see where he'd think I'm making all this up to divert suspicion from myself. Or maybe he thinks I'm nuts. Or both." She looked across the room, away from Charley. "He wants to arrest me. He wants to see me hang."

"They don't hang people anymore."

Amanda rolled her eyes then lifted her cell phone again. "Daggett can stick it. I know somebody who can find that license plate." She punched in a number and put the phone to her ear. "Dawson, it's Amanda. Can you find out who owns a car if I give you a license plate number?"

"Sure. That's an easy one."

She recited the number.

"Hang on. This will only take a minute."

Amanda rummaged in a drawer in Charley's old desk and came up with a pen and piece of paper.

True to his promise, Dawson returned to the phone in less than a minute. "Frank Sturgess, 259 Beale Street, Silver Creek, Texas. Do you want me to see what I can find out about him?"

Her fingers strangely numb, she scrawled the information on the paper. The man was real. He had a name. He lived in Silver Creek. He had her picture in his car. He followed her, spied on her, invaded her life. "Yes," she said, her voice surprisingly quiet considering the turmoil going on in her mind. "Find out everything you can about him."

"I will. Amanda, are you all right? What's going on?"

She started to give him the standard, *I'm fine*, but Dawson was her friend. He deserved better than to have his concerns dismissed so casually. "Things are a little strange."

"Strange how?"

She couldn't think of any reason not to tell Dawson the whole story. Well, the story minus Charley, of course. "The license plate I asked you to look up, it belongs to a man who's been following me. I think it's somebody Kimball hired. He killed Charley, and I'm trying to prove it so I can stay out of prison."

She waited for the expected incredulous response.

"What data do you have to back up your supposition?" Dawson asked in his usual calm voice.

"I've found—uh—information indicating Charley might have been blackmailing Kimball for murdering Dianne Carter. Kimball stole my gun, thinking it was the gun he killed Dianne with, the one Charley was using to blackmail him."

"Can you take that to the police?"

"I tried. That damned Daggett thinks I'm mental. He just wants to prove I did it so he can close the case and be done with it."

"How about the gun, the one Kimball used to kill Dianne?"

"Charley never had the gun. He lied to Kimball about that."

"I see. This information you found, how sure are you that it's accurate?"

"I realize anything Charley's involved in is suspect. But a few nights ago I went out to the mayor's house to spy on him. He caught me, we talked, and he pretty much admitted that he killed Dianne and Charley. So I just need to prove it."

"You went to his house? Amanda, that was very reckless. You could be in danger."

"Yeah, that's a given. Can you do one more thing for me? I talked to Dianne's college roommate, and it sounds like somebody may have been hurt—killed—the night Kimball and Dianne broke up. Can you check on murders in Austin around that time, especially any in the vicinity of the college? It was her birthday their junior year. I don't know the date, but I can probably find out."

"No need. I can find her birthday. I'll get back to you on the murders."

Amanda ended the call and focused on the information Dawson had given her. *Frank Sturgess.*

Charley peered at the words Amanda had written. "What is that? Freak Stings? Amanda, you have the worst handwriting in the world." Charley had a way of bringing her back to reality.

"Maybe you should give up on the vanity thing and get a pair of glasses. Anybody can see that says Frank Sturgess."

Charley frowned, shaking his head. "Don't know him. I thought I knew everybody in this town that would…uh…slide around the law."

"Oh, darn! You missed one. You could have been best buds with this guy. He could have taught you to be a peeping tom, and you could have taught him to be a scam artist. Doubled both your skills."

"I just meant it must be somebody new here, somebody Kimball brought in from out of town."

Amanda drummed her fingers on the desk. "I bet your mother would know all about him. She seems to know about everybody who lives here."

"She does," Charley agreed. "Everybody in town is her friend."

Amanda frowned. "So you admit your mother is a wonderful person. Your whole family is wonderful. Why on earth did you tell me those horrible stories about them?"

Charley's lips clenched shut, and he looked away.

"Fine. I get it. You have no excuse for such despicable behavior. I'm going down to talk to your much-maligned mother about Frank Sturgess."

Amanda got downstairs in time to see Paula and Penny heading out the front door. "Bye, Amanda," Penny said. "We're going to hang with friends. See you later!" They waved and darted out the door.

Amanda returned their waves and continued on to find Irene and Herbert sitting at the kitchen table, heads together, making a grocery list.

"Cokes for Amanda," Irene said, writing on a note pad.

"There's our Coke lady now." Herbert greeted Amanda with a big grin.

Irene looked up, a warm smile on her face. "Hi, sweetheart. How does meatloaf sound for dinner tonight?"

Amanda felt a sudden surge of guilt. She'd accepted the hospitality of this family, and they'd given it so easily, she hadn't stopped to think about the imposition and extra cost she created. "If you're making it, I know it'll be wonderful. But why don't I go pick up some fried chicken or a pizza so you don't have to cook?"

Irene waved a negligent hand. "I love to cook for my family."

"And we love to eat her cooking." Herbert stood, leaned over, and kissed his wife. "I'm going to the hardware store to pick up stuff to fix that toilet stool that won't quit running."

Herbert left, and Amanda took his seat beside Irene. "I'd like to go grocery shopping with you and pay for some of the groceries," she said. "I feel guilty staying here, eating your food, creating extra work for you and doing nothing to help."

Irene looked shocked. "My goodness, don't you dare think like that! You're not causing any extra work. You think after raising seven kids that one more is going to make even a ripple?" She laid a hand over Amanda's and squeezed. "And don't think you're not helping. Having you here is like having a little bit of Charley with us. You're helping all of us cope with losing him."

That made the guilt dig in its heels more deeply. If they only knew how much of Charley was there and how unhappy Amanda was about it, Irene would probably feel very different about Amanda's presence. Though she couldn't change how she felt about Charley, Amanda resolved to figure out something she could do to repay the Randolphs for their kindness.

In the meantime, she needed to do her best to stay alive.

"I have a question. You said you might be able to help me with that information I need to find."

"Of course. What's your question?"

207

"Do you know anything about Frank Sturgess?"

"Frank Sturgess." Irene's brow wrinkled in thought. "I know that name. Just give me a minute." Her brow smoothed and she smiled. "Of course. Frank Sturgess. He's one of Sunny's success stories."

Amanda thought about the scum who'd been following her, spying on her, probably reporting back to Kimball so he could kill her. *I'd hate to see Sunny's failures.*

"He came to town a couple of years ago with his wife and two little babies," Irene continued.

*The scum had a family?* That was doubly creepy.

"Bought the old Renfrow house. He went to work doing odd jobs, but about a year ago, he got in trouble. Tried to rob a convenience store. He admitted he did it. Didn't try to tap dance around it. Said he was desperate, needed the money to support his family. Anyway, Sunny took his case. Got him probation then helped him get a decent job. Him and his wife joined the church, and they've been good members of the community ever since."

*Except for stalking me.* "Do you know where he works?" She'd be willing to bet it was one of the Kimball family companies.

"Can't say as I do. You could ask Sunny."

"That's a good idea, a really good idea." Amanda had become so involved with staying alive and out of prison that Sunny Donovan had slipped to the back of her mind. This could be her chance to find out about her stalker as well as unravel the mystery that was Sunny Donovan.

"I'll give her a call." Irene rose from the table.

"It's Saturday," Amanda protested. "Does she work Saturdays?"

"Probably. If not, I'll phone her at home."

"Oh, don't bother her on her day off."

Irene looked surprised. "It'll be all right. It's not like this is business. I've known Sunny and her mother all my life."

Amanda recalled Charley's comment that his mother was friends with everybody in town. She could easily believe that.

Irene went to the living room where they still had a land line. After a couple of minutes of talking and laughing, she returned.

"Sunny's in her office today. Said if you want to come over, she'd be pleased to talk to you."

Amanda thought of the lawyer's behavior when she'd been at her office a few days before. Irene might be putting a spin on how pleased Sunny would be to see her today.

"Thank you." She stood and gave Irene an impulsive hug, something she'd never done with her own mother. What insanity caused Charley to leave a family like this?

Irene returned the hug. "You want me to go with you?"

"Thanks, but I'll be fine. You get your grocery shopping done. I'll meet you back here later so you can teach me how to make meat loaf."

"Sounds like a deal."

&oc&

Amanda arrived at Sunny's office half an hour later. Charley had tried to talk her out of going, and that made her all the more determined. He refused to come with her, saying he'd go into the dark and wait for her to return. However, she had an eerie sensation that he was following her anyway, just out of sight. Or maybe it was Frank Sturgess again.

For once, she would rather it was Charley.

She parked her bike at the curb and walked across the wooden porch of the old house. Following the example set by Irene when they'd been there previously, she knocked then opened the door and entered. Sunlight streamed through the windows of the small room, resting on the file cabinets, desk and dark computer screen, but Martha wasn't there to announce her.

"Miss Donovan?"

Sunny emerged from her office. Today she wore blue jeans with a white cotton shirt and looked even more familiar than in her going-to-court clothes. She extended a hand. "Please, call me, uh, Sunny."

Amanda reached for the hand, expecting another stiff, perfunctory shake, but instead Sunny grasped her hand firmly though her smile was tentative.

"Sunny, thank you so much for taking the time to talk to me today."

"My pleasure." She turned and led Amanda into her office.

This room was larger than the reception area, though not by much. A wooden desk holding a laptop computer, several files and stacks of papers occupied most of the area. A tall file cabinet sat in one corner within reach of the high-backed chair behind the desk.

Sunny did not take the chair behind the desk, the position of power, but sat in one of the blue upholstered client chairs. Amanda pulled off her leather jacket and settled in the chair beside Sunny. Cozy. Two equals. This woman didn't seem so strange after all. She seemed to be, as Irene insisted, a really nice person. Even a potential friend.

"I understand you know a man named Frank Sturgess."

The blood drained from the older woman's face, her smile changed from tentative to stilted, and her green eyes went wide with an odd expression. Panic?

Oh, yeah. Sunny knew Frank Sturgess.

Did her reaction mean she knew he was an evil man, and she was concerned as to how Amanda knew him, what he might be doing to Amanda?

Sunny recovered almost immediately, a professional mask settling over her face. Too bad. Amanda had kind of liked the real woman who'd sat beside her so briefly, before she mentioned her stalker. "Frank Sturgess? Yes, I know him. He's a former client. Why do you ask?"

"He's been following me."

"Why do you think that?"

She decided to tell part of the truth. Charley's role always had to be edited out. "I saw him following me last night. Then I found his car parked at the Randolphs' place and got his license plate number."

"I see. How did you get his name from the license plate? Have you spoken to the police about this?"

Amanda didn't want to admit that the Dallas cops were ignoring her, so she opted to indulge her new habit and lie. "No. That information is available on the Internet."

That evoked a wry grin. "Of course. Everything is out there on the Internet. So you're a computer expert?"

Amanda laughed at that image. "Not really. I can do e-mail, Facebook, play a few games, the basics. That's the extent of my computer expertise."

"But you found Frank's name by using his license plate number."

"I had help. I have a friend who is a computer expert."

Sunny nodded and tented her fingers. "So you want to know about Frank Sturgess. He moved here when he was laid off from his assembly line job in Fort Worth. He couldn't find regular work, and he made a mistake, robbed the Fast Stop convenience store so he could buy food for his family. I got his sentence commuted to probation, helped him find a job, and he's walked the straight and

211

narrow ever since." She hesitated. "Don't judge him too harshly. He's not a bad person."

Amanda grimaced. "Not a bad person? He stole money and now he's following me and spying on me, and you don't think he's a bad person?"

"He loves his kids. Parents will do anything for their kids, even things that are wrong." Sunny spoke with so much feeling, Amanda wondered if the woman had children of her own. Irene hadn't mentioned a husband or family. Either Sunny had kids or she was a real bleeding heart.

"Where does Sturgess work?"

"Your computer friend didn't tell you?"

"Not yet. He's working on it. I just thought I'd ask since I'm here."

Sunny laughed suddenly, an unexpected bright, tinkling sound. "Hedge your bets. Smart girl. Frank works as a warehouse manager for Silver Creek Financial."

"Is that one of the companies owned by the Kimball family?"

"Yes, it is. Why do you ask?"

Amanda shrugged. "Just curious."

"*Just curious,*" she repeated, her expression and her voice suddenly switching to *lawyer* mode. "Roland Kimball called the police a few nights ago because you were trespassing on his property. Now you think a man's following you, and you want to know if he works for the Kimball family. What's going on, Amanda?"

Amanda's jaw dropped. "Does everybody in this town know everybody else's business?"

"I'm sorry. I didn't mean to upset you. No, not everybody is aware of your encounter with the police. I work closely with local law enforcement. No charges were filed against you, but the officers had to turn in a report. I saw that report."

"No wonder Charley left this town." Amanda didn't realize she'd spoken aloud until Sunny's face clouded.

"Charley, your husband."

"Ex-husband," Amanda corrected automatically.

"Oh? I thought you were still married when he died."

"We were. Legally, anyway. It's complicated."

"Charley was a complicated man."

A few weeks ago, Amanda would have argued with her. Charley hadn't been complicated. He'd been a straight-forward lying, cheating con-man. But over the last few weeks, *complicated* didn't even come close to describing Charley. "Yes. He is…was...complicated. How well did you know Charley?" Might as well plunge right in, ask what she wanted to know.

Sunny sat stiffly erect, her gaze focused out the window. "I represented him in court. He was caught with less than an ounce of marijuana. He had no previous record, so it was fairly simple to get probation for him."

"Probation like you got for Frank Sturgess."

"Yes, like I got for Frank Sturgess."

"Do you consider Charley a success story?"

Sunny studied her for a long moment. "Your marriage to Charley was not a happy one." It was a statement, not a question.

Amanda folded her arms. She'd intended to get information about Charley and Sunny's relationship, not give information about Charley and her. "We had some good times," she said. "At first."

Sunny nodded, her gaze again becoming distant. "Charley could be charming."

"Yes, he could. So, were you and Charley…um…friends outside of court?" She watched Sunny carefully to see what her reaction would be.

Sunny's gaze snapped back to her, and she looked horrified. "You think—Charley and me? Oh, no! No, I helped Charley. I thought he had a lot of promise, that he

213

could straighten up his life, maybe even go back to school, become a contributing member of society." She drew in a deep breath. "I try to help people. Sometimes I do. Frank Sturgess proved that he deserved my help. Charley…disappointed me."

Now they were getting somewhere. "How so? What did he do to disappoint you?"

Sunny smiled tightly. "Attorney-client confidentiality. Did you have any more questions about Frank?"

Whatever Charley had done to Sunny must have been a doozy if neither he nor Sunny would talk about it. Amanda would have to let it go for the moment, but she wasn't giving up. "Frank Sturgess," she said, returning to the thief and stalker who'd turned out better than Charley, "is he having financial problems again?"

"No, he's fine. I'll talk to him and find out why he was at Irene and Herbert's place. I'm sure there's a good reason."

*Yeah, because Kimball paid him to follow me, see if I'd lead him to that gun he thinks I have, maybe even find the right time and place to kill me.* She didn't say that, of course. No point in it. Sunny would think her as nuts as Detective Daggett did if she tried to tell the attorney her Kimball story.

"Thank you." Amanda stood.

Sunny laid a restraining hand on her arm. "Amanda, I have a feeling you're in some kind of trouble, and that trouble may involve our mayor. Talk to me. You can trust me. I'll do anything I can to help you."

The woman seemed so sincere, Amanda had a fleeting urge to confide in her. She could use an ally other than Charley—a flesh and blood ally, a sane ally. But she didn't know Sunny, had only met her a couple of times, and the woman hadn't always acted totally rationally. Besides, there was the skeleton in the closet Sunny and

Charley shared. "I appreciate the offer." She stood and looked at the floor, unwilling to meet Sunny's eyes when she told an outrageous lie. "I'm not in trouble."

Sunny rose to stand beside her. "Let me get you a card with my phone number. I'll add my cell so you can call me at any hour."

"Thank you." In spite of what she might have done with Charley, Sunny Donovan really did seem to be a kind, caring person. She'd tried to save Charley and Frank Sturgess from a life of crime. It wasn't her fault they'd both been incorrigible. Undaunted, she was now offering to help Amanda, someone she didn't know, someone who didn't even live in this town. She might be a bleeding heart, but she was a sincere bleeding heart. She backed up her beliefs with action.

Sunny rummaged for several moments in a couple of desk drawers, finally producing a card. Sunny's desk must be as unorganized as Amanda's if she had that much trouble finding a business card. Sunny scribbled something on the card and handed it to Amanda who looked at the scrawled writing and smiled.

"Is something wrong?" Sunny asked.

"No. It's just that your handwriting is as bad as mine. We should have been doctors." *Oh, that's great. Insult someone who's trying to be helpful.*

But Sunny returned her smile. "That's why God created computers with word processing software."

The two shared a moment of bonding over bad handwriting, and Amanda decided she liked this strange woman in spite of her eccentricities. Or maybe because of them.

"So next time I get caught trespassing, I'll call you."

"Or you could call me before you commit the act, and maybe we can figure out an alternative, legal way to accomplish your goal."

Lawyer talk again. A caring person one minute, a lawyer the next. Rather like her dad. It seemed to go with the occupation.

Sunny followed her outside to where her bike was parked.

"Nice," Sunny said. "I used to ride."

Yes, Amanda definitely liked her. "Really? What kind of bike?"

"Any kind I could afford when I was young. It was my only mode of transportation in high school and college."

"Even when it rained?"

Sunny ran a hand over the top edge of Amanda's windshield and grinned. "Even when it rained. And the smaller, cheaper bikes don't have very big windshields. But the weather's usually good in this part of the country. A little rain, very little snow."

Amanda grimaced. "I don't like riding in the rain, and I can't even imagine riding in the snow. You said you *used to* ride. Not anymore?"

"No. Just when I could afford to get a nice bike, I had to give it up. This is a conservative town, and people expect an attorney, especially a female attorney, to act in a certain way. As you mentioned, everybody knows what everybody else is doing in a small town. So, no motorcycle." She shrugged and sighed, looking wistfully at Amanda's bike.

"That sucks."

"Yes, it does."

"I have a motorcycle repair shop. Nobody expects any sort of decorum or propriety from a motorcycle repair person."

Sunny smoothed a hand over the leather seat. "I used to lust after Harleys, especially the Softail. Would you mind if I took a short ride?"

Amanda didn't hesitate. How could she refuse a fellow biker chick? "Sure." She handed over her helmet and gloves.

"Borrow the jacket too? I think we're about the same size."

Amanda relinquished her jacket, and Sunny put it on. "Nice," she said. "Perforations for cooling, but still armored for safety."

"Charley gave it to me. He probably stole it."

A guilty look flitted across Sunny's face. Because of what she and Charley had done? Or because Amanda would never have met and married Charley if Sunny had let him go to jail for his crime?

"I'll just take a quick spin around the block and be right back," she said.

"Don't let her take it!" Charley appeared at Amanda's elbow.

She ignored him.

Sunny climbed on the bike, fired it up and roared away.

Amanda turned to Charley. "Why not? You think she's going to steal it? You are completely insane. Sunny Donovan tried to help you, and you repay her by badmouthing her?"

"Of course she's not going to steal it. Why would you think that?"

"Then why would you tell me not to let her take it?"

Charley looked frantic as his mouth contorted but remained closed. Was he having some sort of ghostly seizure?

"What have you got against this woman who kept you out of jail and is now offering to help me?"

"I...I did some things to her that weren't very nice."

That confirmed what Sunny had said about Charley disappointing her.

She folded her arms. "You need to tell me what you did to her. It's going to come out sooner or later. Sunny almost told me today." Okay, that might be a slight exaggeration, but she wasn't the one who was constrained from lying. "If you don't tell me, she will."

Charley clenched his lips tightly shut as if the truth might come out of its own volition if he wasn't careful.

"What's the big deal, anyway? I know lots of horrible things you've done. What's one more?"

Charley remained obdurately silent.

The roar of the Harley's engine became louder, and Sunny rode up behind them. She stopped beside Amanda and took off the helmet, a wide grin on her face. "Thanks. That was fun."

Amanda accepted the proffered helmet. She was more than ever intrigued about the secret this woman shared with Charley. This would not be their last visit. "So...you'll give me a call after you talk to Frank Sturgess?"

"Yes, I will." Sunny surrendered the jacket and gloves to Amanda. "In the meantime, don't worry. I'm sure there's a logical explanation. Frank is a good man. You have nothing to fear from him."

Amanda nodded. "I really appreciate your doing that for me. How about I treat you to dinner one evening?"

"No!" Charley screamed, grabbing at Amanda's arms. Cold chills passed through her as Charley's hands did the same.

Sunny climbed off the bike and stood on the curb. "Thank you, but that isn't necessary. Calling Frank will only take five minutes."

"I insist. If not dinner, then how about lunch?"

Sunny shook her head, but Amanda thought she saw the same yearning in the older woman's eyes as when she'd looked at the motorcycle. Perhaps she wanted to socialize. Perhaps she'd felt the same possibility Amanda had of a developing friendship. Perhaps the secret between Charley and her was the only deterrent to that friendship.

"I'll bring the bike, and you can take it for another spin," Amanda coaxed. "Please. Otherwise, I'll feel guilty for taking up your time."

Sunny hesitated, then her face relaxed into a smile. "Okay. Let's go to lunch. You have my phone numbers."

Charley groaned and clutched his head in his hands. "Omigawd, Amanda. You don't understand. You can't do this. Please don't do this."

Charley said *please*? Wow. This must be some scary secret.

Suddenly Amanda wasn't sure she wanted to know. She liked Sunny, thought maybe they could be friends. After all, they had motorcycles and bad handwriting in common. But where had she seen Sunny Donovan before and what would she think of this woman when she finally discovered The Secret?

# Chapter Twenty

Sunday was peaceful. Kimball left no further messages, and she hadn't seen anyone else spying on her. Amanda allowed herself to fall into the soothing routine of the Randolph family. Church in the morning, a relaxed evening with all the family at home.

Sunny called to report she had spoken with Frank Sturgess. He had been coon hunting the night Amanda saw his car. The man was no threat.

Amanda passed a peaceful night and began to consider the possibility that, if she went back to Dallas and left Kimball alone, perhaps he would leave her alone. Maybe if she forgot about him, he'd forget about her. Maybe the cops didn't have enough evidence to arrest her. Maybe Charley would disappear on his own. Maybe, maybe, maybe.

When Amanda checked her bike on Monday morning, everything appeared intact.

Maybe...

"Amanda, you've got a phone call." Irene stood on the front porch, holding the screen door open.

The call must be on the Randolphs' landline since Amanda had her cell phone in her pocket. Who could be calling her on their phone?

When she stepped onto the porch, she saw concern in Irene's eyes. "It's the mayor."

Damn! All the stress rolled back through Amanda, clenching her chest and making it hard to breathe. *Maybe, maybe, maybe...not.* On feet that seemed to weigh a ton each, she walked into the house and over to the phone where Charley stood waiting.

Charley rarely appeared when other people were around. By his presence and the eager expression on his face, she knew he considered this call important.

"Hello?" She held the phone half an inch from her ear so Charley could eavesdrop. He was, after all, her cohort in crime.

"Mrs. Randolph, this is Roland Kimball, Mayor of Silver Creek."

So he was playing the official Mayor Kimball now. His smarmy politician voice rolled through her, sticking in the back of her throat, making her nauseous and angry. "Good morning, Mr. Mayor. To what do I owe the honor of this call?"

"I heard you were still here, and I thought I, as a representative of our little town, should get in touch with you, tell you how sorry we all were to hear about Charley. I'd like to take you to lunch as a gesture of good will."

"Really? Good will? You sure have a strange definition of *good will*. You try to kill me, you threaten me, you send someone to spy on me and you call that *good will*." A gasp from behind told Amanda that Irene had overheard her angry outburst. Damn!

"I'm sorry we got off on the wrong foot, Mrs. Randolph," Kimball said, his voice smooth and cold as ice. "Please allow me to make amends. If you'll agree to meet me for lunch today, I'm certain we can straighten everything out."

Going to lunch with Roland Kimball was not on her list of *Fun Things I Want to Do Before I Die*. However, she needed to do it if she was going to figure out how to prevent his killing her.

"Lunch is okay," Charley advised, "as long as it's in a public restaurant. He won't kill you in front of a lot of other people. Just don't agree to go to his house or anything."

She rolled her eyes in his direction. Did he really think she was that dumb?

"Where?" she asked.

"Anywhere you'd like. But since you're new to town, may I suggest the Round Rock Country Club?"

"The Round Rock Country Club for lunch?" She turned to Irene with a questioning look.

"I've never been there," Charley said. "This should be fun."

*Fun?*

Irene nodded once, woodenly.

"Shall we say around noon?" Kimball asked. "I'll pick you up."

No way was she getting in that black car that looked like a hearse. "I'll meet you there."

"Good idea," Charley said.

Kimball chuckled. "On your Harley? I'm not sure the Round Rock Country Club is ready for a leather jacket, blue jeans and motorcycle boots. If you ride with me, you can dress more appropriately."

"Or we can go somewhere else where my dress will be appropriate."

"I'll meet you there at noon." His voice had lost its cordial tone. "You won't be able to enter the restaurant until I get there to escort you in. Members only."

"I'm familiar with country club restrictions. I'll wait at the entrance."

She hung up.

"Good job! Now we're getting somewhere." Charley gave her a *thumbs-up*.

Irene walked slowly to the sofa and sat down. Amanda considered for a moment if she should run upstairs and try to avoid this conversation. But only for a moment. She could do that sort of thing to her mother but not to Irene. She sank down on the cushion beside her.

"My mama raised me and my three sisters with an iron hand," Irene said. "We went to a very strict church, and Mama made sure none of us girls could go against the church teachings." She shook her head. "I loved my mama, but I didn't like being clamped down like that. I raised my kids with a lot more freedom. I always tried to let them make their own mistakes and learn to fly on their own. And that's worked real good, most of the time. But I've often wondered if I should have been stricter with Charley, insisted on knowing what he was doing instead of respecting his privacy. If I'd clamped down harder on him, laid down the law, maybe—"

"No," Amanda interrupted. "Don't do that to yourself." She glanced toward Charley, expecting him to be gone, but he still stood beside the phone. He looked a little sad. "If you'd tried to rein in Charley, he'd have figured out a way to get around you and do what he wanted. Trust me. Been there, done that."

Irene sighed. "I'm sure you're right. But I should have tried anyway. And now, even if I make you mad by invading your privacy and being too pushy, I'm going to stick my nose in your business. What's going on with you and the mayor?"

"I'm meeting him for lunch today." It was a weak attempt to avoid the question. A useless attempt.

"People don't usually go to lunch with somebody who tried to kill them and then threatened them. Isn't that what you said he did?"

"Don't tell her!" Charley said.

It was a little late for Charley to be worrying what his mother would think about his bad behavior.

She sat quietly for a moment. She didn't want to worry Irene, but there was no way around it since the woman had overheard her comments. She drew a deep breath and told Irene about Charley and the blackmail, Dianne's death and the possible murder in college, the confusion with the guns and Charley's death, the man who'd been outside her window. Everything except Charley's continuing existence.

Tears welled in Irene's eyes, and her hands clenched in her lap. "That no-good rich kid killed Dianne and my son, and he's not in jail?"

"There's no evidence. I have only the, uh, phone call from Charley letting me know Kimball was in his apartment to kill him, and the police don't believe me. They think I killed Charley."

Irene wrapped her arms around Amanda and held her close. "Nobody who knows you believes that."

Amanda returned the embrace, finding her own eyes strangely moist. "You don't know how much it means to me that you believe me."

Irene drew back and wiped her eyes with the back of her hand then sniffed indignantly. "Your husband's dead and those idiot police are trying to blame it on you instead of doing their job and finding the murderer. That's just not right."

"His neighbors overheard me threaten to kill him. But it wasn't a real threat. We were just having a fight."

Irene nodded. "Husbands and wives fight."

"Not you and Herbert."

Irene laughed. "Yes, me and Herbert. In the early years. Before we settled into each other. You and Charley would have got through the fighting if that sorry excuse for a human being hadn't killed him."

Amanda didn't think that would have been even a remote possibility, but she thought it best not to tell his mother.

"Blackmail," Irene said softly. "Charley was blackmailing him."

Amanda looked over at Charley. He had the decency to flinch. "He wanted money to come to Dallas, the big city."

"I guess I shouldn't be surprised. The way Charley left town so suddenly and told us he had to hide, we couldn't tell anybody where he was...we knew he'd done something wrong, made the wrong person mad. And I reckon I'm not really surprised about what Kimball did. I've never liked that man. He's grown from a rich, spoiled brat to a rich, powerful bully."

"I'm sorry about Charley."

"Was my son a good husband?"

Amanda fancied she could feel Charley's gaze on her as he waited for her answer.

She shifted uncomfortably, not wanting to tell a lie and make Charley feel better about their marriage, but not wanting to tell Irene how bad it had been. "We had fun at first."

"I see. So you really were going to divorce him?"

"Yes."

Irene took Amanda's hand. "I reckon it's my turn to say I'm sorry."

"No," Amanda protested. "You don't have anything to apologize for."

"If I'd raised him better, if I'd been stricter..." She shrugged. "Like you said, he was fun. He'd do something wrong, but then he'd get me to laughing. It's hard to punish somebody who's making you laugh."

Amanda looked toward Charley to see his reaction. For an instant, she thought maybe she saw an expression of contrition on his face, but probably not. He smiled and shrugged. "Everybody likes to laugh."

"I know," Amanda agreed, thinking of the times she'd forgiven Charley because he made her laugh, the problems she'd overlooked because they had so much fun. She gave Charley a final glare then returned her attention to Irene. "Trust me, there's absolutely *nothing* you could have done to change Charley."

"Maybe not, but his murderer has got to be punished. Charley did wrong, but that didn't give that awful man the right to take his life."

"That's why I'm going to lunch with him. Somehow, I'm going to get evidence against him."

Irene bit her lip. "You're dancing with the devil, you know. You need to be careful. I don't want to lose you too."

Amanda's heart swelled, and again she found her eyes suspiciously moist. "I'll be careful. You're not going to lose me, not for a very long time."

Her cell phone rang. She pulled it from her pocket. "Dawson, at the shop." She headed toward the stairs and the privacy of her room. "I better take it."

"I found something," he said as soon as she answered. "An unsolved murder."

"The night Kimball and Dianne broke up?"

"Yes. Somebody killed a homeless man in one of the parks out by Lady Bird Lake. The man had been drinking, and it appeared he'd settled down for the night on a bench. An unknown assailant beat him to death with a rock. Weapon of opportunity. The murder has never been solved. The police had no suspects."

"That's the last piece of the puzzle," Charley said.

Amanda sank into the small desk chair and gazed out the window, trying to wrap her mind around this latest atrocity.

"I have one more thing that may be of interest," Dawson continued. "I checked phone records, and Dianne called Kimball for the first time since college a week before she was killed. They talked three times, the last time being a call initiated by him at three minutes after ten o'clock on the morning of the day she was murdered. This would seem to verify your theory that he killed Dianne because she was going to confess to their murder. She must have warned him. I believe this Roland Kimball is a sociopath. Perhaps you should stay away from him."

"I'm meeting him for lunch."

"I don't think that's a good idea, Amanda."

"Probably not, but it's the only one I've got."

"I have some information on Frank Sturgess too." He told her what Sunny had already told her. "Is he still following you?"

"I don't know. I talked to his lawyer, and she called him. Maybe you could get some information on her. She's a strange character. Sunny Donovan, an attorney here in Silver Creek." Amanda dug through her pockets until she located the card Sunny had given her. "Looks like her real name is Suzanne. I guess everybody calls her Sunny because she's the self-appointed purveyor of sunshine in this town." She read off Sunny's office address, phone number and cell number.

"Got it. You haven't asked how business is going, but I am getting some motorcycle repairs done in between my detective work."

Amanda smiled at her assistant's conscientiousness. "Thank you, Dawson. For everything. If I survive this, you're getting a raise when I get home."

She disconnected the call and turned to Charley. "Of all the people you could have blackmailed, you had to pick Kimball. You couldn't blackmail a cheating husband or an accountant who was skimming money or a high school teacher with porn on his computer. Oh, no, you had to pick a sociopath killer to blackmail."

"It seemed like a good idea at the time."

Just as marrying Charley had seemed like a good idea at the time.

ॐ

Amanda arrived at the Round Rock Country Club a few minutes before noon. If the place wasn't ready for a leather jacket, blue jeans and motorcycle boots, they'd just have to get ready. She removed the jacket in deference to the heat and carried it, along with her helmet, as she strode up the wide steps that led to the entrance.

"There he is." Charley pointed toward the top of the steps.

Kimball stood beside the door, waiting for her. The midday sun sitting directly overhead blinded Amanda and obscured his features. Instead of a broodingly handsome man, she saw only a black, faceless shadow looming above, ominous and threatening. She hesitated halfway up the steps, Irene's words ringing through her head—*dancing with the devil.*

She drew in a deep breath. If she could tangle with an amoral ghost, surely she could survive a dance with the devil.

Chin thrust forward, back straight, she continued up the steps until she stood on equal footing with him. "Good afternoon, Your Honor." Then, because she was nervous and determined not to let him know, "Or should I call you *Roland*, and you call me *Amanda* like the other night when I visited you at your house?"

Kimball smiled tightly. "Please call me whatever you like."

Amanda restrained her impulse to say, *How about I call you Monster?* She was there to get information from him, not to annoy him.

Kimball opened the door, and Amanda preceded him inside.

Charley came in with her. "I've always wanted to see inside this place."

Amanda gave him a *Really?* look. She'd grown up going to country clubs in Dallas, places far grander than this, and failed to see the appeal. That told her something about Charley.

The dining room was cool and pleasant with elevator music streaming from the speakers. The waiter pulled out

Amanda's chair. She sat obediently then transferred her helmet and jacket to the empty chair next to her. Kimball sat across the table. Charley took the fourth chair, sitting properly erect.

Kimball ordered the steak lunch for both of them. Amanda didn't protest, but when he requested a bottle of wine, she requested a Coke. She needed all her faculties to deal with him.

They sat quietly until their drinks arrived and the waiter disappeared. Kimball sipped his wine, set it down and folded his hands on the table. "I've been doing some checking, Amanda. It seems you haven't been completely honest with me."

Amanda took a drink of her Coke. Flat and watery. She set down the glass and met Kimball's gaze. "While you, on the other hand, have been completely honest and up front with me?"

He gave her a smug, pseudo-smile. "Of course. I was completely honest when I told you it wasn't a good idea to threaten people who have more power than you do." He sat back, lifted his wine glass and drank slowly, never taking his eyes off her.

Amanda knew that was supposed to frighten her. And it did. But she wasn't about to show it. She sipped her Coke and made a face. "Too bad you don't have enough power to force these people to serve decent Cokes."

"Good one, Amanda," Charley praised.

Kimball set down his glass and leaned toward her, his expression complacent and self-assured. "I have enough power to check the records on safety deposit boxes in Dallas. There isn't one in your name."

Charley swore.

Amanda echoed his sentiment silently.

"Tell him you got it when you went to Dallas and you have it with you now," Charley advised.

Amanda set her elbows on the table and folded her hands under her chin, trying to look smug instead of freaked out. "It's not important where the object of your desire used to be. What's important is that I have it with me now, right here in Silver Creek. I took a little ride over to Dallas a few days ago. Surely your spy told you that. Now I have your little toy with me."

Kimball's features distorted, moving from complacent to fearful to angry, his eyes boring into hers, threatening and cold. Amanda's heart thudded into overtime. An angry Kimball was someone to fear. A frightened, angry Kimball was terrifying.

"And I want to return it to you," she added hurriedly.

The waiter appeared with their salads. Kimball leaned back, his gaze holding hers.

"Amanda, I think you've got him hooked," Charley said. "Go slow and reel him in. Assure him you're ready to give him the gun."

"I don't have what you want in return," Kimball said when the waiter left. "It's at the bottom of the Trinity River."

"I understand," Amanda said. "That's unfortunate, but it can't be helped. I didn't realize the extent of your power." She almost gagged at those words, but knew she had to say them to convince him of her change of heart. "All I want is to never see you or hear from you again. I'm not Charley. I don't want your money. I just want this to be over. Here's my offer. I give back the item he took from you, and we go our separate ways."

Kimball studied her intently as if trying to determine her real agenda. Finally he picked up his fork and plunged it into his salad, lifting a piece of lettuce and shoving it into his mouth.

"Eat," Charley ordered. "Act relaxed. You need him to believe you're in control."

230

Amanda didn't like his peremptory tone, didn't like his giving her orders. Nevertheless, she conceded that it was probably good information, information gained from experience. Charley was, she realized, walking her through his formula for a scam.

She'd thought his assertion that he was going to take care of her was absurd. He couldn't fight for her. He couldn't block a bullet. But he was taking care of her using the only skill he possessed. He was teaching her to run a scam. Part of her wanted to slap him, but part of her was glad to have his expertise at that moment.

She speared a piece of tomato from her salad, put it in her dry mouth and chewed. With any luck, she'd be able to swallow it sometime before night.

"Don't say anything else," Charley said. "Let him be the one to speak next."

Finally Kimball finished his salad, laid down his fork and shoved the plate aside. Amanda had half of hers left but was glad to lay down her fork and cease the difficult task of swallowing around the lump of fear in her throat.

"When?" he asked.

Good question. Amanda had to get possession of a gun before she could turn it over to him.

"Stand up," Charley said. "Pick up your stuff. Tell him you'll call him, then walk out."

Amanda scooted back her chair, stood, picked up her helmet and jacket. "I'll call you." She turned and started toward the door, heart pounding, knees wobbly.

"See that you do," he said quietly. "Soon."

"Keep going. Act like you didn't hear him," Charley said.

She kept on walking though Kimball's words had injected anger into her fear, and she wanted to turn back to him, tell him she'd call when she was damned good and ready, and he could sit on his powerful butt and spin until then. But Charley was choreographing the scene. Charley knew way more about dealing with lowlifes and criminals than she did. In this situation, his field of expertise, she let him call the shots.

As she crossed the parking lot to her motorcycle, she caught a glimpse of a red-haired woman driving away in a red sedan. Sunny Donovan? Could be. It was lunch time, and Sunny was a lawyer. She would likely be a member of the country club so she could entertain clients there. Assuming she had clients of a different class from Charley and Frank Sturgess. Too bad they'd missed each other. She could have used a friendly face while dueling with Kimball.

She climbed on her bike, fired up the engine and roared away. If Charley's friend, Dub, didn't come through with that gun, she had no idea what she would do. Probably fall victim to a fatal accident.

❧⚚❧

Irene was waiting on the front porch when Amanda returned to the Randolphs' house. "What happened? What did he say?"

"Nothing," Amanda admitted. "But I didn't expect much in a public place. I'm going to meet him again."

Irene closed the screen door behind Amanda. "That's not a good idea."

"I have to. Kimball's smart. He hasn't left any evidence. That's why the cops don't believe me. I've got to find some way to prove he killed Charley."

Irene considered her words for a moment. "Let's go in the kitchen and have a glass of iced tea."

She followed Irene to the kitchen and helped her fill two glasses then sat down at the table. This was, she gathered from the times she'd seen Herbert and Irene conferring there, more than a place to eat. It was the summit meeting place where important discussions were held and decisions made. A drink of some sort was, of course, obligatory.

Amanda sipped her tea, grateful for the cool liquid in her hot, dry mouth and throat. She was reluctant to tell Irene the details of what she planned to do. Recently she'd become almost as adept at lying as Charley. Not really something she'd ever thought about adding to her list of skills. *Repairing motorcycles, selling real estate, lying...*

Lying to Kimball was one thing. He didn't count as a member of the human race. And withholding information from her parents for their own good was also justifiable. But she couldn't lie to this woman who'd lost her son then taken his widow into her home and heart. Irene deserved the truth, scary as it might be.

"When and where are you meeting that monster?" Irene asked.

"I don't know." Amanda sat up straighter, girding herself to divulge her frightening plan to her mother-in-law. "I'm going to get a gun like the one he used to kill Dianne, and I'm going to give it to him, but only if he admits to me that he killed her and Charley."

Irene's face paled. "Amanda, that's plumb crazy!"

"Yeah, probably, but it's the best plan we've...I've been able to come up with."

"Even if he lets you out of there alive, what makes you think the police will believe he confessed to you?"

"I'm going to record our conversation on my cell phone. There's an app for that." She tried to sound flippant.

"And what about getting out alive? You got an app on your cell phone for that?"

"Okay, this plan isn't completely fleshed out yet. There are still a few holes."

Irene shook her head. "I can't let you do that. I'm going to talk to Herbert tonight. We'll all put our heads together and figure out something. You're not alone in this anymore. Family takes care of family."

233

Amanda hated that she had brought Irene and soon Herbert into the tangled, dangerous mess of trying to trap Kimball. At the same time, she felt an intense relief at sharing the burden with other people who believed her, who cared about her. Other real people, she amended. Much as she hated to admit it, Charley provided some help. Not enough to compensate for the problems he caused, but he was really good at the sneaky, sleazy parts.

# Chapter Twenty-One

Herbert didn't leave for work immediately after breakfast that morning. As soon as Paula and Penny were out the door, he and Irene resumed their seats at the breakfast table.

"Leave the dishes for now," Irene said. "We need to talk."

Amanda set down the plates she'd carried to the sink and joined them at the table.

"We don't think you ought to take a gun to Kimball," Herbert said. As usual, his lean face showed no expression, but his words were laced with tension.

"I'm not crazy about the idea myself," Amanda said. "But we've got to do something."

"I know most of the guys on the police force," Herbert said. "Went to school with them, hunt with them, play poker with them. I'm gonna talk to them."

Amanda shook her head. "We're accusing the mayor, one of the most prominent and richest men in town, of murders we can't prove. You're probably not going to get a lot of support."

Herbert nodded and slid his chair back. "Don't you worry. We'll take care of the worthless scum that killed my son."

Amanda gasped as she remembered Charley's reference to his dad's shotgun. "You're not...you wouldn't...do anything...illegal?"

Herbert gave her a small smile. "I'm not gonna kill him. I won't deny I've thought about it since Irene told me everything last night. But that's not the right way to do things. I just want to be there when they give him the shot."

"The shot?" Amanda repeated.

235

"Lethal injection. I'd like to see him hang, but I guess I'll have to settle for the shot. I want to see him die like he made my son die. We'll catch him. He won't get away with murder." He squeezed her arm reassuringly then turned and left the house.

"Now," Irene said briskly, "you can relax and enjoy your visit here. The strawberries are just right for picking at the Berkley farm. Let's go get some today, and I'll show you how to make strawberry preserves."

Irene's words were meant to be soothing, to convince Amanda she needn't have any further contact with Roland Kimball, that everything was taken care of, but the anxious expression on Irene's face and the way she twisted her hands in her lap told Amanda her mother-in-law knew it wasn't going to work. Herbert's idea of going to the local police was pretty lame, and they all knew it. They were just trying to talk her out of doing something they considered dangerous.

"Can we have strawberry shortcake?" she asked, going along with the diversion. Might as well pick strawberries. She couldn't do anything else until Dub came up with a gun.

భారత

When her cell phone rang that afternoon, Amanda was stirring a big pot of strawberry jam. She set down the spoon, yanked her phone from her jeans pocket, saw the number was local and felt a flash of excitement that it might be Dub with a gun. She turned the stirring over to Irene and ran from the room while answering the phone.

"Hello?"

"I thought you'd lost my phone number."

Kimball.

Amanda stopped at the foot of the stairs, her stomach doing the familiar Kimball-clenching act.

"No, I didn't lose your number, and I wasn't aware I'd given you mine."

236

"You didn't have to give it to me."

Anger flared at the smug reminder of the range of his power as well as the admission he was snooping in her affairs. No wonder he'd been able to find out she was going on a trip so he could sabotage her motorcycle at just the right time. "Yeah, yeah, I know," she snapped as she climbed the stairs. "You're omniscient and omnipotent around here. King Kimball."

The line was silent for a moment, and she considered asking if he was looking up the multi-syllable words. Probably not a good idea to shoot the rabid grizzly bear with a BB gun.

"I have access to any information I need," he said. "Right now, considering the fact that I caught you in a lie about your safe deposit box then you walked out on me after saying you'd call but you didn't call, I don't think you have anything I need. I think you're just a loud-mouthed bitch trying to cause problems."

She entered her bedroom, closed the door behind her, and looked for Charley. "You're entitled to your opinion. But you may change that opinion when I take this gun to the cops."

"Really? If you could do that, why did you send your father-in-law to tell the cops I killed Charley but you can't prove it?"

Damn!

Where was Charley when she needed him to feed her lies and tell her how to handle this new development?

"I didn't send Herbert anywhere. He's a grown man. He goes where he pleases and says what he wants."

"Who are you talking to?" Charley demanded. "Where did Dad go? What did he say?"

Charley! She never thought she'd be glad to see him. She held the phone away from her ear so he could hear.

"Obviously you talked," Kimball said. "I thought that was part of our deal, you were going to give me the

237

merchandise and keep your mouth shut. Now you've involved your father-in-law."

"You didn't tell him anything," Charley instructed.

"I didn't tell him anything." That was true. She'd told Irene, who'd told him.

"It certainly is an amazing coincidence that he came up with the same story as you, that I killed Charley and Dianne."

"Tell him it doesn't matter what anybody says when you have the only proof around," Charley supplied.

Amanda repeated Charley's words. He really was good at squirming out of tight spots and putting a spin on things. She'd hated that when she was married to him, but it was coming in handy now.

"In that case, I'm sure you'll want to get rid of that item before it causes harm to other people," Kimball said smoothly.

Even though she'd seen that one coming, it still sent icicles through her veins. Not only was her life in danger, she'd put Herbert's and maybe even Irene's lives in danger.

"Tell him you're through playing with him. You'll give him the gun tomorrow night."

Amanda sucked in a gasp, looked at Charley and mouthed, *No gun!*

"We'll get one. Tell him!"

"Fine," she said, trying to sound cocky. "I have to admit, I was kind of enjoying teasing the big, powerful mayor, but you win. Tomorrow night. We meet, I give you the evidence, and this ends. I do not want my in-laws involved."

"Then they'd better keep their mouths shut."

"They will."

"I'll call you tomorrow with a location."

She hung up. "Tomorrow night? Are you insane? What if Dub doesn't come through by then? Where are we going to get a gun? How am I going to bluff my way out of this?"

Charley paced the floor, running his hands though his translucent hair. "We can't go to Smitty's downtown to get a gun. Too much risk Kimball might find out." He stopped and looked at her. "Maybe you could go back to Dallas and get one."

"The creep got my cell phone number. He checked for safety deposit boxes. He found out when and where I was going on that motorcycle trip so he could jack up my bike. This man has a long reach. If I buy a gun in Dallas, he could easily find out. And I don't have the kind of connections you do so I could buy one illegally."

"How about Dawson? Maybe he can find one on the Internet."

"I'll call him." She punched in the number.

"Hi, Amanda. I've been working on the bikes all day and don't have anything on Sunny Donovan yet."

"That's okay. No rush. But, uh, I do need a gun really fast. Can you get one on the Internet?"

"Well, yeah, I can order it."

"How long would it take?" She gave Charley a thumbs-up.

"I'm not sure. A few days, a week or two."

She gave Charley a thumbs-down. "That's too long. Never mind."

"Why do you need a gun?"

"It's a long story. If I live, I'll tell you all about it. In the meantime, can you find a phone number for Dub—?" She looked at Charley quizzically.

"Henderson," he supplied.

"Dub Henderson."

"Give me a minute."

"Why on earth did you choose tomorrow night?" she demanded of Charley while she waited for Dawson to return to the phone.

"We needed Kimball to back off, and I didn't think he would if we told him any later. You're the one who blabbed to my mom and got this thing ramped up."

Amanda drew in a deep breath and told herself to remain calm. Arguing with Charley wasn't going to help matters. His value was in being a con artist. He was worthless when it came to dealing with real situations. She was on her own now.

"I can't find a listing for Dub Henderson in Silver Creek," Dawson said. "Are you sure that's the right name?"

"Oh," Charley said. "His real name is Dwayne. We just call him Dub because who wants to be called Dwayne?"

Amanda heaved a sigh. "Try Dwayne Henderson."

He returned in seconds with a phone number.

Amanda signed off with Dawson and immediately called Dub's number. No answer.

"He's probably still at work," Charley said. "We can try again in an hour."

"Great. I'll just sit here and have a nervous breakdown while we wait."

Somewhere around the tenth time she called, Dub answered.

"I need that gun tonight," she said without preamble.

"No can do. I need a few more days."

"We don't have a few more days. My life is in danger. The lives of Charley's parents are in danger."

Dub was silent for a few seconds. "I could maybe get you one but you wouldn't be able to register it."

"I don't care if I can register it. I don't care if it's stolen."

Again Dub was quiet.

"It's…stolen?"

"We don't care!" Charley shouted.

"We don't care," she echoed. Surely her father would rather she be caught with stolen goods than be found dead.

"Okay," Dub agreed. "Tonight, nine o'clock, Shade Tree Inn."

ॐॐ

Amanda arrived at the Shade Tree Inn a few minutes before nine. Irene had protested her leaving the house at that hour, but she'd assured her mother-in-law she wasn't going to see Kimball. That had only slightly assuaged Irene's concern. She would be up, worrying, until Amanda returned. Amanda left for her rendezvous to buy a stolen gun with a spot of warmth in the middle of all that terror.

"I watched really close and didn't see anybody following you," Charley said as they walked across the lot toward the Shade Tree's entrance.

"Doesn't mean somebody wasn't following me, but I suppose it's marginally better than if you'd seen someone."

"Yeah. Either nobody was there or it was somebody with more skill at following than Sturgess."

"You have a real knack for making me feel better."

The same or similar faces as the ones on Friday night turned toward her when she walked inside then turned back to their drinks when they didn't recognize her. The same scents of stale beer and cigarette smoke greeted her, and the same or similar country music played on the juke box. Familiarity was doubtless an appeal for those who frequented this place.

From the same stool where he'd sat Friday night, Dub lifted a hand. He was nursing a beer while a Coke sat on the bar beside him in front of an empty stool.

Amanda took a seat and lifted the Coke. "Thanks."

"Welcome."

"Be cool, Amanda," Charley advised, taking a seat on the bar and dangling his legs between them. "You don't want everybody in here to know you're buying a gun."

241

Amanda shot him a scathing look. "How was your day, Dub?"

"Fine. How about yours?"

"Good." Didn't count as a lie. She was just observing the social amenities.

Dub took a drink of his beer, and Amanda sipped her Coke.

Amanda hated that she was in a position to need Charley's expertise. However, he'd been helpful with Kimball, and she grudgingly admitted to herself she needed him tonight. She had no idea of the protocol for conducting the purchase of an illegal weapon. She looked up at him, lifting a questioning eyebrow.

"Be patient," Charley said. "Like you know what that word means."

She couldn't retaliate except to shoot him another glare. He laughed happily at her inability to retort.

Dub drained his beer. "Think I'll go outside and smoke a cigarette."

"Go with him," Charley said.

"A cigarette," she repeated. "Good idea. Mind if I join you?"

"Sure."

Together they slid off the stools and moved toward the door. Dub politely opened and held it for her.

Again she felt relief at breathing the clean night air. A person could get lung cancer from just hanging out in that bar.

She followed Dub to the side of the building where she'd seen a man retching on Friday night. Watching the ground carefully, she moved into the shadows with Dub, stopping when he stopped.

Slowly he reached inside his faded denim jacket and withdrew a small package wrapped in brown paper.

From the pocket of her motorcycle jacket Amanda withdrew an envelope containing the amount of cash they'd agreed on. She handed her envelope to Dub, and he handed his package to her.

Dub turned aside, opened the envelope and flipped through the bills, then closed it again and shoved it into his jacket pocket. "Nice night." He took out a package of cigarettes and tapped the bottom until one slid out.

"Yes." She peeked into her bag. It was a gun.

"Take it out," Charley demanded. "I want to see it."

Amanda looked around the parking lot and didn't see anybody else. She withdrew the revolver, bending over to shield it from the sight of anyone who might drive up.

Charley peered at it closely. "Yeah, that should pass, at least for our purposes. Only way he'd know the difference is if he had the serial number."

"Great. That makes me feel so much better," she whispered.

"What?" Dub asked.

"Great gun," Amanda said. "Makes me feel so much better to have protection."

Dub smiled. "I loaded it for you. Unloaded gun's 'bout as useful as a screen door on a bass boat."

Amanda smiled. "True. I don't want to get close enough to pistol whip somebody. Thank you."

"Unload it, Amanda," Charley said. "I don't trust you with a loaded gun."

"You let me know if you need anything else," Dub said. "I hope ole Charley, wherever he is, knows I'm taking good care of his wife."

"I believe he knows," Amanda said.

"Hello, Amanda."

Amanda whirled at the sound of a familiar woman's voice behind her. Sunny Donovan stood there.

"The gun!" Charley shouted. "Hide the gun!"

Amanda realized she still had the .38 in her hand. She shoved it inside her jacket, hoping it hadn't been visible in the darkness. "Hi! Sunny! What are you doing here?"

"I just stopped by for a drink. How about you?"

Amanda studied the woman standing before her. Regal, even in blue jeans and a blue cotton shirt with a classic black leather purse hanging over her shoulder. Sunny did not belong in the Shade Tree Inn. What was she really doing there?

"Hi, Dub," Sunny greeted. Amanda wasn't surprised to find she knew him. Dub had probably used her services. Sunny likely knew more about the secrets in this town than even Irene.

"Hey, Sunny. Buy you a beer?"

"Thanks, Dub. I could use a cold one after spending the day in that hot courtroom."

"Air conditioning on the fritz, or was it just all that hot air from them lawyers?"

Sunny laughed. "A little of both."

Amanda waited, poised to run as soon as Sunny and Dub went into the bar, but Sunny placed a slim hand on her arm. "I'll meet you inside in five minutes, Dub. I need to talk to Amanda first."

Crap. She'd seen the gun.

"Run, Amanda!" Charley advised. "Get away from her!"

Amanda had been considering just that action until Charley suggested it. Instead, she stood quietly while Dub strolled into the bar.

A dog barked somewhere in the distance. Crickets chirped all around them. The night was soft and warm and normal while Charley paced up and down in front of her, going a little higher off the ground with each turn. Nothing normal about that.

"What are you planning to do with that gun?" Sunny asked.

Charley ceased pacing and settled to the ground, folding his arms and watching the exchange intently.

"I have a Right to Carry permit," Amanda replied defiantly. "I'm legal."

"I know that, but it doesn't answer my question. What do you plan to do with that gun?"

"Target practice." Amanda decided she didn't like Sunny Donovan after all. Where did the woman get off, questioning her about something that was none of her business? "How do you know I have a Right to Carry?"

"Amanda, I think you're in some kind of trouble, and I want to help you. Please let me help you."

Sunny Donovan was the self-appointed guardian of the underdog in Silver Creek, and Amanda was her latest project. It was hard to be angry with someone so sincere and determined to help.

"I appreciate your concern, but I've got everything under control."

"What do you have under control?"

Lawyers. This interrogation reminded her of her father. She supposed that association actually made her feel more kindly disposed toward the aggressive, annoying woman. "The gun. My life." She spread her arms wide. "Everything."

Sunny sighed, put her palms together and held her hands to her mouth, studying Amanda intently as if trying to read her mind. Finally she dropped her hands in resignation and smiled. "You're stubborn, determined, independent. I like you. Please, think about letting me help you. If you get in trouble you can't handle on your own, if at any time you realize you're no longer in control of everything, call me. Day or night. I always have my cell phone with me, even when I'm in court."

Amanda grinned wryly. "Even when you're in court? My dad...he's a judge...would throw out any lawyer whose cell phone rang during court."

"I keep it on vibrate when I'm in court." She reached inside her purse and pulled out the object under discussion. "What's your cell number?"

Amanda recited her number as Sunny punched it into her phone.

Amanda's phone rang.

"There." Sunny disconnected before Amanda could extract her phone from her purse. "You have my number in your phone so you can call me without looking it up."

"Okay, okay. I promise I'll call if I get in over my head."

Sunny turned toward the bar, but Amanda put a hand on her arm to stop her, a reversal of their earlier roles. "How did you know I was here?"

Sunny regarded her quietly for a moment, then she smiled. "I didn't. I came to see my client, Dub."

Amanda released her arm, and Sunny continued into the bar.

"I don't believe her," she said to Charley. "Do you suppose she's helping Kimball?"

"No!" Charley protested. "Not for one minute do I believe Sunny Donovan would help a scumbag like Roland Kimball. She would never do anything to hurt you."

But Amanda wasn't so certain. Maybe Sunny thought she was doing the right thing. Maybe Kimball had somehow convinced Sunny that whatever he had in mind for Amanda was somehow in her best interest.

# Chapter Twenty-Two

Amanda returned to find Irene sitting on the sofa in the living room, worry creasing her forehead.

A tiny part of Amanda was pleased Irene cared so much, but the rest of her was dismayed that she was causing her mother-in-law to worry. She didn't want to upset her further by telling her what she planned to do. In fact, she didn't want to talk about it at all. She wanted to get upstairs, hide under the covers and try not to think about the gun inside her jacket pocket...or where the gun would be that time tomorrow night.

"See?" Amanda smiled widely. "I'm fine! Thanks for waiting up. Good-night."

"You're not fine," Irene said softly. "We need to talk. Let's go to the kitchen and have some hot chocolate."

Uh-oh. The kitchen table. Ominous.

Irene heated milk in the microwave and added Ghirardelli chocolate while Amanda sat stiffly at the table. Though the house was warm, she kept her leather jacket on, kept the gun pressed close. Absurdly, she felt if she let it out of her possession in the house, it would somehow spread its influence and involve Irene and her family in the upcoming confrontation with Kimball.

Irene joined her at the table, and Amanda sipped her hot chocolate. "Delicious," she said. "As if you could make anything that isn't."

"Thank you." Irene wrapped her hands around her cup but did not drink. "Herbert and I talked while you were gone. We decided that whatever you're planning to do, we're going to help you. That man has got to pay for killing our son."

"You're going to help?" Images of Irene and Herbert attacking Kimball with kitchen knives, rolling pin,

247

knitting needles and a rolled up copy of *Reader's Digest* raced through her head. "No, you can't. Kimball knows that Herbert talked to the cops."

"I know," Irene said.

"You do?" So much for trying to protect her.

"It's a small town. Everybody knows everything. But this did show us how big a problem we're up against." She shook her head slowly. "I sure didn't think something like this could happen in Silver Creek. It's a good place, a lot of good people. I always knew Roland Kimball wasn't a nice man. I just never would have dreamed something like this could happen."

Amanda nodded grimly. "Kimball thinks he's all-powerful. He thinks he's above the law. He thinks his money can buy him the right to commit murder."

"He's wrong, and we're all going to work together to prove it. Tell us your plan, and we'll figure out where we fit in."

"Agree with her." Charley appeared at her elbow. "You can't argue with my mother. Just agree with her, and then we'll make sure she doesn't know what we're doing."

"Umm...okay." She lifted her cup of hot chocolate and drank, giving herself a moment to think.

Irene looked surprised at the easy agreement. "Where did you go tonight?" she asked. "What are we going to do next?"

Amanda decided to allay Irene's suspicions by telling her the truth up to the point of the actual meeting with Kimball. "I bought an unregistered gun. I'm ready to meet with Kimball, give him the gun and tell him it's the one he used to kill Dianne."

"And you think he's going to confess while you to record it on your cell phone?"

"Exactly."

248

"How do you think you're going to get him to confess to murder? He's been smart enough to get away with it for years. Why would he tell you now?"

Not a good idea to tell Irene she was sure Kimball planned to kill her so he wouldn't be worried about what he told her. "I'm going to appeal to his gigantic ego. Get him to brag."

She did not plan to let Kimball kill her, of course. Dub had put bullets in her gun. And she was almost beginning to believe the purpose of Charley's continuing presence just might be to save her life so she could take Kimball down. But she wasn't going to tell Irene any of that.

"What do you want Herbert and me to do?"

"Tell her you need Dad to bring his shotgun to the meeting," Charley said.

"I need Herbert to come to the meeting. Bring his shotgun, hide and provide backup."

Irene nodded, her jawline firm. "That sounds like a good idea. Herbert used to hunt a lot. He's the best shot in the county."

Amanda finished her hot chocolate. "Tomorrow." She rose from the table, the weight of the loaded gun in her jacket pocket comforting and frightening at the same time.

She climbed the stairs, her footsteps leaden. Was this the last time she'd climb those stairs or any stairs?

*Don't even go there!* she admonished herself.

In her bedroom...Charley's old bedroom...she changed into her night shirt without even checking the shadows for Charley. His seeing her undressed ranked low on her list of things to fear.

She settled into bed and pulled the covers over her head.

Tomorrow.

This nightmare that had begun with Charley's phone call about the gun then progressed through his murder and her almost-murder would end tomorrow, one way or the other.

Tomorrow she'd face Kimball. Beard the lion in his den.

That brought up the question of where they'd meet. She had no doubt he'd choose someplace where he felt comfortable, someplace isolated since he planned to kill her, someplace that would allow for easy disposal of her body.

Would he lure her to the lake the way he'd done with Dianne?

She had no car they could sit in. Not likely he'd kill her in his own car.

Make that—*try* to kill her in his own car.

No, he wouldn't want to get blood on the leather interior of that big, black Cadillac.

So maybe he wouldn't shoot her. Maybe he'd strangle her. Avoid the blood evidence.

Nah. Surely after Herbert's call to the police, Kimball would be careful not to get DNA evidence in his car, and with her hair, she'd be sure to leave lots of long, curly, red DNA.

So would they meet in a clearing in the woods?

She couldn't see Kimball sitting cross-legged on the grass in the moonlight, requesting she hand over the gun. No, he'd want somewhere private.

She sat upright in bed. "Charley?"

"Right here, babe. I'll never leave you."

Yeah, he'd been there, watching, when she changed clothes. "Don't threaten me like that. Hey, are there fishing or hunting cabins around the lake?"

"Lots of them. Why?"

"Does Kimball own one?"

"I don't know. Why?"

"Maybe that's where he's going to take me for the meeting."

"Could be, but there are a lot of cabins around that lake, acres of woods. It's a pretty good size lake."

She snatched up her cell phone. "I know who can find out."

Dawson answered on the fourth ring.

"I have something really important I need you to find for me."

"Okay."

"Can you search real estate records and see if Kimball owns some property close to the lake where Dianne Carter's body was found?"

"Yes, I can do that."

"Kimball or his dad or his wife or her family. Anybody related to him."

"Okay."

"I need it in the morning."

"No problem. Do you want to know what I found out about Sunny Donovan?"

At that point, Amanda wasn't very interested in Sunny Donovan and whatever mess she and Charley had got into, but she didn't want to sound ungrateful. "Yes, of course."

"Born in Silver Creek, Texas. Her father was killed in a hunting accident when she was three years old, and her mother never remarried. The mother only had a high school education, so it was difficult for her to raise Sunny by herself. She often worked two jobs, developed health problems, but she was determined to get her daughter educated. Sunny got a scholarship to UT Austin where she studied law, then she went back to Silver Creek to practice so she could be close to her mother and help her."

That all aligned with what Irene had told her. "Any connection to Charley?"

"She was his lawyer when he got arrested on a drug charge. Got him probation."

"That's it?"

"Nothing more that involves Charley, but I did find one thing that's kind of interesting. Sunny interned her senior year at your dad's law firm."

The connection was interesting, but Amanda couldn't see how it related to Charley or why it would be part of a big secret. Lots of law students had interned at her father's firm over the years.

She frowned into the darkness. What about those fleeting suspicions she'd had concerning her dad's odd behavior, the way he'd withheld knowledge of Charley's family and repeatedly bailed Charley out of trouble? Almost as if Charley had a hold over her dad.

Crazy, irrational thought...had Sunny learned something about her dad during her internship, something she'd told Charley that had allowed him to blackmail her father?

Even as the thought formed, she dismissed it. Her father had nothing to hide. He was the quintessential upright, uptight citizen.

"Thanks, Dawson. I really appreciate all your help." A lump suddenly and unexpectedly formed in her throat. "You've been my friend as well as my assistant. I know I can always count on you."

"Yes," Dawson said. "Of course you can count on me. And I am your friend." He was silent for a moment. "Are you okay, Amanda?"

Amanda laughed shakily. "Sorry. I guess I'm a little emotional tonight. I'm meeting Kimball tomorrow to give him the bogus gun, and it's made me kind of nervous." Made her think about things like never climbing the stairs to this bedroom again, never seeing her father or mother or Dawson again.

"That's why you want to find out if Kimball has access to some property where he might take you? Dianne was killed in her car out by that lake."

"I don't have a car. We can't have an intimate conversation and gun exchange on my motorcycle. If he thought the lake was a good spot for murder before, maybe he'll think that again, but this time he's going to need somewhere private. There are some cabins out by the lake. It's a long shot. But I'd feel a little less nervous if I had some idea of where we're going to meet. Maybe alert the cops." *So they can find my body.* She had no illusions that either the Silver Creek Police Department or Detective Daggett would give any credence to anything she had to say *before* her murder.

"Amanda, you shouldn't meet this guy, especially not alone."

"I know. But I have to. I don't think there's any doubt he's the one who jacked up my motorcycle, hoping I'd die. He thought Charley had already told me about Dianne's murder. He's going to keep trying to kill me until he succeeds or I stop him. And now it's gone beyond that. Irene and Herbert are in danger."

"That's a pretty bad state of affairs. I'll check on any real estate Kimball's family owns that could be used for, uh, nefarious purposes. Is there anything else I can do? What about that gun you asked me about?"

"Got a gun."

"You've got a gun? Maybe I should come down there."

Amanda added the image of Dawson wielding a thumb drive to her images of Herbert and Irene assaulting Kimball.

"Thanks, but I need you there at your computer. That's how you can be of most help to me."

Again Amanda stretched out in bed, trying to empty her mind of the images racing through her brain. Kimball,

Dawson, Kimball, Irene and Herbert, Kimball, her mother and father she might never see again, Kimball…

"Charley?" She spoke his name softly this time, amazed to find she actually wanted him to be there.

"Still here." He stood at the window, his back to her. "Just checking to see if anybody's out there."

"And?"

"I don't see anybody."

No reason for Kimball to have her followed now. She was coming to him. "Good," she said. "Go to sleep."

"I don't sleep. I'll stay here all night and watch over you."

Good grief. He couldn't pass up a chance to do the melodrama thing.

That one time, she was glad he was watching.

෴

The only way Amanda knew she'd slept at all was that sometimes the scenes rushing through her mind became surreal. Kimball was evil, but he didn't have horns. She herself did not have twenty-one bullet holes in her chest. Kimball couldn't fly through the wall into her bedroom the way Charley did. When the sun finally rose, she was glad to get out of bed and stop trying so hard to sleep.

Breakfast was strangely quiet. Though Amanda was certain Penny and Paula didn't know what was going on, they seemed to sense the tension in the air and were subdued.

The clink of silverware on plates replaced conversation as they ate. Almost simultaneously the twins slid their chairs back, picked up their empty plates and put them in the sink.

"Bye, Mama." Paula planted a kiss on her mother's left check while Penny planted one on the right. They completed the ritual by doing the same to their father.

Then, to Amanda's surprise, the girls came over to her and repeated the farewell procedure before dashing out.

When the front door slammed behind the girls, Herbert stood, walked over to his wife and kissed her, then came to Amanda's side. He placed a comforting hand on one shoulder and leaned over to whisper in her ear. "It's gonna be okay. We're here."

She put their lives in danger, and the family responded with love. Amanda's heart swelled, and she blinked rapidly to get rid of the excess moisture in her eyes.

Maybe Charley wasn't really their son. Maybe Irene's baby had been switched at the hospital, and somewhere in Silver Creek a depraved, psycho couple was raising a kind, loving son who should have gone home with Irene and Herbert.

Dawson called shortly after nine o'clock. She went upstairs to take the call.

"Cardinal Corporation owns a cabin on Silver Lake. Benjamin Montgomery, father of Catherine Montgomery Kimball, owns Cardinal Corporation."

A chill darted down Amanda's spine. "That's it. That's where he's going to take me." *That's where he thinks he's going to kill me.*

"It's not on the lake. It's back in the woods. Montgomery's dad had it built in 1962. He was a big duck hunter. He died in 1980. It's possible nobody's been there since then. I didn't find anything to indicate there are any hunters in that family. Looks like they only do things that make money."

"I don't suppose this cabin has a street address one can find on a GPS."

"No, but I can give you the legal description."

"I guess that'll have to do."

As soon as she finished talking to Dawson, Amanda called Detective Daggett. Though she assured herself she had the situation with Kimball under control and could handle it on her own, and though she knew Daggett wasn't going to believe her, she had to try one more time.

Surely, she thought, Daggett would be in the office at ten thirty on a weekday.

He wasn't.

"Can I have him call you?"

Amanda sighed and gave the receptionist her number. "I need you to give him a message."

"Go ahead."

"This is Amanda Randolph. I've spoken with him before about an individual in Silver Creek, Texas. Today I'm meeting with that individual and turning over to him a gun he thinks was used in a murder. Just in case I don't survive this meeting, I want Detective Daggett to know what happened to me." Perhaps the last sentence was a bit melodramatic...or perhaps not. "I don't know where we're meeting, but it may be in an old hunting cabin on Silver Lake. I'd like to give you the legal description. That way, at least maybe he'll be able to find my body."

She read the description. The woman assured her that Detective Daggett would get her message.

"I don't know why you bothered to call him again," Charley said grumpily. "He's not going to help you. He's not even going to talk to you. Not that it matters. You don't need him. I'm here, and I'm going to take care of you."

"Like you took care of me while you were alive?"

"Haven't you ever heard of giving somebody a second chance? Maybe this whole situation is to teach you about forgiveness."

"You better hope that's not right, or you'll be stuck here forever."

Amanda started to put her phone in her pocket, but hesitated, suddenly overwhelmed with an urge to call her parents.

Ridiculous, she told herself. Her dad was working, and her mother was doubtless busy being Beverly Caulfield. Not like she'd never have the chance to talk to them again. She was *not* going to be murdered tonight.

She slipped her phone into her pocket and headed downstairs.

"Would you help me turn the mattresses?" Irene asked when Amanda walked into the living room.

"Turn? Uh…sure. What? Turn the mattresses?"

"To keep the wear even, I turn the mattresses twice a year."

Somewhere between turning the mattresses and dusting the jars of canned fruits and vegetables, Amanda decided Irene was creating work to help keep her mind off her impending rendezvous with Kimball.

All day they turned, dusted, cleaned and cooked, and, in spite of Irene's efforts, Amanda's imagination created an endless litany of potential disastrous scenarios for the evening.

The cell phone in her pocket remained obdurately silent.

The twins returned from school, and Herbert came home from work. Dinner was another quiet meal. Amanda dutifully shoved bites of spaghetti into her mouth, chewed and swallowed. She had no doubt the food was delicious, but on that night it tasted like cardboard and was just as difficult to chew and swallow.

After dinner, Paula and Penny went upstairs to do their homework. Irene, Herbert, Amanda and Charley settled in the living room to watch television. Though the TV was occasionally on during the evenings, it rarely received the complete attention of four people. Well, three people and one ghost.

Herbert and Irene exchanged a few remarks about their day. Amanda could not summon the energy to attempt any sort of conversation.

The windows were dark, the TV the only light in the room when her cell phone finally rang. Irene gave a small shriek and half rose from the sofa.

Amanda pulled the phone from her pocket and looked at the display. "It's him."

"This is it, babe. Showtime." Charley sounded excited.

"Hello?" Was that squeaky, high-pitched voice coming from her?

"Are you ready for our meeting, Amanda?"

"Waiting with bated breath for you to say when and where."

"The *when* is soon. As to the *where*, I'll let you know. You need to get on your motorcycle and go downtown. When you get there, stop in front of the courthouse and call this number. I'll give you further directions at that time."

Amanda didn't like the sound of that. Kimball was taking all possible precautions to be sure she came alone and that nobody knew where she was going.

"Oh, good grief," she bluffed. "We're not going on a scavenger hunt. We're supposed to be two adults meeting for mutually profitable business reasons."

"We're playing by my rules. I'll tell you where when you need to know."

"Excuse me? *Your* rules? I'd say you have more to gain from this meeting than I do so we're not playing by your rules. Tell me where to meet you or forget the whole thing."

"Are you sure about who has the most to gain? You have an item I may or may not want while I have the power to make your life and the lives of your family and friends easy or difficult."

There he went again, boasting about his stinking *power*. Threatening her and Herbert and Irene. Amanda no longer felt exhausted and drained from the day's tension.

This arrogant piece of dung had to be stopped. All her fantasies of doing away with Charley paled next to what she wanted to do to Kimball.

"With that much power at your command, you should be able to designate a meeting place and share that information with me without the slightest concern of interference."

"You have a bad habit of running your mouth when you shouldn't. We don't need anyone at this meeting but you and me."

He wasn't going to tell her. "If you're that terrified of my friends, I'll humor you." She hung up, determined to have the last word even if that word was ineffectual.

She looked up to see Irene and Herbert sitting on the edge of the sofa, watching her intently.

She forced a smile to her lips. "Game on."

"Where are you meeting him?" Irene asked.

"He wouldn't say. I'm to go downtown then call him, and he'll tell me where."

"I don't like this," Herbert said. "If we don't know where you are, I can't get there to help you."

"I'll call you as soon as I find out. In the meantime, don't worry. Remember, I have a loaded gun and I know how to use it." She lifted her cell phone. "And a recorder. I'll get his confession, you'll get to see him on trial, sentenced to death and given the shot."

Herbert and Irene exchanged worried glances.

"Let's go!" Charley sounded delighted with the evening's prospect of adventure.

No need to fear for your life if you're already dead. Amanda, however, was still alive.

So far.

# Chapter Twenty-Three

Amanda brought her Harley to a stop in front of the Silver Creek courthouse. The moon had not yet risen. Only the faint light of the stars and a few street lights relieved the total darkness. Familiar trees and buildings lurked as mysterious shadows. The streets and sidewalks were deserted. Only Billy Earl's Roadhouse showed signs of life with its neon words flashing, lending eerie colors to the white columns and steps of the courthouse.

Things were only going to get more eerie. Amanda pulled off her helmet and gloves then reached into her jacket pocket. Her fingers passed over her cell phone and continued to the hard metal of the gun. She'd put the hammer in another pocket at the last minute. Maybe it wasn't as effective as a gun, but it couldn't hurt to have a backup weapon.

She took out her phone. In the darkness the screen glowed like a spotlight. If Kimball had lured her there to kill her, this should make her an easy target.

"Do it, babe," Charley encouraged, moving close. "Call him. You've got a gun, a hammer and me. We're ready for His Honor, The Murderer."

Easy for him to be ready. What could Kimball do to a ghost?

She drew in a deep breath, straightened and sat erect on her bike. Locating Kimball's incoming call on her phone, she hit the icon to return that call.

His phone rang five times. Was he not going to answer? Had this all been a sick head game? Was he even now sighting in on her, preparing to shoot her?

She looked around the square, half expecting to see Kimball lurking in the shadows. Billy Earl's sign flashed, splashing red light over her, and for a moment, she imagined a red spot on her chest, a laser sight from a gun.

"Amanda, how good of you to call."

The sound of his oily voice made her sit even straighter, turned her anxiety to resolution. Her jaw clenched. "*Roland*, you're so irresistible, I simply couldn't wait to see you."

"When you see a black Cadillac turn the corner, follow me and turn off your cell phone."

"Why? Are you afraid the signal will interfere with your navigation equipment in that hearse you drive?"

"We don't want to take the chance that anybody's tracking you."

"Don't do it!" Charley advised.

"No problem," Amanda replied to Kimball. "I wouldn't want anybody to know I'm hanging out with a guy like you anyway. It would ruin my reputation."

She disconnected the call.

Charley looked at her in alarm. "If you turn off your phone, you won't be able to record his confession!"

Amanda gave him a withering glance. "Of course I'm not going to turn it off. Have you forgotten all the times you ordered me to do something and I let you think I was going to do it just to shut you up?"

Charley considered that, his forehead wrinkling. Before he could respond, Kimball's Cadillac rounded the corner.

Amanda shoved her helmet onto her head and her hands into her gloves. The bike roared to life, and she took off after Kimball.

He drove slowly, twisting and turning through the streets of Silver Creek, residential as well as downtown. *Trying to be sure they weren't followed?*

It was a pleasant night, but Amanda failed to enjoy the leisurely ride. She wanted to get to wherever they were going, wanted to confront this evil man, wanted to get this over with. She was tired of living in fear, checking her bike every morning before she dared to ride it, looking over her shoulder and out her bedroom window for prying eyes. Much as she liked staying with the Randolphs, she wanted to be able to go home without worrying about being arrested. And she wanted to know that Irene and Herbert weren't in danger from dirt bag Kimball.

After driving in circles for fifteen minutes, Kimball turned into the woods surrounding the lake. Ice crystals stabbed Amanda's heart as she followed the black Cadillac along a single lane dirt road. Judging from the amount of grass and weeds growing in the middle, few people came that way.

The car stopped.

No cabin. Nothing around them except trees.

Amanda braked to a halt several feet from the Cadillac. When she turned off her bike, the headlight went out. The darkness was complete. She could barely see the outline of the black car. Her burgundy red bike was black, the chrome dull with no light to reflect from it. Silence reigned. No creature of the night rustled through the leaves or called from the trees. She was alone with a killer.

"Wonder why he brought us out here." Charley's voice was loud in the silence. "This is kind of creepy."

"I'm sure he brought us here so we can have a nice, quiet, uninterrupted talk," she said. "Or a nice, quiet, uninterrupted murder."

The driver's side door of the Cadillac opened, spilling bright light into the darkness, illuminating the interior of the car, silhouetting the man inside. Kimball, wearing black slacks and a black knit shirt, slid out, stood and closed the door behind him, returning the world to darkness.

He smiled, his thin lips pressed together tightly as he came toward her. His dark eyes were empty holes in his shadowed face. Amanda pressed her hands against her jacket, feeling the reassuring outlines of the hammer and gun.

"We walk from here." Kimball turned away from her and started through the trees.

Amanda put down her bike's kickstand. When she removed her helmet and gloves, the night air on her skin reminded her of how vulnerable and exposed she was.

"Charley?" she whispered.

"Right here, babe. I got your back."

"You'll pass right through my back," she muttered. Nevertheless, having him there was irrationally reassuring.

Forcing her feet to move, one in front of the other, she followed a few yards behind Kimball. Only when she had taken several steps through the underbrush did she realize they were on an overgrown path that had not seen much use in a lot of years.

"I don't think this is the way to a rich man's hunting cabin," Charley said, echoing Amanda's fears. "Surely he'd have had a better road to get there."

"Where are we going?" Amanda asked.

"Some place private."

"Really? I thought maybe you were taking me to a five-star restaurant where I'd get to meet all your friends."

Charley laughed.

Kimball didn't.

For several minutes they walked in silence, the only sound the crunching of leaves under their feet and the rapid pounding of Amanda's heart. At one point when Kimball went round a twist in the path and disappeared, Amanda pulled her cell phone from her pocket. No signal. That explained why Kimball hadn't checked to be sure she'd turned off her phone. He'd known they were going somewhere it would be useless.

But he hadn't counted on all those apps Dawson had downloaded to her new smart phone, those apps she'd insisted she'd never have occasion to use. She set the phone to record and put it back in her pocket. She could only hope they got wherever they were going and had a meaningful conversation before her battery died or her memory card filled up.

Finally they reached a clearing with the remains of what had once been a small, badly-constructed cabin. Large cracks separated the rough-hewn boards that looked as if they'd never seen paint. One small window gaped wide with its wooden cover hanging askew beneath the opening. Glass had never been a part of the structure. What remained of the roof was flat. It looked like an attempt by someone with limited funds and no experience in construction to create a rudimentary shelter.

Even in its heyday, Amanda couldn't imagine Catherine Montgomery Kimball's grandfather hanging out there. Certainly he wouldn't have brought his friends to this place for a weekend of drinking and shooting.

Kimball continued to the front door, grasped the short rope attached to one side, and pulled on it. One hinge was broken, and the door sagged when opened.

"Who does this place belong to?" Amanda asked.

"I have no idea, but I don't think the owner is going to complain," Kimball said. "I'd say he doesn't use it often."

So her meticulous recitation of the legal description of the Montgomery family property to Detective Daggett had been to no avail. If Kimball killed her here, Daggett would never find her body.

Only one solution to that. She wasn't going to let Kimball kill her.

She followed him inside, stepping on the rotting boards, around the holes in the floor. A spider darted across a web hanging directly in front of Amanda's face. She gasped and turned her head away in time to see a mouse skitter through a hole in the wall.

"Nice place," she said. "Come here often?"

Kimball crossed the room, picked up an ancient kerosene lantern and lit it. That told her he'd been there recently enough to keep the lantern fueled.

The small flame cast flickering, ominous shadows over his face as he turned to her.

"I believe you have something you want to give me."

Amanda unzipped her jacket halfway, reached into her pocket and pulled out the gun, holding it tightly in both hands lest he try to take it from her by force. "If you mean the gun you used to kill Dianne Carter, yes, I have it right here."

He said nothing, merely extended his hand.

"Why'd you kill her?"

"Who?"

"Dianne. The woman you shot with this gun Charley rescued from the garbage bin where you dumped it. You and she dated. You cared about her at one time. Why kill her?"

Kimball took a step closer, and Amanda took a step backward. "I didn't come here to talk." His voice was rough, the smooth oil gone. "Give me the gun."

Amanda held the weapon behind her back.

"You killed my husband, you've put me through hell, I may even be arrested for murder. I deserve to know what started all this."

"Deserve? You deserve nothing. Give me the gun. *Now.*"

She was doing this all wrong. Suddenly she remembered her reply when Irene had asked how she intended to get Kimball to confess. Amanda had replied that she'd appeal to his arrogance.

"You wanted her back, didn't you? She dumped you in college, and with all your money and power and country club membership, you couldn't get her back. She loved her husband, a man who couldn't even get into the country club. That made you really mad, didn't it?"

Dark fires flamed in Kimball's eyes. It was probably just a reflection of the lantern flames. Or maybe not. Whatever the cause, it was freaky. Amanda had to force herself to remain in place, not back away. She was getting to him. Soon he'd be pouring out his guts to her cell phone.

"Take off your jacket," he ordered.

"Don't do it!" Charley said. "Don't let him get hold of your phone!"

"You sick pervert," Amanda said. "I'm not taking off anything for you. Dianne didn't either, did she?"

Kimball's thin lips stretched into a semblance of a smile. "You don't know anything about Dianne. She wasn't the saint everybody in town thought she was."

"Ask him if Dianne enjoyed killing the homeless man," Charley directed.

That was taking a chance. They had no positive proof that had happened. But she had to bow to Charley's superior knowledge of this sort of situation.

"Are you saying Dianne enjoyed herself the night you two killed that homeless man?"

Kimball's eyes turned to bottomless pits where not even the lantern light reflected.

"She didn't enjoy it, did she?" Amanda pursued, terrified and encouraged by Kimball's reaction. "She refused to take part. She thought you were a sick, evil man. That's when she broke up with you. Never wanted to see a disgusting man like you ever again."

Kimball moved toward her. "Give me the gun." His words held a faint echo, as if they'd been dredged up from the depths of hell.

Amanda stepped away from him, backing into the wall. She couldn't get any farther away. He stood inches from her. His garlicky breath blew hot on her face.

"Back off," she ordered. "Did nobody ever tell you not to eat garlic or onions before a close encounter?"

"Give me the gun."

The situation was getting out of control. She brought the gun from behind her back and pointed it at him, inches from his stomach. "I said, back off. This gun is loaded, and I'm not soft like Dianne. I wouldn't have any problem killing you. In fact, I'd enjoy it."

Her father had impressed on her that she should never point a gun at anyone unless she was ready to kill that person. Tonight was the first time she'd known she could do that, kill a human being. Well, she wasn't sure Kimball qualified as a human being.

"After all you've done to me," she continued when he said nothing, "I'd take great pleasure in emptying this gun into your gut and then, if you're still breathing, I'll happily pistol whip that smirk off your face and through the back of your skull."

"Give. Me. The. Gun."

"I will if you back off and get out of my face."

With surprising speed and dexterity, Kimball grabbed the hand that held the gun.

"Watch out, Amanda!" Charley's warning came a little late.

Panicked, Amanda squeezed the trigger, but Kimball pushed her hand sideways and the bullet went harmlessly through the opposite wall.

"Bitch!" He twisted her wrist with one hand while trying to wrest the gun from her with the other.

Amanda struggled to keep the gun, clawing at his fingers with her free hand.

"Leave her alone!" Charley dove between the two of them, pummeling Kimball. At least, Amanda assumed that's what he was trying to do. His hands passed through the man.

Charley must have made some impact, though, because Kimball looked startled and momentarily loosed his grip on her wrist.

Amanda yanked her arm free and tried to aim the gun at Kimball again. He recovered and slammed her against the wall, his body holding her in place. Charley appeared behind him, wrapping an arm around and through his neck. Again Kimball looked startled but did not release his grip on Amanda. She squirmed but was pressed so tightly between him and the wall, she couldn't move. She hung on to the gun, but he twisted her wrist until her fingers loosened their grip. He yanked the gun away from her.

From the corner of her eye, she could see Charley futilely trying to grab the weapon from Kimball.

Finally Kimball stepped away, shoved her against the wall and pointed the revolver toward her. "Now," he said. "Take off your jacket and hand it to me."

"Don't do it!" Charley exclaimed, still grappling for the gun. The only evidence that he had any effect was when Kimball shuddered and brushed that hand as if brushing off a spider.

Charley was trying. She grudgingly gave him credit for that. But essentially she was alone in a tumble down cabin in the middle of nowhere with a murderer. Not exactly the way she had planned for the evening to go.

"What choice do I have?" Amanda asked of Charley, her words quiet and dispirited.

"None," Kimball responded. "The coat."

She hugged the jacket more closely. "Why? You've got the gun. Our deal is finished." She edged toward the door, hoping he'd let her go, hoping she could escape with her life and her recording. Though Kimball had not made a confession, surely she had enough to convince the cops to investigate him.

He moved with her, the gun still pointing toward her.

"Give me the jacket. As soon as I check the pockets, you can have it back."

Damn. She'd be lucky to get out of there with her life. It seemed there was no chance she'd get away with her recording.

Slowly she unzipped her jacket. Maybe she could grab the hammer.

And then what?

Gun trumps hammer. He could shoot her from across the room while she had to get up close and personal in order to beat his brains out with a claw hammer.

Nevertheless, after slipping one arm out of the jacket, she reached inside with that hand and closed her fingers over the handle of the hammer. She slid her other arm from the sleeve, yanked out the hammer and tossed the jacket into Kimball's face. The gun exploded, the bullet screaming past her head and slamming into the wall behind her.

She surged forward, throwing herself at Kimball, swinging the hammer toward the hand holding the gun. She struck him a glancing blow, not enough to crack a bone but enough that he dropped the revolver and cursed.

Her jacket slid to the floor between them as he grabbed her with one arm. She swung the hammer wildly, trying to connect with some body part, any body part. But Kimball wrapped his arm around her neck and twisted her so her back was pressed against him.

"Lift the jacket with your foot," he growled, his mouth against her ear.

When she didn't respond immediately, he tightened his grip on her throat.

"I'm trying!" Charley said, standing in front of her, his fingers of cold air on her neck telling her he was doing all he could to dislodge Kimball's arm.

Amanda slid her foot under the jacket and lifted it a couple of feet off the floor.

"Drop the damn hammer and get it."

Amanda reached down, snagging the jacket with the claw end of the hammer and lifting it.

Kimball took the leather coat. "Now drop the hammer." His arm tightened around her throat.

She dropped the hammer. It fell to the floor with a thud of despair.

He fumbled with her jacket, feeling inside the pockets until he found the cell phone.

Lifting it with his free hand so both he and Amanda could see the recording icon, he laughed. "I knew it. I knew you'd do something dumb." He tossed it to the floor and ground his heel into it.

"Okay, smart bitch, now that you're not recording anything, you still want to know about Dianne?"

Amanda tried to squeak out that she could care less about Dianne at the moment, but Kimball squeezed her throat so tight she was unable to speak.

Charley paced back and forth in front of them. "Don't let him tell you. If he tells you, he'll have to kill you."

"Does anybody else know about the homeless man?"

"Tell him no!"

Amanda tried to shake her head, but her movement was constrained. "No," she croaked.

Kimball's grip relaxed a little.

"He's smiling!" Charley said. "That crazy man is smiling while he's killing you!"

"Killing that man was fun," Kimball said, the tone of his voice confirming that he was, indeed, smiling. "We were stoned. Yeah, Saint Dianne did drugs. She did anything I told her to, except she didn't want to kill that worthless old man. She freaked out on me that night. Then she got religion. Married that wimp Carter and convinced the whole town she was pure as the virgin snow."

His arm around her neck tightened again. Amanda's fingers flew to her throat, trying to pry him loose.

"Be still. You wanted to know all this so badly, pay attention. Things were fine until a couple of years ago when she got on a guilt trip. Wanted to confess her sins, tell the world we killed somebody, take her punishment."

"What do you care?" Amanda croaked. "Your family owns the town."

"Sure, I could have kept it from ever going to court. But that bitch I'm married to would have freaked, and so would my old man. They're no saints, but they want everybody to think the whole family is. They sit there on their money like they own me. They'd never have supported me as governor if Saint Bitch had talked. So I shot her. And everything would have been fine if your worthless husband hadn't found this gun."

"I'll get help!" Charley shouted and disappeared through the wall.

Amanda would have liked to make a sarcastic comment, but he was already gone and she could barely talk anyway.

"Are you going to shoot me like you shot her?" she asked Kimball.

"No. I don't want the two deaths linked. I've had time to think and plan this time. You're going to be easy. Thanks to your habit of riding around town on that motorcycle, nobody's going to be surprised when you end up in a fatal crash, out riding the rough roads around the lake. Run the bike into the trees, throw you down beside it. A broken neck will seem like part of the crash injuries, assuming they ever find your motorcycle or your body out here. This would have been a lot easier if you'd died the first time."

Anger blended with Amanda's fear. "You admit you jacked with my bike!"

"Your husband wasn't very smart. He told me you were taking a long trip. With my connections, it was easy to find out the details. Getting into your bike shop the night before was easy, almost as easy as getting into your apartment. I figured you'd be up in those mountains by the time you lost all the brake fluid and your tire came loose."

"But I didn't die. Did that tick you off, having your plans ruined. I'm the loose end, aren't I? You thought I'd die and be blamed for Charley's murder, but I'm still alive."

"Not for long. Yes, you would have been blamed for his death. You are being blamed. I wore motorcycle gear so everybody would think I was you. Then you came over, and that made it even better. Everything would have been perfect if you'd just died like you were supposed to. You'd be dead, Charley would be dead, you'd be blamed for his death, and I'd be the next governor of Texas."

He tightened his arm around her neck. Amanda couldn't breathe. She was going to die after all. She thought of her mother and her father, of Herbert and Irene, and she felt tears in her eyes at the thought of never seeing them again. Even worse, she'd soon be on the same plane as Charley. Surely if they were both dead, they would no longer be married. Surely she wouldn't be stuck with him forever.

Suddenly Charley came through the wall again, smiling, exultant. "Don't worry, Amanda! Your mother's here! And she's got a gun!"

Her mother? Out here? The oxygen deprivation must be getting to her. She couldn't conceive of her meticulous mother, every hair in place, tripping through the rough terrain in a pair of thousand dollar heels, carrying one of the guns she deplored.

# Chapter Twenty-Four

"Omigawd!" Charley shouted. "He's going to kill you before she gets here!" His cold fingers brushed her throat as he tried ineffectually to pry Kimball's arm from her neck. Blackness crept around the edges of her brain.

"Amanda! Lift your right foot and shove your heel against his knee!"

The blackness edged closer, making Charley's words only a muffled noise.

"Amanda! Suck it up! Stop letting this creep have the upper hand! You never let me! You like him better than me?"

If that wasn't just like Charley. She was dying, and he was trying to start an argument.

"*Lift your right foot!*" he repeated. "*Shove your heel against his knee!* I'm not going to shut up until you do!"

Wearily Amanda lifted her right foot.

"Hard!" Charley demanded. "Push as hard as you can!"

Mouthy Charley. Amanda lifted her heel to Kimball's knee and pushed.

"Hard!"

One final push, and she'd give herself to the blackness, stop fighting it.

Abruptly the pressure around her neck released and somebody screamed. She fell to her knees, gasping and coughing.

The screaming turned to cursing.

"Amanda! Over here! Get over here, away from the window!"

Amanda didn't want to go anywhere. Her throat hurt. She couldn't stop coughing.

Somebody pushed against her, grabbed her shoulder.

Couldn't be Charley. Had to be Kimball.

She jerked her shoulder away and rolled to the side.

"Good girl!" Charley applauded.

*Good girl?* Like he was training a dog? She struggled to her feet and fell toward him. As soon as she got her strength back, she'd strangle him.

A shot exploded through the open window.

"Don't move, Mayor Kimball." The voice was familiar, soft-spoken but firm. When she had time to think, she was sure she'd recognize it.

"That bitch tried to break my knee," Kimball said.

The front door flew open. "I'll break more than that if you move one muscle." Herbert stood in the open doorway, a shotgun leveled at Kimball. Irene appeared from behind him, pushing through the door and coming toward her.

"Stand down! Everybody drop your guns! Police!"

She was definitely hallucinating from oxygen deprivation. Detective Daggett and two uniformed cops could not be coming through the doorway.

Another figure came in behind them. "That's my daughter! Get out of the way!"

"Daddy?" Amanda tried to push to her feet. Her father's arms surrounded her, holding her up.

"Are you okay?"

"I guess. What are you doing here?"

"On your feet." Daggett stood over Kimball, his gun aimed at the man's head.

"I can't. That damn bitch broke my knee."

"Then you better figure out how to crawl."

"We were so scared." Irene wrapped an arm around her on the side opposite her father.

"I was afraid we'd lost you when you set off through the woods." Herbert held his shotgun pointed toward the ground.

"You followed me?"

Herbert shrugged and grinned shyly. "Yeah. It was hard to keep up when you all were going round and round the town, and then I had to track you through the woods. That part was easier. Been hunting these woods all my life. Reckon those skills came in handy tonight."

Two uniformed cops from the Silver Creek force dragged Kimball through the door, and Daggett came over to her.

"Are you okay? You probably ought to go to the hospital to get checked out."

Amanda shook her head. "No." The word hurt as it came up her sore throat. She coughed twice and tried again. "No. I'm okay. What are you doing here? You didn't believe me. You wouldn't take my calls."

Daggett raised his eyebrows. "I never said I didn't believe you. If I'd taken all your calls, I wouldn't have had time to do any work and track down this scum."

"You did believe me?"

Daggett shrugged. "Your story was a little strange, but I've heard stranger. My gut told me you didn't kill your husband, and that meant somebody else did it. After all you told me, I had to check into this guy's background."

Anger sent adrenalin surging through Amanda, masking her pain and giving her energy. "You could have made my life a lot easier if you'd bothered to share that with me!"

"I never discuss an ongoing case."

Amanda glared at him. "But I guess you're going to want me to discuss your ongoing case when you take that monster to trial."

Daggett grinned crookedly. "I figured you'd be downright eager."

"You got that right. I was trying to record his confession since there's no evidence, but he smashed my cell phone."

"No problem. Your lawyer friend got it all." He nodded toward the window.

Amanda looked in that direction. The moon had risen, and she could see Sunny Donovan quite clearly, standing outside looking in, clutching a Glock. With her other hand she lifted a small metallic device and smiled. Good grief. The whole town of Silver Creek was there along with part of Dallas.

"Sunny? What are you doing here?"

Sunny looked sheepish. "Keeping track of you, but after you spotted Frank following you—"

"Frank? The man Kimball hired to spy on me?" Had Sunny and Kimball been working together after all?

"Kimball didn't hire Frank. Frank followed you as a favor to me. But he's not very good at it. After you caught him, I had to figure out something else. Remember when I rode your bike? I palmed a couple of tracking devices from my desk drawer and put one on your bike then another in the lining of your jacket."

Amanda recalled the day in Sunny's office when she'd fumbled in her desk drawer for a long time before finally producing a card.

"Why?" she asked. "Why were you tracking me?"

"I knew you were headed for trouble."

"Good thing she did," Daggett said. "I almost didn't find you with that legal description you left for me. That's about five miles from here, cross-country."

"We found him wandering around, lost as a goose in a snowstorm," Irene said. "Hadn't been for Herbert being able to track so good he can follow a squirrel through the treetops, he wouldn't have found you."

"She's right," Daggett admitted. "Those shots got us in the right vicinity, but Mr. Randolph took us the rest of the way. You are one lucky lady to have so many people looking out for you."

"And me," Charley added. "I'm looking out for you too." Amanda's attention snapped to him. "Yeah, I'm still here. Guess our business isn't finished yet." She could tell from the guilty look on his face that he knew exactly what other business remained. She wasn't sure she wanted to know.

Seeing Charley reminded her of his strange announcement that her mother was there with a gun.

"Where's Mother?" Amanda asked.

"Waiting in the car," her father answered. "You don't think she was going to walk through the wilderness in her best heels?"

"No, of course not." Maybe she hadn't heard Charley right. She had been under a lot of stress, emotional as well as physical. Not every day a girl almost got killed.

"She'll be very upset by now, worrying about you. Can we go, Detective Daggett?"

"Sure. Bring her in tomorrow so we can take her statement. She probably ought to go to the hospital, but good luck with that." He turned and left the cabin.

"I'll fix her something for that throat," Irene offered.

"Hot chocolate would be good."

Irene laughed. "We can have some of that too."

"Dad, how did you know where to find me?" Amanda asked as they started toward the door.

"Dawson called me. He told me what you were planning to do and about the cabin where he thought it would happen."

"He told? Geez! You can't trust anybody."

Her father looked at her strangely then looked away. "Fortunately Sunny planted those tracking devices on you and your motorcycle since that wasn't the cabin you ended up at. Your mother and I came in with Sunny."

Amanda looked toward the window and saw Sunny still standing there, watching. Amanda thought she saw tears in the woman's eyes, but it was probably just the flickering lantern light.

"Come with us, Sunny," her father said quietly, and Sunny nodded. "There's something we need to talk about."

"I'll ride Amanda's bike," Sunny said. "You and Beverly can take her to the Randolphs' house in my car."

*Beverly?* Oh, yeah. Sunny had interned for her father's law firm. Apparently she'd been a friend of the family.

৵৹৶

Surrounded by her family, one friend and one ex-husband, Amanda sat at Irene's kitchen table and sipped hot chocolate. Her throat was still sore, but Irene had concocted some kind of vile brew and insisted Amanda drink it before she could have a cup of hot chocolate.

After all the stress and worry of the last few weeks, it was hard to believe it was finally all over. She wasn't going to prison. Kimball wasn't going to kill her. Kimball wasn't going to become the governor of Texas. Charley was still around, but she was so deliriously happy at the moment, even his presence didn't upset her.

Her mother and Irene fussed over her, each trying to outdo the other in pampering—offering her more hot chocolate, hot broth, a warm scarf for her throat. Under ordinary circumstances, she'd have run from the room screaming, but at that moment she was thoroughly enjoying the pampering.

Her father and Herbert drank coffee and discussed Kimball's sins and how much time he was likely to spend in prison.

Charley and Sunny sat quietly watching.

That was the only dark spot in the otherwise glorious evening. What secret were Charley and Sunny going to confess, and how did her father figure into it? He'd told

Sunny to come with them, that there was something they needed to talk about.

During her second cup of hot chocolate, Judge Caulfield cleared his throat. As if he'd slammed his gavel, everyone stopped talking and turned their attention to him. "Herbert, Irene, could we have a few minutes alone with our daughter?"

Herbert and Irene exchanged confused glances, but Irene said, "Sure."

Amanda expected Sunny to leave the room too, but she remained. She'd been right. Whatever secret Sunny and Charley shared involved her father. And her mother, apparently. She squirmed in her chair and looked at Charley. He refused to meet her gaze.

"Mandy, your husband was not a good man," her father said.

"Yeah, there's a reason I was divorcing him. Several of them, in fact."

Charley continued to look at the floor, not rising to the bait.

The judge drew in a deep breath and sat upright in his chair as if steeling himself for a blow. "I have not been totally honorable, either."

Amanda slid back her chair and started to rise. "I don't want to hear this."

"No, you don't want to, but you need to."

Amanda returned to her chair and wrapped both hands around the ebbing warmth of her cup.

"You know about Charley blackmailing Kimball. Well, he was also blackmailing me."

Amanda took a big swig of the cooling chocolate, savoring the feel as it went down her sore throat. But the pain in her throat didn't compare to the pain piercing her heart. Her fear about her father was confirmed. He wasn't the paragon of virtue she'd always believed him to be. She sat quietly, waiting for but not encouraging this confession.

"He asked for money, but I refused to give it to him. I would not do anything illegal. I did, however, bail him out of jail repeatedly and arrange for legal representation." He drew in another deep breath then let it out. "You asked why I didn't tell you about Charley's family. We didn't want you to come to Silver Creek to meet them."

"They're wonderful people," Amanda protested.

"Yes, they are. That's not the point. We were afraid of what you'd find out if you came down here."

The cup containing the last few dregs of chocolate and milk had gone ice cold in her hands. Or maybe her hands had gone ice cold around the cup. "What were you afraid I'd find?" she forced herself to ask.

For a few moments everyone was silent. The grandfather clock in the living room ticked loudly in a grim, staccato rhythm.

"Charley came to Dallas specifically to find you," the judge said.

Amanda's heart, so happy a few minutes ago, clenched into a small, hard knot. She'd ceased to love Charley long ago, but it hurt to hear their marriage, their relationship, had all been part of a scam, that Charley had never loved her, had only wanted to get close to her father in order to blackmail him.

"It's true," Charley whispered. "I came to Dallas and looked you up. But I swear I fell in love with you as soon as I met you. Remember, I can't lie now."

Amanda glared at him, barely able to resist the desire to tell him to shut up in spite of all the people around them.

"It was my fault." Sunny spoke for the first time. "When I defended him, got him off on the drug charge, he broke into my office and went through my files."

So that's where Sunny came in.

But they still hadn't told her what the horrible thing was that her father had done. Had Sunny defended him in court for some crime? That didn't seem likely since he had his choice of just about any attorney in Dallas.

Her mother, sitting beside her, reached over and took her hand.

Yikes. This was going to be really bad. She couldn't recall her mother holding her hand since she was about five years old. Maybe four. And maybe it had been her nanny, not her mother.

"When Sunny was in law school, she interned in my office."

Amanda looked at the anxious faces around the table. "Dawson told me that. It's public information."

Her father no longer looked like the judge. He looked like a scared father.

"Your mother and I were having some problems. We separated for a while. Sunny and I...we had a relationship."

Amanda's jaw dropped. She looked at her mother to see if she was going to kill the both of them. Her mother's expression didn't change. She continued to look sad and caring and frightened. She already knew.

"I got pregnant," Sunny supplied. "I was young and broke and still in law school and had no idea what I'd do with a baby. My mother said we'd manage, but I couldn't do that to her. She'd worked hard all her life to take care of me, and her health wasn't good. You've seen her. She's frail. She deserved to rest, to have me support her for a change. I didn't want to make my mother's life harder, and I didn't want my baby to grow up struggling as hard as I had to."

"So you had an abortion?" Amanda asked. People did it all the time, but it still felt strange to think her father's child, her sibling, had never been born.

Sunny smiled weakly. "No. I loved my baby from the moment I knew she was on the way. I gave birth to her. I held her once, and then I gave her up for adoption to a loving family who could give her everything. I've regretted it every day, wished every day I'd had the courage to keep her, wanted to hold her in my arms and watch her grow up. She's an amazing woman, a daughter any mother would be proud of." She hesitated, then added, as if to herself, "But she's had a good life. Better than I could have given her."

Amanda wasn't sure if it was the quiver in Sunny's voice, the tears in her green eyes or just her words, but a really improbable thought crossed her mind. As soon as it did, she suddenly realized why Sunny looked so familiar, where she'd seen her face before.

In the mirror.

"I'm your mother," Sunny said softly.

"Too," Beverly amended. "She's your mother too."

Amanda looked at each face around the table.

Her father, the judge, the man who'd been the rock of her life. He'd lied, cheated on her mother...well, on his wife.

Her mother, the woman who'd raised her. She'd never felt really close to her mother. They'd been too different. Oddly, she now felt closer to her than ever before. Her mother had taken in the love child of her husband. She'd cared for her, even loved her in spite of their differences.

And Sunny. The woman she'd liked instinctively the first time she'd met her. The woman she'd wanted to have as her friend. The woman who'd given birth to her and then given her up.

She stood slowly. "I think I need to go to bed now."

No one spoke as she left the room.

���⌖࿐

"I found the files Sunny had on you," Charley said.

282

Amanda sat on the edge of the bed, unable to lie down and unable to get up.

"She kept track of you. Talked to your dad. He sent her pictures. Even got her into your high school graduation ceremony. She kept everything. She had an entire file cabinet in the back room. It was always locked, so I knew something important was in there. I broke into her office one night and got into the file cabinet. She even had your original birth certificate, so that's how I knew."

Amanda looked at him, the man she'd once thought she loved, the man who had betrayed her so completely. "So you decided to come to Dallas, marry me, blackmail my father, and live well on the proceeds."

Charley put both hands in his pockets and looked at the floor. "Marrying you wasn't part of the plan. I married you because I loved you. But, yes, the rest is true. I was going to meet you then go to your dad and threaten to tell you about Sunny if he didn't pay me. He refused. But by then, I was in love. Not that loving you kept me from using you. Your dad wouldn't pay me, but he did keep his mouth shut about me, and he did bail me out of trouble whenever I got caught." He lifted his head and looked her directly in the eye. "I'm sorry."

*I'm sorry?* Amanda watched him, expecting him to disappear at any moment now that he'd reached such an epiphany.

A knock sounded on the bedroom door. Amanda jumped. Charley disappeared.

"Amanda?" It was Irene. "Can I come in?"

"Of course."

Irene entered the room and came over to sit beside Amanda. "How you doing?"

"You heard?"

Irene nodded. "They told me. That's a lot to take in all at once."

"Yeah," Amanda agreed. "A lot."

283

"Your daddy's a good man. Everybody makes mistakes, especially when they're young."

Amanda laughed. "I don't fault him for his relationship with Sunny. You've met my mother...uh...my..."

"Mother," Irene supplied. "She's still your mother. In fact, you're a pretty lucky lady. You have two mothers and one mother-in-law and we all love you. You're not mad at Sunny for giving you up, are you? She was trying to do the right thing for everybody. Sunny's like that."

Amanda thought about it. Sunny was right. She'd had a good life. She couldn't imagine not having her mother and father and even her sister. "No, I'm not upset with her. I like her. I think she likes me. But I don't know if I can ever think of her as my mother."

"You don't have to. Just let her be your friend."

"I think I can do that."

"Then you're okay with everything you found out tonight?"

Amanda considered that question. "Yeah, I guess I am. In fact, I understand my mother better than I used to. She's more complex than I realized."

"So there's only one person you can't forgive," Irene said. "Charley."

Amanda nodded. Even though Charley had said he was sorry, she couldn't seem to forgive him. He'd done too much, caused too many problems, hurt her too much. "He's the only one whose motives were bad."

"I'm sorry." Irene unconsciously echoed her son's words.

"Oh, Irene, you don't have anything to apologize for. Except maybe you didn't check your babies close enough, and they switched your son for the son of the psycho couple who lived across town."

Irene laughed. "I'm afraid he's mine. I just kinda lost control of him when he was, oh, about a week old."

"I can believe that."

"Do you want me to go downstairs and tell everybody to go home, give you some time to deal with everything?"

Amanda thought about it. A night alone to think about all of it would be good. On the other hand, she didn't have a lot to deal with. All she could do was accept the new relationships. Nothing had changed except she finally knew Charley and Sunny's secret. The three people waiting downstairs were probably freaking out about what her reaction would be.

She stood. "No. Let's go downstairs and figure out who's going to be stuck with me for Thanksgiving dinner."

"No contest." Irene smiled. "We want you down here for Thanksgiving. I'll be making pecan pies."

Amanda looked around the room before leaving it. Was Charley really gone or just *in the dark*, waiting until she was alone? Surely with his murderer going to prison and all his secrets out in the open, Charley could go on into the light.

Still no sign of him as she walked down the stairs.

Kind of weird to think of his finally being gone.

Maybe she'd miss him.

Nah.

When she entered the kitchen, all conversation ceased and everyone turned anxious gazes on her.

She walked first to stand behind her father and wrap her arms around his neck. "Dad, I guess you learned your lesson about cheating on Mom. Look what a stubborn, problematic daughter you got out of the deal."

Her father pressed his hands over hers. "I regret hurting your mother and Sunny. But I can't imagine my life without you."

She moved from her father to her mother. Maybe one arm around the shoulders would be more appropriate.

Nope. She wrapped both arms around her mother's neck. "Mom, I'm not sure I could have done what you did. But I'm really glad you did. I couldn't have asked for a better mother. Maybe we could go shopping soon and get me some decent clothes." That last sentence was hard to say, and Amanda wasn't sure she could actually do it. But she'd try. She didn't have to wear the clothes after they bought them.

"It took me a while to forgive your father," Beverly said. "You were the deciding factor. We were on the list to adopt. We didn't think we could have children. Then he told me you were on the way." She shook her head. "I wasn't sure I could go through with it until I saw you the first time with that red hair and red face, waving your fists and screaming at the world. I loved you immediately." She patted Amanda's hands. "Your face is a lovely porcelain color now, but the rest hasn't changed."

"Is my sister adopted?" Amanda asked. That would explain a lot. Maybe her sister's birth parents had taken too many drugs.

"No. I gave birth to your sister. She was a wonderful surprise when we'd given up on having children. We never tried to adopt a second child. You were all we could handle."

Amanda laughed. "I know."

She moved on to the last remaining person. Sunny. Instead of hugging her, however, she sat down next to her. Perhaps this woman had given birth to her, but she didn't really know her, didn't feel comfortable being familiar. In fact, she felt downright uncomfortable, and Sunny looked downright terrified. For a moment, both women remained silent.

"If you want to come visit me in Dallas," Amanda finally said, "I've got plenty of motorcycles you can choose from, and we could maybe ride together."

Sunny burst into tears, leaned over and wrapped her arms around Amanda.

"I'd love to ride motorcycles with you," she said through her sobs.

Amanda tentatively returned the embrace. She didn't think Sunny would ever be a mother figure, but she was pretty sure the two of them would be friends. Good friends. Maybe even best friends.

Sunny sat back and wiped her eyes. "I'm so glad you inherited my love of motorcycles, but I'm sorry you inherited my bad handwriting."

Amanda smiled and looked around the room. Everyone, including Irene who stood in the doorway, was happy and smiling.

Irene walked over to the table. "After all the bad things Charley did, I'm sure the good Lord will forgive him because of the good that's come from his death. We found Amanda, and she found Sunny, and everybody's happy. Now that his killer will pay for what he did, Charley should be able to rest in peace."

"I hope so," Amanda said, her words perhaps more fervent than the situation called for.

"You can just keep on hoping." Charley appeared across the room. "I'm still here." He waved his hands wildly. "No white light. Nothing. I'm stuck."

Amanda dropped her head into her hands and groaned.

"Are you okay?" Irene asked. "Let me get you another hot chocolate."

"I think I need something stronger," Amanda said. "I think I need a Coke. Maybe two or three of them."

Was she never going to get rid of Charley?

THE END

## About the Author:

I grew up in a small rural town in southeastern Oklahoma where our favorite entertainment on summer evenings was to sit outside under the stars and tell stories. When I went to bed at night, instead of a lullaby, I got a story. That could be due to the fact that everybody in my family has a singing voice like a bullfrog with laryngitis, but they sure could tell stories—ghost stories, funny stories, happy stories, scary stories.

For as long as I can remember I've been a storyteller. Thank goodness for computers so I can write down my stories. It's hard to make listeners sit still for the length of a book! Like my family's tales, my stories are funny, scary, dramatic, romantic, paranormal, magic.

Besides writing, my interests are reading, eating chocolate and riding my Harley.

Contact information is available on my website. I love to talk to readers! And writers. And riders. And computer programmers. Okay, I just love to talk!

http://www.sallyberneathy.com

CPSIA information can be obtained
at www.ICGtesting.com
Printed in the USA
BVHW040158040821
613609BV00021B/297